RARY

14
10/2022

WITHDRAWN

Love

FROM

Mecca

to

Medina

Also by S. K. Ali

Saints and Misfits
Love from A to Z
The Eid Gift: An Adam and Zayneb Story
Misfit in Love

Love
FROM
Mecca
to
Medina

S. K. ALI

SALAAM
READS

NEW YORK LONDON TORONTO SYDNEY NEW DELHI

An imprint of Simon & Schuster Children's Publishing Division
1230 Avenue of the Americas, New York, New York 10020

This book is a work of fiction. Any references to historical events, real people, or real places are used fictitiously. Other names, characters, places, and events are products of the author's imagination, and any resemblance to actual events or places or persons, living or dead, is entirely coincidental.

Text © 2022 by Sajidah Kutty
Jacket illustration © 2022 by Mary Kate McDevitt
Jacket design by Lucy Ruth Cummins © 2022 by Simon & Schuster, Inc.

All rights reserved, including the right of reproduction in whole or in part in any form.
SALAAM READS and its logo are trademarks of Simon & Schuster, Inc.

For information about special discounts for bulk purchases, please contact
Simon & Schuster Special Sales at 1-866-506-1949 or business@simonandschuster.com.
The Simon & Schuster Speakers Bureau can bring authors to your live event. For more
information or to book an event, contact the Simon & Schuster Speakers Bureau at
1-866-248-3049 or visit our website at www.simonspeakers.com.
Interior design by Hilary Zarycky
The text for this book was set in Adobe Garamond Pro.
Manufactured in the United States of America
First Edition
2 4 6 8 10 9 7 5 3 1
Library of Congress Cataloging-in-Publication Data
Names: Ali, S. K., author.
Title: Love from Mecca to Medina / S.K. Ali.
Description: First edition. | New York : Salaam Reads, [2022] |
Sequel to: Love from A to Z |
Summary: Adam and Zayneb embark on the Umrah, a pilgrimage to Mecca and Medina, in Saudi Arabia, but as one wedge after another drives them apart while they make their way through rites in the holy city, Adam and Zayneb start to wonder if their meeting was just an oddity after all.
Identifiers: LCCN 2022009868 (print) | LCCN 2022009869 (ebook) |
ISBN 9781665916073 (hardcover) | ISBN 9781665916097 (ebook)
Subjects: CYAC: Marriage—Fiction. | Muslims—Fiction. | Islam—Fiction. | Mecca (Saudi Arabia)—Fiction. | Medina (Saudi Arabia)—Fiction. | Saudi Arabia—Fiction. | LCGFT: Romance fiction. | Novels.
Classification: LCC PZ7.1.A436 Lp 2022 (print) | LCC PZ7.1.A436 (ebook) |
DDC [E]—dc23
LC record available at https://lccn.loc.gov/2022009868
LC ebook record available at https://lccn.loc.gov/2022009869

To Jez, who loves and lets be

There are no happily-ever-afters.
There is only a story that begins anew each day.

BERTHA FATIMA PRESENTS A STORY BOX FOR YOU TO OPEN (FOR HER)

BERTHA FATIMA CHEN-MALIK, FIRST OF HER NAME, HAD BEEN AN indoor cat her entire life. She liked cozy nooks that fit her just so and, really, any box, container, or basket that held her snug like a constant hug.

Wide-open, roamy spaces gave her a strange sort of feeling, like she was expected to do so much, when all she wanted to do was curl up and live inside her dreams, amid eating meals—balanced properly between crunchy and soft cat foods, that is.

All this to say she absolutely loved her catsitter Layth's rental, an alcove room inside an old house, and wanted to live in it forever—or at least longer than the month she'd be spending there, soon coming to an end.

It was a wonderful size, with space enough for a comfortable queen bed, a wide desk, a closet, a little sitting area designated by its one burgundy wing chair with a small round mahogany pedestal table tucked next to it, and a tiny but functional kitchenette. Attached to the main space was a private bathroom with a sloping roof, which had the perfect little nook, under the slope, for Bertha Fatima's litter box. Bertha Fatima was ever fastidious and stationed herself religiously in front of her litter box, to meow plaintively, to ensure it was cleaned often.

To the human eye, the best part of Layth's place, perhaps, was that it looked and felt like the office of a person who thought a lot. Like the study of a brilliant academic. Or even Sherlock Holmes. Or Agatha Christie, actually.

This was in part because its deep teal wainscotted walls were lined with identically hued teal bookshelves, ones that weren't fully outfitted with books currently but held a wide variety of objects belonging to the homeowner, like framed butterflies, the fake (hopefully) skulls and bleached carcasses of small animals, leather books, and several antique items Bertha Fatima greatly enjoyed sniffing, with her lips parted slightly, to investigate and ascertain their long-ago and faraway origins.

However, other than giving us a picture of where Bertha Fatima spent her days, these items, which tell someone else's story, are of no further interest to us.

We are here, after all, to absorb the story of Bertha Fatima's human parents, Adam Chen and Zayneb Malik, a tale that moves through three continents but ends in one.

So let us fix our gazes on an item placed on the shelf more recently, an object more important than those belonging to the homeowner: a wooden box the size of a large shoebox, carved in florals and paisleys, inlaid with mother-of-pearl.

The box holds a museum of two lives (belonging to the aforementioned Adam and Zayneb) and the lives of those they interacted with as they journeyed to the center.

Museums are of vital importance to Bertha Fatima's parents.

A manuscript, *The Marvels of Creation and the Oddities of Existence*, housed in the Museum of Islamic Art in Doha, Qatar, is what drew Adam and Zayneb together in the first place, inspiring them, separately, to journal the marvels and oddities they witnessed in their respective lives, including the marvel of meeting each other. And now, while they still marveled and found things odd, we no longer need to peek in their journals to discover where they ended up.

The journals closed when A and Z came together in love—*for good, forever.*

Or so they say.

For, alas, they weren't together now. Physically. Mentally.

Nor spiritually. And since I, the compiler of their marvels and oddities previously, am most interested in their souls and how they grew (or didn't), I have taken it upon myself to curate a collection of items—mementos, to be precise; souvenirs, to be banal; testimonials, to be profound—from a recent trip they took.

A trip that changed the course of their future. (And future relationship.)

The story-box museum had been mailed to the alcove room, and Layth, the catsitter, had placed it on the teal shelf as the package was addressed to Bertha Fatima and he figured he'd give it to Zayneb when she came to pick the cat up—hopefully soon.

Then he'd left for the day.

So now Bertha Fatima sat beside the box, her head held high and still, her front paws primly together on the dark shelving—not in contentment nor ease, mind you. It was, rather, with deep curiosity (twinged with melancholy), of which she only allowed a smidgen to show on her furry face.

Because this truth remained: While she absolutely adored the abode she currently lived in, she adored Adam and Zayneb even more.

And her unwavering and solemn gaze—at you, dear reader—was fraught with questions: Will she be away from her parents much longer? Will they become a family again?

And, frankly put, *How could they so brazenly deposit her with a catsitter for an entire month? Where exactly in the world were they right now?*

She, without opposable thumbs, awaited you, kind reader, to unbolt the ancient lock (faux thirteenth century) and open the carved wooden box and take out the first artifact—belonging to Adam's sister Hanna—to begin the storytelling.

We will then give the reins to Adam and Zayneb, to share their respective perspectives.

Bertha Fatima must know what is going on.

She must know whether she will, one day soon, find a home once again with her beloveds, hopefully reunited.

PART ONE

And the earth—We have spread it out wide, and placed on it mountains firm, and caused [life] of every kind to grow on it in a balanced manner, and provided thereon means of livelihood for you as well as for all [living beings] whose sustenance does not depend on you.
—Surah 15:19–20

THREE WEEKS EARLIER

HANNA STARED AT THE TEENY GOLD ARABIC CALLIGRAPHY THAT skirted a quarter of an inch from the top of the black plastic cube set on a glass platform.

Perhaps gazing at the souvenir Kaaba could ignite the feeling of being in Mecca with her dad this past summer.

Alas, no—all it did was make her want to run to get a magnifying glass to see if any of the Arabic words on the souvenir were the *actual* ones from the *actual* Kaaba in Mecca. She sighed and put the Kaaba back in its blue velvet pouch.

She would have to start at the start.

She pulled the laptop from the coffee table onto the couch she was lying on, stomach down, and began two-finger-typing the introduction for her social studies project.

The Mecca That Started It All
By Hanna Chen, 8B, Ms. McMann,
Doha International School

The mecca of basketball is Madison Square Garden. The
mecca of fashion is Paris (or New York or Tokyo, depending

on who you ask). The mecca of movies is Hollywood. Or, for a lot of people, Bollywood (which is in India). Or Nollywood (which is in Nigeria). (But for me, the mecca of movies is Japan, because of Studio Ghibli.)

I hope you get what I'm trying to say. In case you don't, I'm saying there's a common thing here: It's that they all use the word "mecca."

What people mean by the word "mecca" is a place where lots of people, thousands, millions (maybe even billions as well [maybe in the future]) gather for a certain thing. Like basketball or fashion shows or making movies.

But I wonder if people even know where the word "mecca" actually, *originally* came from.

It came from Mecca with a capital *M*, the place in the Middle East where people have been gathering for thousands of years to visit the first site of worship in the world still standing (according to Muslim people).

For this project on a place that the world doesn't know enough about, I'm going to talk about Mecca, the real city. The city that started the trend of using the words "the mecca of" something.

In this essay, I'll share some photos of Mecca in the olden times (meaning around the seventh century). But the pictures themselves won't be from the olden times. They're actually from my brother's project

"Adam!" Hanna lifted her head up from the couch. "Adam!"

When there was no answer, that sensation in her stomach began, the one that felt like she was getting pinched with mega-big hands from the inside. She set her laptop on a cushion and jumped off the sofa to run upstairs, anxiety pressing harder as she headed to her brother's workroom.

She knew he'd told her not to worry, that he was taking his medication, that his multiple sclerosis was under management, but Hanna was never satisfied until she saw for herself. That he was okay. Always.

The workroom door was ajar, and she peeked inside. Seeing only Adam's worktable with his latest project spread out, a 3D map, and not him, she pushed the door open wider.

He had earbuds in. And he was sitting on Hanna's old pink chair, talking to the laptop on his knees, his back to her.

Hanna came up behind him to find out who exactly he was chatting with.

"Zayneb!"

The girl on screen immediately smiled wide, her big eyes lighting up on seeing Hanna. She was beautiful in a breezy, effortless way. Her hair lay center parted into curls that framed her long oval face, the ends reaching down to her waist. Under a shaggy gray cardigan that slipped off her shoulders, she wore a white cotton sleeveless crop top, its scooped neck revealing smooth dark brown skin and a tangle of thin necklaces, including one that had a tiny golden goose hanging from it.

Zayneb, who'd been playing with the goose, her forehead furrowed as she explained the latest drama in her life to Adam, now dropped the pendant to wave at Hanna.

Adam tapped his earbuds to disconnect them from the laptop before turning around to his little sister. "There's something called knocking?"

"I called you a thousand times," Hanna responded, still smiling at Zayneb. "What's the exact date you're getting here to Doha? You're coming for Thanksgiving, right?"

"Yikes, Hanna. I don't remember saying that." Zayneb lifted her cardigan up on her shoulders and pulled down her top. Her midriff just hanging around for Adam's view was one thing, but she wasn't too sure about Hanna seeing it.

"But you said you guys are gonna spend Thanksgiving together?" Hanna turned to Adam.

Adam leaned back in the chair and rubbed his face, hoping it hadn't turned red when Hanna crept up like that—when he'd been staring at Zayneb and the way she'd let her cardigan fall away so artfully.

She was in Chicago, so far from him, when all he wanted in the entire world was to be with her right now.

And, actually, for all time.

He set the laptop on a side table and leaned farther back into the pink chair, almost sinking into it. Then he crossed his arms.

"I'm so sorry. I just don't have enough of a break from school to spend all the time I want to with you in Doha, Hanna," Zayneb said. She was buttoning up the cardigan and trying hard not to glance at Adam's face—an action she knew would set her off in peals of laughter.

Adam could tell Zayneb was avoiding his gaze.

Adam loved Hanna, but her mini-auntie ways often interfered at the exact moments when Zayneb and Adam were trying to enjoy some time to themselves.

It drove him bonkers that Hanna hadn't realized they didn't need her "chaperoning" them, or finding out—and being in charge of—all their plans, or just being an oblivious third wheel.

His little sister knew that he and Zayneb had had their nikah done—she'd been there at the ceremony—but she sure acted like she didn't understand what that meant.

For Zayneb, though, this was the least of her troubles.

She preferred this trouble—this "Auntie" Hanna—over the turmoil that was waiting on the other side of the door to the bathroom she was in right at the moment.

"So you guys are *not* seeing each other?" Hanna bent and jutted her head in front of the laptop screen, blocking Adam's view of Zayneb completely. "At all?"

Adam sat up and leaned to the side and caught Zayneb's eyes from over Hanna's shoulder.

They smiled at each other, a secret dancing in their eyes.

Only a few more weeks.

Insha'Allah.

Rent the Hidden Bloom Cottage—
Perfect for a Fall Getaway!

Follow a trail of autumn leaves through a tunnel of trees bending in joy toward each other and find your awaiting love nest!

The Hidden Bloom Cottage sits in the midst of an old forest in Sussex—renowned for its deer-hunting grounds in the Middle Ages, for being the home of Christopher Robin and Winnie-the-Pooh, and now, a protected, sacred space for wildlife and . . . lovers.

A well-stocked kitchen opens onto a cozy sitting room, containing a love seat laden with quilts and blankets, facing a fireplace (supplied with ample stores of wood), above which sits a wide-screen TV, surrounded by bookshelves housing books—new and classics—and a plethora of both traditional board games and video games for the included Xbox and Wii systems. (We just love this room and couldn't stop ourselves from offering such a verbose description!)

Just off this charming, hygge-ful space is the master bedroom: a lush, intimate oasis of peace and comfort. You and your special one will be enveloped in a canopied, curtained, four-poster bed fit for royalty, with an en suite bathroom similarly tastefully decorated. The room opens via French doors to a traditional English garden where seasonal blooms put on a show well into autumn while you partake of your specially delivered afternoon tea, sandwiches, and cakes on the patio.

£350 for the week; £150 for a three-day weekend

ARTIFACT TWO:
ADAM'S WOODEN SAND TIMER
INTERPRETIVE LABEL:
OUR PERSPECTIVE SHIFTS WHEN WE ZOOM IN

I STAYED OUT OF THE WAY AS HANNA MOVED AROUND THE TABLE taking photos of my 3D map for her social studies assignment. As soon as she left, I approached the table and knelt a few inches away to look at the whole thing at eye level.

If I brought my hands up to the sides of my face and cut off my peripheral vision, a slightly magical transformation took place: I was transported 1,400 years back in time.

There was a kneeling clay camel among the palm trees of Medina off in the distance, and here, closer to me, was the simple cube-shaped Kaaba in Mecca. And in between lay the route, strewn with glow-in-the-dark sand so that when the lights were off, you could still see it.

I squinted my eyes in an attempt to place myself squarely in the middle of the dusty path, with the rugged mountains of Mecca behind me.

I almost felt it, that I was back there, back then, moving forward to safety, to those waiting for me with arms open wide.

But it was impossible to ignore the small matter of *was the map visually accurate?*

My attempted scale map of the journey from Mecca to Medina

that constituted the Hijrah, the migration of the prophet Muhammad, peace be upon him, to a new community, was neither an art project—with the creative license that comes with that—nor a commissioned one.

Had it been the latter, I wouldn't have been worried about the accuracy.

No one had handed me a file with specs for this task. I didn't know if the dunes I'd molded out of foam before covering them with sands from the shore outside our backyard here in Doha were like what the Prophet and his companion had trekked by. I'd just tried my best after poring over the maps various scholars had recorded after the Prophet walked the earth.

But, really, how could this be an assigned task when no one wanted my work anymore?

I got up, holding on to the table carefully to do so, and took a seat in the bright pink shaggy chair, a hand-me-down from Hanna's room.

The last time someone had hired me to make something, anything, was back in January. Ten months ago. And I'd finished and shown that commission in September.

About a month ago, I'd stopped refreshing my inbox hourly, stopped checking my spam folders, stopped dropping by all the freelance sites I had accounts on to check for messages that hadn't somehow also made it into my e-mail notifications.

I'd decided to just ignore the fact that I was jobless—well, actually *gig*-less, since I never have had a full-time job.

Instead of mulling this sad state of events, I'd chosen to travel back to the year 622 CE via a map.

It started with the idea that molding and baking tiny bricks to make a tiny Kaaba would somehow make me forget I wasn't needed by anyone. That there was currently $120 remaining in my account. And some money left in an account Mom had reserved for me in her will that I was afraid to check in on in case it would constitute a shock I couldn't handle right now. I'd been dipping into it freely these past four years; Mom had said it was for me to use for experiences, not school, not living, not trying to be independent. *For Adam to have fun,* she'd said.

I just knew there was enough to rent the Hidden Bloom Cottage for an entire week with Zayneb. I'd already put the deposit on that trip.

Dad thought this 3D Hijrah map spread on the table was an actual job someone had paid me to do.

He came downstairs after work sometimes to check on its progress, beaming with pride as he circled the table, coffee cup in hand, seeing it all come to life.

I hadn't told him it was a commission. But, yeah, I liked that he thought it was. Then I didn't have to tell him a certain thought that had been weaving through my mind lately: *Maybe I'd been wrong to drop out of college in freshman year.*

Dad had been so kind to be open-minded about me leaving school, saying yes, you have my blessing, it's a good idea for you to explore things other than university, *so, Adam, go make stuff.*

Four years later, I was making stuff nobody asked me to, spending hours doing so—but not making *money.*

In three weeks I would be with Zayneb for Thanksgiving break.

Accomplished, beautiful, brilliant Zayneb, with a huge future ahead of her.

Zayneb, whose parents thought I was working hard and earning a living, who'd told me they admired how "I stood on my own two feet."

Instead, I had a map that took me nowhere.

Before I started worrying again, I pulled my laptop to me, opened a browser, and looked at our Thanksgiving break cottage, Hidden Bloom. As soon as I clicked the video walk-through of the place, its soundtrack filled my ears, a cover of "You Are My Sunshine."

It was the song sung at my mother's funeral, and whenever I'd heard it before Zayneb came into my life, I couldn't prevent my eyes from tearing up with the remembrance of Mom's casket, of the feeling my nine-year-old self carried into church that day: *I didn't get to say goodbye.*

But then I learned Zayneb associated the song with happiness. That that's how she'd learned it at school.

And the whole vibe slowly changed for me.

Spending a week with my sunbeam Zayneb was a de-stressor, the pure, organic, good-for-your-health kind.

An e-mail notification popped up on my screen as I imagined curling up with her on the cottage sofa, just staring at the perfection of her face before kissing all of it.

Re: Fixed Stars; and Grains of Sand proposal

Adam, thanks for the follow-up. The Map of Fixed Stars was quite a draw at the gallery. Your audio guidebook paired nicely.

Regarding your pitch of a Grains of Sand exhibit, our team agrees it doesn't fit into the vision we're developing

**at the moment. We'll make sure to reach out should it make
sense at a later date.**

I closed the message.

If you took a grain of sand and magnified it, it wasn't sand any longer.

It was an otherworldly object—sometimes snail-like, sometimes appearing as tiny starfish, sometimes resin lumps trapping minute creatures, or even jewel-like clear orbs, each different.

Each grain told a story of the land it lay on and circulated through, of spaces it had nestled into, ignored and stepped on.

It was a storehouse of memory, of every person who walked by it, of conversations, of revolutions.

I'd envisioned capturing the beauty of sand through an exhibition showing large-scale models of different grains from sample locations around the world, assembled in huge sand-timer cases.

But, again, no one wanted me to.

I closed my laptop abruptly, and even though the rest of the line "I hung my head and cried," from the song on the cottage website, got cut off, it aptly summed me up at the moment.

I put the laptop away and knelt by the map to shut the world out with my hands again, to try to place myself on that dusty path to Medina once more.

My breathing immediately slowed.

To be clear, I'm not saying it was simpler times back then—how could it have been when warriors from several tribes were after you as you fled your home seeking refuge?

I guess I just liked that the map in front of me presented the idea of a destination.

Somewhere to settle, to make a future.

I only had Zayneb as a destination of sorts.

But, like you couldn't capture a beam of sunlight, she also couldn't be held on to.

My arms came away empty every time we went our separate ways.

With a jolt, a breath drawn in abruptly, I came back from Medina to my twenty-first-century circumstances and saw reality: My arms were empty—*of anything.*

I had no future to present Zayneb with, no prospects, nothing to settle into.

And I didn't have a courageous heart to tell her this truth.

ARTIFACT THREE:
ZAYNEB'S GOLD GOOSE PENDANT
INTERPRETIVE LABEL:
FROM HIGH IN THE SKY, ALL WE SEE IS THE BIG PICTURE

AFTER SLIDING THE LAST HIJAB PIN INTO PLACE, I UNDID THE TOP button of my gray cardigan for some space to stuff the ends of my head scarf into. Then I stared at myself in the mirror.

I was a liar.

Not an outright liar but the highly sophisticated kind. The kind that let her person—Adam—think that *his* person—me, duplicitous me—always spoke to him from the bathroom at home (which he never asked about; like, why are you always in the bathroom?) when really I was at school.

Adam didn't know I practically lived at school now.

I slid my arms into backpack straps and took a deep breath before placing fingers on the handle of the door that opened onto a hallway leading to Sigmund Commons. This hallway was empty and quiet, like the bathroom—hence my choice of the spot for my early-morning chats with Adam—but when I left it, I'd step into the mouth of the beast.

Was I exaggerating?

Nope. I was actually *understating* the state of my life currently.

After a beautiful summer spent with Adam and our families, I now found myself on the most-wanted list on both campus media websites and was completely unhoused, with my anxiety pet, Bertha Fatima, taken away from me. And I absolutely hated roses.

The part of the campus where I spent the most time was covered in roses. The alum who bequeathed all her wealth to the university had been a rose connoisseur, so there were altars to her all over the place, but especially leading up to Sigmund Hall and its grounds. There were so many varieties that some even bloomed into late fall.

They taunted me, those roses. *Stop and smell us! Pause and admire us! Sit and bask under us!*

And that, there, was the real reason I hated roses.

They reminded me that my parents laid all my problems on the fact that I refused to "stop and smell the roses"—as they'd *literally* said aloud when they drove me up to campus at the start of the school year.

If they knew the things going on in my life currently, they'd say it was all because I was doing too much. Then they'd throw in something about roses again.

As if life were as simple as soft petals arising from a stick of sharp thorns.

Anyway, flowers were an easy nemesis when the real culprits in your life had faces.

Even if I didn't know what those faces looked like.

I had absolutely no idea who was feeding lies about me to two rival campus media outlets, both of which were accusing me of mismanaging the funds of a student club I'd led in my junior year of undergrad at the same college where I was now studying law. Each news site was trying to outdo the other at posting more insidious things about Zayneb Malik.

People saying things about me shouldn't technically be stressful because I didn't care what others thought of me.

But Professor Lincoln Mumford *did* care what others thought of me, and he held my future in his hands, so whenever I glimpsed my name in a new online notification, I couldn't quell the panic that arose.

Professor Mumford ran the externship program at the law school. He was the one who decided which students got placed with which international organizations in second-year law.

I wanted to be placed with the International Criminal Court at The Hague. That's why I chose this school in the first place—it's the only one in the country that has externships at The Hague.

My grandmother, Daadi, died in an illegal war when I was seventeen, and I wasn't over it. And I didn't think anyone should be over it.

There was no significant news coverage. She wasn't even named.

And I just know she would have been if she'd been a white woman who'd been bombed from the sky. That sounds horrible. But why does it seem to sound less horrible when it's brown or Black people who get killed like that?

As one of my favorite writers, Teju Cole, put it, Daadi was an "unmournable" body.

As I put it, I don't think anyone should be okay thinking some lives are not worth fighting for, that brown and Black people dying don't count as much.

Even on an international stage, such bombings were simply pooh-poohed away: *oops, collateral damage; oops, miscalculated drone target; oops, took out a whole wedding. Oops, "profound con-dolences" and "sincere apologies" for millions of innocent people killed while we try to rebrand imperialism.*

But now my chances to fight to change this status quo, to be accepted into the international human rights law stream at school, were dwindling.

I could just feel it.

Each time there was a new report about me looking shady, I imagined Professor Mumford clicking his tongue and erasing another letter of my name on the list of potential student placements at The Hague, like a reverse hangman game.

He'd think, *How can someone dishonest represent the university in such a prestigious international setting?*

And then, if the bad press involving me didn't cease, Professor Mumford's next thought would most probably be, *You know what, let me just completely erase the possibility of Zayneb Malik, International Human Rights Lawyer.*

But instead of the reports dying away, they were increasing.

Just this morning, I'd gotten messages from a writer asking for "my comments" on the newest article to be published. And then I could swear I'd seen some guy who looked like a wannabe reporter walking quickly behind me earlier, before I ducked into the bathroom. For my "cozy" call with Adam.

"Bismillah," I whispered almost on autopilot as I stepped into the hall clutching the goose pendant hanging on my necklace, a gift from Adam.

No one around.

I pivoted left abruptly and headed the opposite way from the Commons. It was a significant detour from the path to my morning class, but I could afford to be ten minutes late if it meant I'd avoid faces. The Commons would be full of faces with eyes that had seen too much of me in campus news.

Footsteps behind me. "Zayneb."

I turned. It was the guy I'd seen before. Green sweatshirt, jeans, short haircut, phone with plug-in mic held out—ready to record.

"*Campus Daily* is printing a story about the MSA's mismanagement of funds. Do you want to share your side in a feature with the *UpBeat*?"

"I'm going to class."

He shrugged, like he wasn't a student himself. "Can I record?"

"No, because I have nothing to say. I was MSA president two years ago. The mismanagement was from three years ago." *And that's why I'd become the subsequent Muslim Student Association president in the first place. To stop terrible people from ruining the world.*

"Yes, but you were on the admin team that year."

"I was on *that* admin team for exactly one week. I resigned."

I still had no idea who'd tipped them off that I'd been an admin—so briefly—that scandalous year.

That was the year the then-president began our first meeting swearing all of us on the "sacred council" to secrecy, *that we were a team no matter what, that what happens behind closed doors stays there, that we were chosen to make decisions for people who couldn't,* etc., etc.

I'd bolted the minute I heard that cultlike talk and worked hard to offer another way to run things, guaranteeing my election as president the following year.

But now someone was feeding lies about me to campus media. Who? And why?

"Permission to record?" The guy was relentless.

"Can't you go write about something else?"

"Everything breaking news is mine."

"So I'm breaking news?"

"Yup. And I'm trying to make news editor."

"How can it be breaking when it's about something years ago?"

"There's more to the story. Like the fact that you raised money yourself during your presidency."

"Yeah? It's called charity?"

"But was it authorized charity?" He looked at me triumphantly. "That's the breaking news campus senate is investigating *right now*. And you can tell me all about it."

While practically running back to the bathroom, I glanced behind to see if the guy was following, but he was just staring after me. Probably mentally composing a new headline: *Zayneb Malik, Hiding from the Truth.*

The peace I felt as soon as I stepped into this bathroom was incomparable. This was where I always spoke to Adam, so it had his peaceful aura.

Maybe that's why I considered this *my* bathroom.

That, and the little detail of not having a place—with a bathroom or even a bedroom—to call mine.

ARTIFACT FOUR:
ZAYNEB'S ATLAS BEETLE IN A
SPECIMEN DISPLAY BOX
INTERPRETIVE LABEL:
A SHELL KEEPS THE WORLD
AWAY FROM THE PRECIOUS STUFF

A COUPLE OF WEEKS AGO I'D LOST MY SPOT IN THE APARTMENT I'D been sharing with three other friends since my last year of undergrad. I'd thought I'd be able to hang on to the place through law school. I shared a room with Mariyah, the quietest person on the planet, totally dedicated to doing her master's in chemistry *and* baking fabulous desserts—the perfect person to have around while studying.

But then the rent went up, and I'd been too stressed (dealing with stupid stories about me online in the *Campus Daily* and its "edgy" rival, the *UpBeat*) to pass on all the notifications about the rent increase to Mom and Dad, too worried that if I spoke to them, they'd hear the mounting anxiety in my voice, and so the other girls ended up finding someone else to take my place.

So now, while I waited for a vacancy to open up somewhere, I was paying to sleep on a friend's couch that came with a terrible bathroom situation. I had to agree to not take showers at their place to be allowed "in."

A few times a week, I dragged myself to the campus gym to mime working out in front of the watchful employees in order to score access to showers. It was either put on that performance or walk around smelly.

Of course, with the way things were going in my life, it just had to be that no one at my new place was okay with a cat around. I had to ask my friend Layth, who worked in an animal sanctuary in Ecuador but was in the city for the month, to take care of Bertha Fatima. Petting her had been my one heart-rate stabilizer.

My heart was now in constant panic mode.

And if I didn't sound like Eeyore from Winnie-the-Pooh enough, there were also the weird tics that had started attacking my body that I kept telling myself I'd check with a doctor but I never got around to.

My right eyelid would start feeling a sensation, after which I'd imagine a sheet of paper, edge first, approaching it. At first slowly and then quickly, over and over. And then my eyelid would start flickering. To avoid a cut from the nonexistent paper.

Once I mastered getting over that tic, another one would start somewhere else on my body. And then at another spot.

I knew it was stress.

And that's why I couldn't tell my parents—about the tics, about the apartment, about the wild stories about me. They were of a common mind on the source of my stress; they both belonged to the Why Do You Have to Do So Much, Zayneb? school of thought.

They would lecture me on "life balance" and to "remember the important things in life," and then, yes, bring up those awful roses.

I couldn't even tell Adam everything.

I didn't want to make him sadder than he'd been when I'd brought up the club funds mismanagement allegations.

Plus, he was all the way across the ocean—maybe two oceans away, I don't know.

He was just too far to sink into, to ask to hold me, to ask to kiss my tics away.

So I decided to beetle, which in my head is a verb.

It's when you fortify your armor to face a world that doesn't let you step onto a level playing field if you're different from the dominant culture around you. Beetling meant looking straight into your eyes in the mirror and swallowing any expressions of sadness, pumping your arms (your pincers), and then fixing an *Excuse me, are you talking to me?* gaze on your face before stepping out into the world.

Adam knew I thought I was a beetle, but he didn't know why.

Before we got nikahfied, he and I had this mindless game we played where we would ask each other if we were one type of something in the world, which one would we be—what type of cookie, movie, bird, etc.—and it couldn't be what we *wanted* to be but what we actually were.

The game came out of Adam giving me a wooden goose when it was time for me to leave Doha after we fell for each other on my visit to the city. He carved it for me because I was protective of the Muslim ummah, like geese are of their communities, and he'd loved that.

After I flew back home, Adam and I began getting to know each other more. Tentatively.

Like by my asking him what candy, what TV show, what perfume he thought he was. Adam would ask me what tree, which mountain, what kind of cloud (I snort-laughed at that one), all natural stuff.

For flowers, I said I was a Venus flytrap, always ready to *bite* anyone who needed to be put into place. Adam said he was a succulent, if those were allowed to be called flowers, because he didn't need that much attention and liked being in the background.

"What about if you were an insect?" Adam had asked me after the flower question.

That was an easy one for me—a beetle. But I didn't tell him why, because I still wasn't sure how much he could know the truth of me yet.

I'd learned early I was like a beetle—that I wore a hard suit of armor, one I'd developed to stay strong in all situations, because my insides were so soft that if I or anyone examined them too long, we'd see it was all just mush. That I was squishable.

Almost every day I had to tell myself that I was worthy. Of being loved, respected, and living a beautiful life.

Because deep down in that mushy space inside me, maybe because of years of being seen as unwanted by the world outside my home, I didn't believe it.

Which is ironic for someone who wanted to fight for the worth of others.

I was really late for class now.

I had to go through the Commons.

I gritted my teeth and opened the bathroom door once more, but this time turned right and speed-walked.

"Where did the money that you fundraised go? Under your term as president?" Oh great, the *UpBeat* reporter had waited for me.

My phone buzzed. **You sure you're ok**

A text from Adam as I ran away again from this guy who believed he worked for CNN.

I'm great!

You had this I'm far away look

That's because I AM far away :)

"Was it to an international organization? When you promised to serve the student body?"

Sorry Hanna took over our call this morning

    Lollll

"Or did some of it go on a trip you took abroad this summer?"

There's nowhere to escape her

Except England, Squish. I couldn't help adding my secret nickname for Adam.

"When you traveled to Istanbul?"

We gotta keep that cottage a secret

    Hidden Bloom: hidden from Hanna

"Is it true you met with the leader of an international charity in Istanbul? Mahmoud Abdul-Lateef?"

I stopped texting and turned to his obnoxious green sweatshirt. "Who told you that?"

He just shrugged.

But I didn't need him to answer.

There was only one person who knew I'd met Mahmoud in Istanbul.

Murie.

The girl I was crashing with currently, the first friend I'd made at law school.

ARTIFACT FIVE:
ADAM'S ONE QATARI RIYAL
INTERPRETIVE LABEL:
THERE'S SAFETY IN NOT DIGGING TOO DEEPLY
INTO THINGS

Hanna held out a big envelope. "You're the only one who hasn't paid up, Adam, and the race starts in fifteen minutes."

I put a hand in the back pocket of my pants to touch—and not get out—my wallet. "How much did I say again?"

"One hundred and fifty riyals." She pushed in the sides of the envelope with her fingers so that it made a gaping mouth, awaiting my contribution. "And thank you, sir, for such a generous pledge for fighting the extinction of precious species!"

"Oops, is it okay if I give it to you on the way home? I don't have that much on me right now." I'd have to stop by the bank. And take out forty dollars to cover that amount in Qatari riyals. Which meant I'd have less than one hundred dollars to my name.

But then again, giving charity doesn't decrease wealth according to Islamic tradition, so I should be good.

As long as I didn't touch my bank account again.

And Dad didn't find out.

Because then he'd worry and replenish my account and "take care" of me, forever, perhaps—which would prevent me from ever moving forward to Zayneb.

Dad can never find out I've got nothing.

I looked up at him, wearing track pants and T-shirt, with a bullhorn in his hand. It was the weekend, and he didn't need to be in his regular headmaster-of-an-international-school mode, sans suit, but for Hanna, he'd do anything.

We were at the Corniche, the boardwalk on the waterfront along Doha Bay that stretches for seven kilometers, five of which were going to be run today by a group of students from Doha International School, Dad's school, to raise money for the World Wildlife Fund. Hanna helped organize it because animals were her number one passion.

We'd been "training" for it for the last month or so, with Hanna and Dad running, and me walking, with some attempts to jog a bit on the cooler evenings. Hanna had printed out and presented me with a bunch of articles that stated that supervised running and other cardio exercises were good for MS patients; it was compelling reading, but I didn't know just how many of those patients cited in the reports actually lived in a hot country like Qatar. Heat exacerbates MS symptoms, so I avoided going out during the day until the end of November, when temperatures began dropping.

The feeling of pins and needles attacking my legs if I walked longer than fifteen minutes in hot weather wasn't something I looked forward to.

I knew I'd have to soon move away from Qatar for more optimal conditions.

Chicago always stood out in my mind as a potential home.

But that would mean broaching the topic with Zayneb. Again.

The last time we'd talked about it, it hadn't gone the way I'd envisioned.

It was right before we departed from each other this summer

in Istanbul, her to take the flight back to Chicago, while I waited another hour for mine to Doha.

We'd been seated by her gate, my left arm around her as she leaned against me and scrolled through her e-mails, adding things to her to-do app. She was starting school a week after returning from our Istanbul trip, so the list was long.

"Yessss! Mariyah says the landlord's okay with Bertha Fatima staying with me in the apartment!" She tipped her head back to catch my eyes. "Our baby! She misses you so much!"

Bertha Fatima had been my cat when I was in Ottawa briefly in the spring before she became Zayneb's. I missed her, too. "Maybe it's time for us three to reunite?"

"How? We can't take her to England with us for Thanksgiving. Hanna will have a breakdown. You know what she thinks about the trauma of flying pets."

When Zayneb took the cat, Hanna had insisted that Zayneb *drive* Bertha Fatima from Ottawa to her parents' home in Indiana. Zayneb had quickly complied, in part due to the deluge of documents Hanna had e-mailed detailing all sorts of nightmarish scenarios involving animals and airplanes.

Zayneb said it took weeks for the images of gaunt cats lost in airports to leave her brain.

"No, I mean what if I come to Chicago?" I clarified now. I wanted to actually say, *What if I move to Chicago?* but then she'd sit up abruptly and say, *Why? Is everything okay, Adam? Everything okay with work? Your projects going well?*

Doha was my base for making the art I showed throughout the Middle East. It made sense for me to stay there.

"Chicago for a visit?" She did sit up to twist herself to look at me. "After England?"

I nodded. Then added in a tentative voice to gauge her reaction, "Or, even before?"

"What do you mean? Don't you have projects to work on?" She pulled on one end of her hijab to let it fall in front of her shirt and then secured it tighter under her chin before flipping the end back behind her. Her trademark *I'm processing what you just told me* move. "What about the *Fixed Stars* exhibit? I thought that was due soon?"

"Hey, are you saying I can't take time off for my family? Bertha Fatima hasn't seen me in months now." How Zayneb kept track of my project due dates on top of her own deadlines was beyond me. "She'll forget what her own dad looks like."

"Not the way you FaceTime her incessantly." Zayneb laughed, which was a win, which meant she'd moved on from her previous worry—*why would Adam want to come to Chicago?*

But then she began to frown. "My parents will be like, why are you and Adam getting together beyond holidays? They'll think it's too much."

I tried not to show how that gutted me, but my shoulders and eyes and ends of my mouth have minds of their own and totally betrayed me.

"Oh no, Adam, I'm so sorry!" Her eyes, those beautiful eyes I wanted to look at always but especially whenever I felt scared, like right now, immediately filled with tears, and she reached out to hug me. "I didn't realize how that would sound!"

I let her cuddle into me but then drew away to shake my head and shoot her a small, mischievous smile. "No, it's okay. A combo of Bertha Fatima *and* me *is* too much. We'd drive you up the wall."

"You'd never." She put her head back on my chest. "But yeah, it's better for both of us—I mean all three of us—to focus on things we need to get done. Before we *really* move in together."

I tucked in a curl of hair that had crept out of her hijab for her. "And that would be when Bertha Fatima is . . . how old?"

I tried not to hold my breath as I waited, hoping she wouldn't say *three years older, when I'm done with law school.*

"When our baby is seven years old, insha'Allah."

Our Bertha Fatima was currently four.

The kids and some of their family members taking part in the World Wildlife Fund race ran as soon as Dad sounded the bull-horn, with Hanna taking off even faster—first, running backward to encourage everyone following. Dad joined at the rear, and then there was me, walking behind them, trying hard not to think about Zayneb and Bertha Fatima and the fact that I was already lagging way behind in this race, and others, too. Like the one where I get to the finish line of being with Zayneb for good.

Whenever I felt down, I used to be able to switch to seeing the good in every situation—like right now the way the waters of Doha Bay moved rhythmically in soothing waves. Reminding me that with hardship comes ease, as promised in the deen.

Reminding me that the hard parts of life ebb and flow, that someone will commission something from me any minute now, that I wasn't forgotten in the art world on this side of the globe, that I'd see Zayneb soon, that I could then push away this sadness growing in me—without having her ear to whisper-deposit it into when the day was done, when it got too much to hold.

But today I couldn't see the ebb and flow.

I just saw that I'd be with Zayneb for only a week, and I'd never ruin that restful, happy week for her with my problems.

I saw that she couldn't help carry them when her plate was full, when our vacation was to provide her with space to set her load down for a bit.

So I just saw that I was alone and that the beautiful horizon across the water was far away and that there were no current plans to build a bridge for me to tentatively cross the divide, into her—hopefully—open arms in Chicago.

ARTIFACT SIX: ZAYNEB'S PAPER SNOWFLAKE
INTERPRETIVE LABEL: *SPLIT-SECOND DECISIONS CAN REVEAL BEAUTY . . .AND STRIFE*

I WAITED FOR MURIE ON THE COUCH. WELL, IN MY SLEEPING BAG. Which I was only allowed to spread on the couch after ten thirty p.m. to stake my claim on it as a sleeping space, in case the other three girls wanted to sit and enjoy the couch before then.

So now it was 10:40 p.m. on Thursday, and no one was even in the apartment.

I just had two questions for Murie when she decided to show up.

1. Murie, did you tell campus media that I met Mahmoud from that charity in Istanbul?

2. How could you?

A part of my brain tried to intrude on this plan to grill Murie, saying, *Slow down; think things through. What if she gets mad* and then you don't have any place to stay near campus? *What if then you have to go* out there *to find an overpriced apartment from which you'll have to pay to commute to school every day?*

I squashed that pip-squeaky voice because I just wanted to see Murie's face when I asked those questions.

Murie was currently campaigning for student government, for the position of treasurer. It wasn't really campaigning, because it was an uncontested race, but she still wanted to make a splash.

She had her eyes on an entry-level position at a huge corporate law firm in town, Bertram & Benedict, and she'd told me that after studying the students who went on to work there, she saw that serving on student government was a common denominator. "I'm going to start from year one!" she'd said.

Lucky for her that no one else was running for treasurer this year.

There were a lot of positive write-ups about her on both campus news sites, and when I looked up who was writing all about her in the *UpBeat*, I discovered it was the green-sweatshirt guy. His name was Tyler Hunt.

That's when it started to make sense.

She must have been answering his questions about me, too. Because he was on the *Zayneb Malik, Scoundrel* beat as well.

The side of my right eyelid started flinching, the precursor for the tics soon to invade my face.

I sighed and picked up the huge tri-fold project board that served as my "cubicle space" designator when I studied at the apartment kitchen table and propped it on my stomach now. Along with a suitcase with my clothes, and a big crate holding some of my course textbooks and readings, it was the only thing that made the place feel like home for me.

The board was covered on the outside in Qur'anic verses and Hadiths and on the inside with inspirational sayings and quotes I'd collected over the years. They were glued onto a background made up of big paper snowflakes that I'd cut out for a fifth-grade project on Wilson Bentley, the pioneering photographer of snowflakes. It was the first A-plus I'd ever received after a string of bad grades from the moment I entered school (*Zayneb is a loud child who moves from one task to another without paying attention* was a common comment on report cards), so the project board had a special place in my heart.

The interior of the board also had a big precious photo of Adam in a bow tie after the opening of his first art installation in North America, in his hometown of Ottawa, smiling while holding Bertha Fatima, also in a bow tie.

I now lay this beautiful thing on my face and breathed it in, trying to still the tics.

The door to the apartment opened. A giggle from Sasha, one of my roommates, followed by a laugh, a male one. "The couch?" he asked.

"Yup," Sasha giggled.

I sat up, holding the board in front of my face to cover the fact I didn't have a hijab on while a strange man was present.

Sasha let out a yelp even though I waved hello high above the board. "Oh my god! Zayneb!"

"Sorry, just didn't want you guys sitting on me." I turned the board to face her before lying down again. The back of the board said stuff like *AND SEEK HELP THROUGH PATIENCE AND PRAYER* and *CALL UPON ME AND I WILL ANSWER* and *WHOEVER DOES AN ATOM'S WEIGHT OF GOOD WILL SEE IT* and *IF THE DAY OF JUDGMENT ERUPTS WHILE YOU ARE PLANTING A SAPLING, CARRY ON AND PLANT IT* in big black letters, and I just knew it was killing the vibe for Sasha and her friend.

Which made me smile behind the project board because I'm mean like that.

"Is it already ten thirty?" Sasha's voice sounded disappointed.

Really? She was just going to stand there making me feel bad for being on my rented couch?

"Ten forty-five now," I pointed out.

"My room's a mess," she whined.

And I have no room. And I'm paying for this couch.

"I didn't know you guys had a new roommate?" The guy's voice sounded deflated, like my project board was getting to him. I smiled bigger.

"She's crashing here until she finds a place," Sasha said, all the giggles gone now. "Which is supposed to be by the end of November, right?"

I sat up again. "Hopefully. But also, I'll be away the week of Thanksgiving, so you can party on the couch all you want."

Ugh. Actually, I didn't want them *partying* on it. It was, after all, my bed.

"Is there a reason she has that Bible board on her face?" the guy asked.

"I observe hijab and you're a guy and I'm supposed to know when guys are coming into the apartment."

"Well, excuse us for invading your privacy," Sasha said. "Let's go, Lars."

"But we can't go to my place—the guys are watching a game," Lars moaned.

"Let's just hang outside."

"Why can't we just hang out on that other chair there?"

Oh wow, Lars was an asshole.

"Because she's on the couch."

"Yeah, and she's not on the chair."

I heard him shuffling to the armchair, Sasha following. Were they drunk? Partially?

I shifted and lay on my side with the board facing them on the chair. I lifted the board up higher so that the final big Qur'anic saying, *AND YOUR LORD IS EVER-SEEING*, was also visible.

I suspect their backs were to it, because all I heard were smacking noises. I squished the two folded sides of the board into my ears and willed sleep.

Lately, even though I was living with people, I felt so unbelievably lonely.

I woke up the next morning to a horrific sight. Lars and Sasha were sleeping on the floor partially clothed.

I picked up my project board and wore it around my head lest Lars woke up. After picking out an actual head scarf from my suitcase and using the bathroom quickly, I prayed Fajr behind the couch, asking Allah to forgive me for the conditions I was living under, and for praying Fajr late, and then went to Murie's door.

"Yes?" Her voice was upbeat and chipper. She was part of the four a.m. club—extraordinary people who woke up at four a.m. "to conquer themselves before they conquered the world"—so she'd already been up for three hours now. I had no idea how she woke up that early when she went to sleep after midnight most days.

"It's me, Zayneb."

"Come in!" She opened the door herself. "You poor thing! I saw Sasha and Lars out there when I got in. I'm so sorry. Do you want me to talk to them?"

Did I?

No.

I didn't want Murie to talk to anyone.

I followed her into her bright, artfully minimalist room. It had a white bed over which an oak shelf held a neat array of plants, several with cascading leaves. A desk beside the bed had only an open journal and pen, and, opposite all that, a wall flush with white cabinetry hid all her things. She invited me to sit on her chair while she crossed her legs on the bed, the journal in her lap now.

Just like how her auburn bangs were long and neat but partially covered her eyes, Murie was part enigma, part open book.

She and I had become fast friends when we were the only two in our assigned one-L cohort who skipped orientation week activities involving alcohol—me because of Islam, her because of having a mother struggling with alcoholism. Over several bubble tea dates, she told me she'd toyed with becoming Muslim after seeing how it had transformed one of her previous boyfriends. And then we'd both gone on a perfectly synchronized rant, finishing each other's sentences, about all the Islamophobia in society; she understood a lot due to volunteering at a civil rights organization in high school.

I liked her right away because she was eye-on-the-prize oriented. She told me she'd known what she wanted to be since she was twelve years old, when she'd helped find the papers her bankrupt father needed to provide his lawyer with to go after the company he worked for. "I searched his devices, printed stuff, and got those papers in order, and I just knew I was meant to do this: bring order to disorder, showing the way forward to win, while getting paid."

I told her about finding out how Daadi had died, how it had set me on a course of righting things using systems in place, like the law, methodically. I told her that after deciding this, everything had become clear, like I would always know what to do.

Like when the Muslim Student Association had a corrupt leader, I knew I had to step in the year after and lead it ethically, by the rules. And how when I found out that the money the past MSA president had mismanaged was actually supposed to have been sent to a charity in the Middle East, I raised that amount and sent it on. And then I met the leader of that charity to get updates on his work when I was in Istanbul.

I had shared all this with Murie.

And now, in campus media, it was all coming out twisted. Like I'd sent the money to some terrorist organization.

Which was a blatant lie.

That was the enigma part of Murie: After we became friends, when I'd talk about these things, she'd listen without speaking and just absorb it all. No conversation, even when I'd seek out her opinions. And that felt like I was talking to a therapist, so I'd just keep going, and pretty soon she was stuffed with all my secrets; and then I realized she'd offered me none of her own.

I hadn't even known she was running for treasurer until I saw her face up on a banner, along with others in her slate. Her response had been "Oh, I didn't tell you? It's something I have to do to get into Bertram and Benedict. Remember my plan to land there starts in year one?"

I swiveled the chair to face her squarely now. "Murie, who told the *Daily* and the *UpBeat* about me meeting Mahmoud from Mercy for All in Istanbul?"

She stopped twirling her pen in her fingers, and I could see her eyes narrowing under those bangs. "How would I know?"

"Well, you're the only one here who knows about me meeting Mahmoud." I straightened my legs and crossed them at the ankles. I was ready to stay here as long as I needed to, to get the truth. "That's why I'm asking you."

"Are you trying to say *I* told them?" She lay her pen down in the middle of the journal and closed it.

We haven't even started learning how to cross-examine and conduct trials—that's next semester—but somehow I already knew that movement of hers was a sure giveaway that she wanted this conversation *closed*, like the journal. "I didn't say that. I'm just asking you how they'd know something I only told *you*."

"Again, how would I know?" She leaned her back into the wall and stared at me.

"Well, someone must have told them."

"They could have researched things."

"There's nowhere to research that I met Mahmoud." I tipped my head as though I was considering her carefully. "And you sure are giving a lot of breaking news about yourself to Tyler."

"Z, have you found a place for December?" Now she leaned forward. "I think the stress of not having a place of your own is getting to you. I can't imagine what it feels like to have Sasha and Lars going at it right under your eyes."

"Are you telling me to leave the apartment?"

"No, just reminding you of your promise you'd be out soon."

"Oh wow. I guess I hit a nerve then?" I stared right back at her. "The agreement was until I found a place."

"And you said you'd have a place for December." She raised her eyebrows. "Is there anything else? I have to change now, so I need my room?"

I stood up. "Must be nice, all the awesome press you're getting as a one-L student running for government. Uncontested."

"You have until December tenth to find something. Right before exam week." She got off her bed and opened her door. "You'll feel better when you have your own space, I promise."

I left her room without sharing my reply. *I'll feel better when I find out the truth.*

Then, because I didn't get the truth from her, I did something to shake her.

45

Standing right outside her room, I pulled my phone out and signed up to run for treasurer against her.

And I messaged Tyler, the green-sweatshirt guy, promising him my first interview if he promised to tone down his *Zayneb Malik, Scoundrel* pieces.

He responded right away.

I guess he was all about "the scoop," wherever it came from.

I stepped out of the apartment and opened my voice recorder app. As I walked, I told Adam what had just happened, without telling him what had just happened.

Basically, I collected all the things I wanted to share with him but couldn't share with him until we had time spread out like green fields in front of us, so much time that we could just talk in that open way when you know without a doubt that the person with you accepts and loves all of you.

I had so much collected on this voice recorder app since school started.

And I was going to share it all at Hidden Bloom.

ARTIFACT SEVEN: ADAM'S AJWA DATE SEED
INTERPRETIVE LABEL: CONVERSATIONS ARE THOUGHT SEEDS

WITH MY HAND ON THE RAILING, I GOT OFF THE BLEACHERS TO FIND a secluded spot. It was almost time for Zayneb to call, and I didn't want everyone watching the basketball game to also watch Zayneb.

She never observed hijab when we spoke and wouldn't appreciate a bunch of strangers seeing her like that.

On the court, where her team was huddled for a pep talk from the coach, Hanna looked over at me for a moment as I made my way down from the bleachers. I held my phone in the air. She gave me a thumbs-up.

Once upon a time, Hanna and I had played basketball together. I was the one who'd taught her to love the game.

Now, other than shooting baskets with her in front of our house occasionally, I didn't have anything else to do with her favorite sport. She'd become so good that she played in the junior Doha team run by the Aspire Club.

Zayneb and I wanted to get her NBA tickets when she next came with me to visit Zayneb in the States. When I brought that up as an idea, Hanna had said, "But would it be at Madison Square Garden? The mecca of basketball? That's where I want to go."

We'd promised to take her to the "mecca of basketball" one day.

I ducked under the bleachers and waited for Zayneb to Face-Time.

After waiting ten minutes, I called her.

It rang and rang.

I tried a few more times and then went back to my seat to watch Hanna play the rest of her game.

Zayneb sometimes missed our chat sessions, but she'd always text before or right after explaining herself. This time, though, there was nothing.

I looked at her social media to see if she'd shared anything new.

I'm running for treasurer! was in her Instagram stories above a picture of her posted by the *Campus Daily*, her campus news site. Under a dark green scarf—one of her campus colors—her smile was big and confident.

I clicked the post and read the caption: *Former student club president accused of mismanaging funds, Zayneb Malik, now running for treasurer.*

Yikes, why did they have to include *that* under a candidate announcement post?

I scrolled the comments, eyes growing wide in disbelief as I saw there were more people piling on Zayneb than wishing her well.

I closed the app, my heart sinking for my Zayby.

When we got home, Hanna exited the car and looked from me to the basketball rim hanging off the carport. "Around the world?"

I nodded.

We played until we both won a few rounds each, and, as I leaned on the car to watch Hanna dribble the ball to the back of the carport to put it away, I noticed Dad was outside, the front door open behind him.

"Adam, that was pretty good." He looked impressed.

I laughed. "It's just ball."

"Still." He swung the door open wider, and I followed him into the house. "I'm just happy to see you feeling so good."

"Yeah, well, it's a remission period." I kept it short. I don't know why, but I still wasn't comfortable talking about my MS too much with Dad.

Actually, I did know why: Mom had had MS, and her experience with the disease had been a quickening of attacks before she passed away.

Anything that involved me giving Dad a status update on my MS, especially if it was a worsening period, always made me anxious. Because I knew it would make *him* anxious.

But I figured I shouldn't be so closed when I was feeling well. I stopped myself at the foot of the stairs and turned to Dad, who was making his way to his office at the end of main hallway. "I *am* feeling good," I called out. "Really good."

He turned around, his face immediately filling with joy. "And just in time for your trip."

Hanna, who had come in and begun running up the stairs for her usual shower after basketball, stopped mid-step at the word "trip." "What trip? Who's going on a trip?"

I tried not to groan. I'd been attempting to keep news of our getaway *away* from Hanna until the last second.

Dad looked at me and made an *oops* face before pivoting toward his office.

"No one." I had to go to the workroom, to my map. To shake off Hanna.

"No, tell me. Are you and Zayneb going somewhere? She said she didn't have time at Thanksgiving." She followed me up the stairs. "You guys just went to Istanbul in the summer. Not fair."

"And you just did Umrah in the summer. Not fair."

"That's not the same. That was an act of worship. Not this secret place you're going to with Zayneb."

"Hanna, that's enough." Dad was back, now at the bottom of the stairs, his face stern—well, as stern as he could get it to be when he was staring at Hanna. "Go take your shower, and then you have to prep for your Qur'an class online. Don't be late."

Hanna stomped off to the bathroom, and I exchanged glances with Dad. Then we both took off to our respective, peaceful work spaces.

I'd texted Zayneb several times and got no reply.

She was probably busy because she was running for this new position, treasurer—something I'd known nothing about until seeing her post it.

I took a seat on my desk chair and stared at my phone. I hoped she was okay.

Couldn't she have called me to let me know this was happening, that people were trying to wreck her chances as soon as she threw her hat in the ring?

I could have helped her. Supported her emotionally, I mean.

Was I feeling bad because she wasn't calling me back or because she didn't tell me or because I couldn't really save her from the trouble that always seemed to follow her because of her bravery?

It could also be because I felt left behind.

I always knew that life with Zayneb would be like this. Her running ahead, trying this, trying that. Me, constantly catching up on her adventures.

I wanted her to do all the things she wanted to. It made me

happy to see her all consumed and glowing with purpose.

But now, knowing that she was getting busier when I had literally nothing to do was opening some kind of gap in me. And I kept wanting to fill it with . . . *her*.

Which was cringey.

She'd run away from me if she saw how much I wanted her, how she was the only thing going on in my life.

Even the pages of the sketchbooks here on my desk lay empty now.

I needed to find something else. If not a job, some other thing to take me to a job. Because sitting here wondering what Zayneb was doing wasn't taking me anywhere.

I abruptly swiveled in the desk chair and rolled myself to the worktable.

When in turmoil, make something.

Leaning forward, I dribbled more sand on the wide strip of glue-tape I'd contour-cut and pasted on the shore of the Red Sea, about fifty miles from Mecca on my map.

There was a knock on the door.

"Yes?" I called out hesitantly, hoping it wasn't Hanna, mid-shower, dripping wet, asking about my trip again. I wouldn't put it past her.

"Can I come in?" Dad.

He opened the door once I answered in the affirmative. "I wanted to watch," he said, pulling Hanna's old chair close to the worktable.

I nodded. "Maybe you can tell me if this part makes sense. The amount of date trees I've placed close to Medina." I pointed at the palms I'd assembled in parts of the city. They each had small clusters of dates I'd made from rolling the tiniest bits of clay—all made on Steady Hand Days, when hand tremors didn't show up to make everyday tasks challenging, let alone delicate art projects.

It was a good date harvest according to my map, which meant there had been lots of Steady Hand Days lately.

"Looks great to me. It's a desert oasis city, so yes, lush back then too according to historical sources. And its dates—ahhh, there's nothing like them. Remember the ones we brought back?" Dad closed his eyes after saying that, like he could still taste them.

I nodded again, thinking of the small dark ones, Ajwa, that were my favorite from the varieties Dad had brought back from Umrah this summer. I'd saved a few pits to plant one day.

He was quiet for a bit, watching me brush off the excess sand from the edge of the Red Sea. "I was thinking."

"Yeah?"

"Since you're feeling so good, what about Umrah?" He waited until I looked at him before going on. "The Umrah trip I'd promised you and Zayneb as a nikah gift?"

"That we're doing next year?"

He was quiet at that. "Well, I was thinking this year."

"When? I'm going to visit Zayneb's family at winter break, remember?"

"I was thinking the week of Thanksgiving break."

I stopped sweeping sand, my brush paused in the air. "But we're going to that cottage near London, the one I found for Zayneb."

"Yes, I know. I meant if you hadn't paid for it yet." Dad sat back, his hands in his pockets. He looked like he was in a very cool ad—in a khaki thawb, his typical weekend wear, sitting on a super-shaggy bright pink chair, his expression uncertain. "Shaykh Murtaza, remember Uncle Murtaza from London? He's leading an Umrah group leaving at the beginning of that week."

I resumed brushing sand away. I didn't know how to think about what Dad had just asked me.

Umrah instead of the cottage?

"I'm not sure what Zayneb will think of this," I said, knowing she'd been looking forward to a cozy time together. *I'd* been looking forward to being with Zayneb, wherever she was.

"The weather in Mecca and Medina will be tolerable. And you're feeling good. And Shaykh Murtaza knows about your MS. And he's already promised me they would make sure everything would be accessible and planned properly."

"You already talked to him? As if I'm coming?" I knew the irritation showed in my voice. "I don't know if Zayneb will be okay with this change of plans."

"Well, I wanted to check if it was viable before I spoke to you," Dad said, softening his voice. "Don't you want to be there with Zayneb when you're strong? She'll probably feel the same way."

I set the tin I'd collected all the extra sand in on the table. And then looked at Dad. He was in the same cool-ad pose, but this time his face looked even more uncertain. Maybe bordering on *sad*.

Uh-oh. Was he remembering Mom?

Neither of them was Muslim when she was alive, so there was no way he was thinking of having gone on Umrah with her.

"I just don't know how you'll feel next year. I just think you'll have the best experience when you're feeling your best." Now he definitely looked melancholy. "You know how there can be a wave of symptoms suddenly. At the moment, the sea is calm."

Ah, so he *was* thinking of Mom.

I looked at the map. I always took it for granted I'd visit Mecca and Medina eventually, mainly because Dad had promised the trip to me and Zayneb the day we got our nikah done, when we'd become a couple, and Dad keeps his promises.

But yes, I also didn't know what state my health would be in when we were actually ready for him to fulfill his gift. "I've only paid the deposit on the cottage, but it's refundable if I cancel in time. But that trip is something we've been looking forward to."

"I'm not going to pressure you. If you're inclined toward taking me up on my offer, try to let me know your thoughts this weekend. Shaykh Murtaza says he'll need to know by Monday whether you're interested. He can expedite everything for you and Zayneb." Dad got up from the chair and went to the door. "Talk it over with her. I'm sure she'll be on board for your health."

Before he closed the door, I asked him to turn off the lights, my preferred ambiance to process things.

I wanted to sit and think without anything cluttering my thoughts.

I wanted to explore why this idea of Dad's—a beautiful idea—was creating disquiet in me.

But, as if on cue to support Dad, the glow-in-the-dark sand lit up on the Hijrah map, showing the route from Mecca to Medina.

My eyes were immediately drawn to the path revealed.

The more I stared at it, the more a realization lit up inside me, too.

Maybe, in trying to get a commission, I'd been focusing on the wrong thing all this time.

Maybe I need to explore everything I can still do while I have the chance.

I had to seize Dad's offer while I could use my own legs to walk around the Kaaba in gratitude.

I was sure once I explained this to Zayneb, she'd understand.

Another thought sprouted in my head: Going on Umrah was better than putting all my hopes in Zayneb rescuing me from falling into this hole growing inside me. Which would be the state of things at the cottage—where she'd temporarily fill the void, but then, when we went our separate ways again, it would just reopen.

ARTIFACT EIGHT: ZAYNEB'S BROWN KNIT SCARF
INTERPRETIVE LABEL: WE OFTEN FIND FRIENDS
WHEN WE'RE NOT LOOKING FOR THEM

SOMEHOW MY OLDER SISTER, SADIA, ALWAYS SHOWED UP WHEN I
needed her calm serenity. She didn't even know about my living-
on-a-couch situation (and I would never tell her as it would definitely leak to my parents, who thought I had an actual room while
I was waiting for a new apartment opportunity to open up), but
she'd still made sure to get a hotel room with two double beds
when she came up to Chicago for a shopping weekend.

So for one night, I'd get to sleep on a real bed.

And get away from Murie's deathly stares. Ever since she found
out that her run for student government was no longer uncontested, she'd iced me out completely, and I welcomed the freeze
with a smile on my face.

I loved Sadia so much—though not so much when we were
growing up and everybody always pointed out what an obedient
oldest sibling she was. But ever since she helped broker the possibility of me and Adam in Mom and Dad's eyes, of the A-and-Z
coupledom making sense, I'd become a huge Sadia fan.

At every chance she got, she'd pointed out amazing things
about Adam, so much so that Mom and Dad started to repeat
them, and then, voila, just like that, earlier this year, Dad sug-

gested we should be getting our nikah done so we could actually hang around each other like a real couple.

Paying attention to how Sadia had supported me made me realize how big her heart was and how she hadn't been "the obedient child" to be irksome but because she loved our parents and wanted them to be happy—like she loved me. (I loved our parents too, but it wasn't in a blanket *yes, sir, right away, sir!* way. If that had been the case, I wouldn't have been trying to get into international human rights law right now and would have *yes, sir, right away, sir!ed* their suggestion to study real estate law instead.)

Sadia had helped negotiate my happily-ever-after like it was her own.

The wedding itself was going to be once I was done with law school. Then, insha'Allah, we'd find a place and move in together.

Because we were so far apart, Adam and I had decided we'd set up getaway visits during every break. Some of them would be with our families, but a lot of them would be just us.

Like the Hidden Bloom Cottage over Thanksgiving week.

Which was why I was at a Macy's sale this Saturday morning with Sadia. I wanted to make sure I got some nice warm outfits for November in England.

Nice warm outfits under which I'd have on cool underwear for Adam's eyes only.

(But that part of the shopping I'd do when Sadia wasn't hovering around.)

"What about a hat? It might get too cold just for a hijab, and these are cute." Sadia held up a beanie-style knit hat in mustard yellow.

"Too loud." I spotted the scarves sales rack. "I want a big *scarf* scarf. Like those blanket ones."

"I'm not into the hijab-with-a-scarf thing. It's too much layering for my taste."

"But my taste is all cuddly and cashmere, so envelop me in the biggest scarf ever!" I couldn't wait for the England trip. The cottage description was my vision of heaven: hygge on overdrive. I visited the Hidden Bloom Cottage website whenever I wanted to deep-breathe. I reached into my pocket for my phone now to show the cottage to Sadia again.

Oh. Right. Sadia's phone-free injunction.

She'd arrived on Friday night, whisked me away to her hotel, and made us lock our phones in the hotel safe.

She was a therapist and insisted that optimal socializing in person required phone-free hands.

Yup, she was scary sometimes.

"This is the biggest thing here." Sadia emerged from an aisle. "But it's not on sale."

She was holding a brown scarf so big and so soft that even from afar, I already felt enveloped in its embrace.

"That's my scarf. I feel like I've known her all my life. I feel like we're getting reunited." I almost stumbled over my own feet in my attempt to run over and snuggle into the scarf. Once its arms were around me, I sighed. "Home. My friend. Her name is Scarfy."

"Oh wow, it's real cashmere. But, again, it's not on sale." Sadia glanced at the price tag. "This is too much, Zu-zu."

"Don't show me the price." I turned away and closed my eyes to imagine this scarf hugging my neck and shoulders in conjunction with Adam's arms draping over me (one arm would be around my back, and his other would be across my front so that his hands met and clasped each other perfectly at my waist) as we walked the crisp cool streets in Sussex and, also, as we walked the old-growth forests filled with crisp, cool leaves, because I was pretty sure Adam would want to go into nature. I wouldn't even need a light jacket with this scarf *and* Adam. I turned back to Sadia. "It can be in place of a jacket. Remember I was supposed to get a fall jacket, too?"

"How is that a jacket?" Sometimes Sadia acted like she was eighty.

Which was precisely the reason I succumbed to acting like a little kid around her.

"Haven't you heard of doing things with blanket scarves?" I reached for my phone again. "Oh, great, I can't even show you all the magic you can do with big scarves. Because I have no phone."

Adam.

I was supposed to call Adam this morning!

"We need to get back to the hotel, Sadia. I missed my call with Adam." I began heading to the cash registers but then stopped because Sadia hadn't moved. "Can we? Go?"

"But we're not done."

"But Adam—"

"He'll understand. Zu-zu, you only have two and a half weeks left until your trip." Sadia was at the coats rack already like the excellent mom she's going to be one day. "Here are some nice, warm jackets."

"Okay, then you explain to Adam that you jailed my phone." I took my scarf friend off and lightly tied two corners together at each end, which made instant arm holes, and stuck my arms in. "See, a jacket."

I twirled for Sadia and the mirror on a post nearby. It looked good with my jeans. Add some nice boots and I was set.

"All right then, I'll buy it for you," Sadia said. "I've never seen you this excited about a boring scarf. It's kinda grandma-style."

"No, I'll buy it myself. It's the happiness I need right now." I took it off and added it to the sweaters I was going to try on in the dressing room. Which was right next to the lingerie section. "Let me try Scarfy with these tops I might get. Then meet you at the registers near where we came in?"

She nodded. "But I'm getting that scarf for you, Zu Zu. In return, you'd better send me a cute picture of you wearing it at the cottage."

Before I reconvened with Sadia, I snuck off to another register and paid for some little outfits to wear at Hidden Bloom, for just me and Adam.

Then I hid that bag beneath the clothes I was going to buy under Sadia's supervision at the other register.

Sometimes sisters—even adorably kind sisters—didn't need to know that you were planning a very sexy week with someone you hadn't kissed for months now.

The truth is, this was one of the major reasons Adam and I had getaways.

It's hard not being with each other when you'd waited all your life to be with one person only, but then when you found that one person, you had to stay away from each other for four long years due to being in different parts of the world and due to your parents not being totally in agreement that you made sense for each other, and then when it finally happened, when you finally came together for real, then you realized the logistics of your lives meant that you couldn't move in together or even see each other every weekend.

When the logistics of your lives meant that you saw each other only through a screen, when all you wanted to do was reach through that screen and stroke their arm, touch their face, snuggle into their chest, and melt into them, then you made sure that a huge chunk of your together time when you were *actually* together was spent exploring each other.

I just wanted to wear all the sexy clothes and stay hidden with Adam in Hidden Bloom.

As soon as Sadia's car drove off, and I'd waved to her enough, I put my purchases down in front of the low-rise building that housed the apartment that housed my rental couch and sat down on the front stoop to power my phone back on. The streetlights were already on as it was past Maghrib.

"Zayneb!"

I glanced up. It was Ava, my third roommate, who I rarely saw but who was always trying to connect with me—while I tried to avoid her because I seriously couldn't handle another thing now, even if it was getting to know someone.

Only Ava would call to me from across the street a block away, where she'd just parked her car. That's how enthusiastic she acted whenever she saw me on campus somewhere.

She was practically never at the apartment as her parents lived in the suburbs and she often ended up staying there after weekends, driving into the city for school on most weekdays, for weeks at a time.

She must be incredibly privileged, because she'd spent so much time decorating her room in a dark academia style—all dark wood furniture, moody paint, and tons of books and cute little antiques—to have just been, like, buh-bye to the place.

I loved her room's aesthetic.

I was secretly praying that she realized she didn't need a bedroom and would let it go—to me.

Then maybe I'd be her friend.

Ugh, I'm so mean. And such a user. In guilt, I looked up at her and smiled and waved before glancing down at my phone. Seven messages and missed calls from Adam.

I forgot to tell him Sadia was spending the day with me. I needed to call him back.

"Do you have a couple minutes? To catch a quick coffee?" Still breathing heavily from sprinting over, Ava took a seat beside me. Her curly ginger hair spilled to graze her shoulders from under her shearling bucket hat. "My class doesn't start until six."

"Actually, I'm about to make a call." I flashed my phone as some sort of evidence. Then I saw her face. It was splotchy and tearstained. "Is everything okay?"

She didn't reply. Then shook her head. "There's something I've been trying to talk to you about. But not here." She looked behind her at the building.

Following her gaze, I realized she was looking at our third-floor apartment window.

It was all so mysterious. "Okay."

"Finally," she said as soon as, with hot drinks in hand, we slid into our chairs at Houston, We Have a Problem, the café at the corner of our street. I placed my Macy's bags down by the wall under the window, unwound Scarfy (which Sadia had wrapped around my neck herself, while muttering "grandma"), and set it on the back of my chair. Ava kept her hat on and hugged herself into her sweater, her bowl-cup of tea steaming on the table in front of her. "I've been trying to talk to you for weeks now."

"But you're never home."

"That's what I want to talk to you about, actually."

I stirred a sugar cube into my mug of coffee, pretending to be intent on doing so, while silently saying a dua. *Please, Allah, let her say,* Can you take over my lease?

Even if Murie was going to be livid at the idea of me living there longer, this could be a transaction between me and Ava. I didn't need to involve Murie, didn't even need to see her around the apartment if I kept to my room. I looked up. "Did you want someone to take over your room?"

"Uh?" Ava, both hands around her cup as she lifted it to her lips, now paused the action. "Take over my room?"

"Yeah? Because you're never there?" I said encouragingly. I took a sip of my still-piping-hot coffee and burned my tongue but decided to not get too upset about it. *I just want Ava's room. I can suffer for it.* "If you need me to, I can take over your lease."

She put her steamy tea bowl back on the table. "No, no. I need my room."

"Oh." *Then why am I here when I could be talking to Adam right now?* I went back to stirring my coffee to cool it, willing Ava to get whatever she wanted to say out. "What's up, then?"

"It's about Lars. You know, Sasha's boyfriend?" Ava made a face.

Oh God. She was going to involve me in Dating Drama. Maybe Lars had been her boyfriend before? And she couldn't stand to see him around, with Sasha? "Yes, I recently met him. Sort of."

"He's part of a hate group. A well-known white supremacist one. He shares some terrible posts online."

"Just gross." I joined Ava in making a face. "I sensed asshole alert as soon as I heard him for the first time."

"The stuff I saw—Holocaust denial, horrific antisemitic conspiracy theories, Islamophobic cartoons—it's all vile. And whenever

I come back to our place, I'm always worried he's inside. I feel literally sick." She took off her hat and put it on the table and patted her hair down. "And when you moved in with us, I got more worried."

Without the shadow cast by the rim of her bucket hat, I noticed her round red glasses perfectly matched her hair. And that her eyes were earnest and frank. It was those little details that made me instantly move my radar closer to "she's all right" from "why does she want to talk to me?"

"Because I wear hijab?" I elaborated for her, partly because she was the type of conversationalist who was reflective and so chose her words carefully, and, by filling in for her, it helped move us—well, impatient me—along, and partly because I wanted her to know I saw her kindness. "And you were worried he'd act up? And take it out on me?"

"Yup. The first day he came over, he saw my Star of David necklace and made a comment. It just instantly put me on guard. And that's when I googled him." She began stirring her tea. "The next time Sasha invited him over, I was home, and I decided to take the mezuzah down from my bedroom door."

"Sorry, I don't know what that is. Something religious?"

"Yes, I had it outside my door. It has Jewish prayers in it."

"That's horrible. I'm so sorry, Ava." I was horrified and also disappointed in myself that I hadn't noticed anything. "How come I didn't even know this was happening under my nose? I guess I should have paid more attention."

"No, you come back to the apartment so late. And like you said, I'm never there." She raised her eyebrows and then gazed into her tea bowl as though she was seeking something in it. "Anyway, I just wanted to warn you."

"Is that why you're not there? At the apartment?" I held her gaze when she looked back up at me. "Is it easier to be at your parents'?"

She didn't say anything for a long moment, which answered my question.

I tried to put her at ease. "Because honestly, if that had been me who had noticed Lars was a bigot, and my parents lived nearby, I'd do the exact same thing."

"Yeah, okay, it's easier," she admitted. "I don't want it in my headspace. He started coming around more often, and it takes such a toll to deal with it. To even think about dealing with it takes a toll, you know? But I did report it to student safety."

I sat back, angry. And hurt for Ava, that she had to tiptoe around her own place and take precautions, *like literally not living in a space she paid for.*

And, I realized, I'd slept on the couch a few nights ago not realizing a white supremacist lay just a few feet away. "Ugh, we need to get him out of the apartment." I took a long sip of my coffee and looked through the café window at the dark streets. "Maybe with exams coming up, we can say nobody's allowed to bring people back to our place?"

"Sasha's name is the main one on the lease. She wouldn't agree to that."

"Does she know? About who she's with?"

"I'm pretty sure she doesn't know. I've never told her. She's kind of defensive about him. Once Murie made a comment about what a dick he was, not about his hate stuff but just other shit, and Sasha made it seem like it was just a hookup. Like she wasn't really into him. Because you know her dad is the head of a school board, right? She could never be linked with Lars seriously if she found out the truth."

"What about Murie? What does she think?"

"I didn't really get into it with her. She ran the free speech club in undergrad, and somehow I don't think she'd see things in the same light. She's a card-carrying libertarian." Ava glanced at her phone. "Oh shoot, I gotta run, my class is on the opposite side of campus and my books are in the apartment." She took an impressively long gulp of her tea and then set it down. "Let's talk again? Put your number in and I'll text you."

I took her phone, sent myself a text, and then leaned forward as she put on her hat and buttoned up her sweater. "Ava, it's not just you who has to deal with this. I'm in too, okay? Even if I don't see that Larsehole much, know that I'm working on dealing with him."

"Thanks, Zayneb."

"Well, thanks for giving me the heads-up."

She nodded and smiled at me before making her way to the door and then shot me another smile at the café entrance, and I thought, *As soon as I lost one friend, maybe Allah granted me another. Someone who actually thought about protecting me, not throwing me under the bus. Someone thoughtful and kind.*

I finished my coffee slowly and walked back to the front stoop to call someone else thoughtful and kind: Adam.

As the phone rang, I calculated the time difference.

Uh-oh, three a.m. now in Doha.

"Hello?" Adam, all groggy. "Zayneb, are you okay?"

"I'm so so sorry, Squish! For calling you so late and for missing our time. Sadia was here and you know her and phones." I felt guilty all of sudden, remembering restful sleep was important for managing his MS. "Sleep now, and we'll talk at our regular time tomorrow?"

"No, I'm glad you called." He cleared his throat. "I kept trying to reach you because . . . something exciting has come up."

"Really?" I stood up and hopped down one step, and started pacing, excited already. "I need happy news. Gimme, gimme."

"So remember how the cold is better for my MS? Like cooler weather?"

"Yeah?" I stopped walking. Was this about some new air-conditioning he's getting at his Dad's? Sometimes Adam told me the most boring news that he thought was unbelievably exciting.

"Well, remember my dad wanted to give us an Umrah trip as a wedding gift?"

"Yeah?" I started walking again. OMG, maybe Umrah at winter break? Oh, but wait, Adam was supposed to come spend the break with our families, including at my parents' house because my brother Mansoor and his wife Hodan were expecting their first child in early December.

"He wants to give it to us this year, insha'Allah. Our Umrah trip."

"But we're supposed to spend winter break at Springdale. Remember, Mansoor and Hodan are having their baby? We're going to be an aunt and uncle?"

"No, not at winter break."

"Then when?" I frowned. "I have no other breaks." There's a silence at the other end. "Squish? Adam?"

"My dad meant that on Thanksgiving break, we go on Umrah."

I took a moment to go over that in my mind. "Wait, how does that work? We go to Hidden Bloom for part of the week and then part of the week we go to Umrah? But that would be only like three days?"

"No, he meant . . . my dad meant that instead of staying in

England, we'd meet there and then go to Umrah with this tour group from London, led by a family friend, a Muslim scholar."

Now I was silent.

Adam let me be silent.

For a long time.

He didn't say *Zayneb? Zay-by?* his nickname for me, which was a play on "baby." He just waited.

I sat back down on the stoop and the shopping bags knocked over and a bag inside a bag fell out. I bent over and shoved the small bag quickly into the bigger one before its contents spilled all over the steps.

While thinking of Umrah, a religious pilgrimage to Mecca, I didn't want to look at the tiny, sexy clothes I'd purchased.

For a trip Adam didn't want to go on.

"Are you saying we should cancel Hidden Bloom for Umrah?"

My voice was flooded with waves upon waves of disappointments. And I didn't even care that they were swelling enough to crash against Adam's ears.

ARTIFACT NINE:
ADAM'S HAPPY FACE BALLOON, DEFLATED
INTERPRETIVE LABEL:
THINGS POP WHEN YOU DIG IN YOUR HEELS

WHY HAD IT FELT EXCITING WHEN DAD HAD LAID IT ALL OUT AT dinner last night? When I'd asked him for more information? And when Hanna had acted the part of a travel agent, pumped that Zayneb and I weren't going on a "secret trip" but one which Hanna herself had been on?

The way Dad had presented it had made me almost giddy, which I hadn't felt in a long time. Performing Umrah during daytime temperatures that were tolerable, ending in cool nights, the pilgrimage led by a kindly, deeply spiritual and thoughtful leader, who would personally make sure I was okay in terms of my health, with a group of young people around my and Zayneb's ages to spend the days with as we explored Mecca and Medina, two of the oldest, most visited places on earth . . .

It had sounded magical.

Now with Zayneb aghast on the phone, it actually sounded like a pin moving in slow motion to pop a big happy-faced balloon. And it felt like the remains of that limp, deflated balloon carcass lay plastered on my face as I tried to speak through it to reach Zayneb's heart.

"Dad meant—" I stopped. I kept hiding behind Dad.

But the truth was that I'd gone to bed last night with a happy-balloon smile on my face thinking about spending time with Zayneb in such a special place.

"I want to go," I said simply. "I want to go when I can still walk on my own. When I can even try to touch the Kaaba, maybe. When I'm feeling as good as I am today."

"Oh, yeah." Her voice was small but also a bit more energized sounding. "You're right."

There was a sigh attached at the end of her words, and I closed my eyes.

Was I holding Zayneb back? Because she had to mold her life around my needs sometimes? "Listen, Zayneb, I'm going to get some sleep now. Let's talk tomorrow."

I had to hang up because at that end of *my* words, there was a catch in my voice I couldn't deny. The emotions welling in me were at the point of spilling over.

When I woke up, I lay in bed for a long time trying to remember Zayneb. Like her actual presence. Like how, when she was around, it didn't matter where in the world I was; I felt like it was home.

I guess I was trying to remember this because, very recently, I'd started to feel more tense when I thought about talking to her. The opposite of home and safety and comfort.

It felt like something I'd potentially say could take her off her game. Which I didn't want to happen—when she already had to grapple with the first year of law school, the accusations of mismanaging funds, and now running for student government (which she hadn't mentioned to me yet).

It also felt like I couldn't share how stagnant I'd been feeling. How if she found out that I was at a standstill in my life right now, something inside her would loosen, and while she'd become quiet and try to be supportive, her eyes would lose that glean of contentment that they had whenever they turned to me.

And now, after our call, I was sure I'd upset her, added to her stress, with the news about changing plans from Hidden Bloom to Umrah.

So I stayed in bed thinking of how to reverse her emotional state so we could go back to being comfortable with each other.

But I also didn't want to change the Umrah plans.

Besides my physical state being more optimal now, there was also the fact that my spiritual state was the opposite of optimal.

I'd become worried about my job situation to the point I was scared I'd fall into despair soon—which was something Dad always warned me about. *A believer never despairs about the mercy of God.*

Maybe *I* could just go. Just me.

To Mecca and Medina. And then spend time with Zayneb later.

Because it felt like I was meant to go to Umrah at this time. That I was being invited to visit this most sacred place.

How could I say no?

For the rest of the day I helped Hanna with her homework, sat with Dad to go over the paperwork needed for Umrah, and worked on the Hijrah map while listening to one of my favorite craft podcasts.

And then, suddenly, it was time for my call with Zayneb.

Morning for her, evening for me.

I took my phone outside into the backyard to reduce the potential of anyone hearing us.

I was going to bring up the idea about splitting our vacation time.

Zayneb and I hadn't really fought before—just had occasional miscommunications that got cleared up pretty quickly—but in the state I was in right now, I was pretty sure I was going to dig in my heels.

I wanted my way. And I also didn't want her to change her feelings on my account. I wanted her to do whatever *she* wanted to do, to take care of things she needed to right now.

I wanted her to be happy.

But I wanted to be happy too.

"Assalamu alaikum, Squish." Her voice sounded solemn.

"Walaikum musalam. Ah, you're calling on the phone."

"Yeah."

"Why not FaceTime?"

"Oh sorry, I'm kind of a mess now and don't want you to see."

"I've seen you in every state, Zayneb."

"It's kind of noisy here at the apartment too, so I'm in the hall and have on my hijab so it's nothing special, you know?"

"What about the bathroom?"

"Someone's in it."

"Okay, well, I guess I won't see your face when I say something you might not like."

"Um. What do you mean."

"So, I love you. And I want you to not stress and to concentrate on all the things you have happening and all the studying you're supposed to be doing and taking care of yourself, so I understand that you're not up for Umrah at this time. But I'm going to go. Because I don't know if I'll be in this state of health next year."

"Why would I not like that?"

"Because I'm going to go. Insha'Allah."

"That makes me happy. I don't get why you'd think otherwise. Let's go."

"Even if you can't go, I'll be going." I couldn't help but say this part softly, to lessen the blow. "I think it's okay we split up on Thanksgiving break and do our own things. We're not always going to connect or agree on what we want to do and that's okay."

There was no sound from the other end.

When she spoke, it was with a muffled voice, and I knew her enough to recognize she was holding back tears. "But then who will make sure you're okay?"

She wanted to be there to help me.

Again, I got that squeeze in my gut as another truth announced itself: She saw herself as my caretaker.

That would essentially be the trip for her.

"Zayneb, the Umrah group that's going is comprised of some people I knew from the mosque while I was studying in London. They're my friends. And the leader knows my condition. I'll be okay."

"But, Adam." Her voice was breaking. "I'm sorry, but I can't talk now."

She hung up.

And even though there was a rip in my heart, I didn't feel like calling her back.

These last couple of months had shown me I actually had to "stand on my own two feet," as Zayneb's parents have always said, even if it was with exactly nothing in my hands.

I'd just raise those empty hands in prayers when I got to Mecca and ask Allah to provide for me as only He can.

Provide for me so that I wouldn't make Zayneb's life more difficult than it needed to be. I loved her too much for that.

ARTIFACT TEN: ZAYNEB'S ELECTION FLYER
INTERPRETIVE LABEL: STAND OUT OR STAND BACK. JUST DON'T STAND IN THE WAY

I HAD TO CONVINCE ADAM TO COME TO HIDDEN BLOOM WITH ME.

Which was hard to do when Mecca and Medina called him.

Was I being like Shaitan? To plot to take him off the Umrah route?

No, I was trying to be a good partner.

Adam going to Umrah without me felt painful. I needed to make sure he had everything he required on a trip that arduous. Because he didn't like to stress people, he wasn't always committed to ensuring his needs were met.

He couldn't go without me.

I'd be so worried.

And then there was the matter of him suggesting we split up for our own respective trips.

Which, I just knew in my gut, was the first step to rolling out lonely-couple syndrome, when you feel alone in a relationship— perhaps for the rest of our lives. When we each do our own things and have nothing in common.

Which I'd read could happen to opposites-together couples.

A life of searing separateness.

Whenever I came near to thinking of that possibility, I immediately teared up.

Oh no, we were *absolutely* going on a trip *together* at Thanksgiving break.

I was going to make sure of it.

But before I could put all my efforts into convincing Adam, I had to get things off my plate.

I had to shake up Murie.

The first time I saw Sigmund Commons, I wanted to move into it. A huge circular domed room, its dark walls lined with arched entrances to different areas of campus, with paths crisscrossing from one hall entrance to another, creating several slice-of-pie-shaped spaces in between that were filled with chairs gathered around low tables, it was always humming with life. At any given moment there were crowds of students in conversation with one another, or taking their places at the edges of the paths to deliver speeches, rap, perform comedy routines, or canvass for votes. To just engage with one another.

Like I was today.

I'd roped my old roommate Mariyah and another former roommate, Claire, into handing out postcards that said *Zayneb Malik for Treasurer* on one side with my credentials on the other. It felt kind of middle-schoolish, but I needed to be in people's faces to present the real me—in case they'd heard of the campus-media me.

Basically, after public humiliation, I needed to hit the ground running with my head scarf fluttering proudly in the wind behind me. "Still I Rise," like Maya Angelou poetically proclaimed.

That would be the new narrative I'd fashion.

I adjusted my burnt-orange jersey hijab now before walking up to a table of four students who were sharing a container of fries and talking. They appeared to be in a good mood.

"Hi, guys. I'd just like to introduce myself. Zayneb Malik, running for treasurer." I tried to hand the postcards out, but only one person took theirs, so I left the rest on the table. "I'm open to and available for any questions you may have!"

"The question is, are *we* available?" said one of them, repositioning their baseball cap.

I laughed. "Good point. My socials are on the card, so feel free to say hello and ask any question that may arise before the election in three weeks!"

"Oh! Oh! I have a question!" the person who took my card said, waving their hands in the air like we were in second grade. "Did you or did you not steal funds from your club?"

They all laughed.

I joined in on the laughter. "Good question! Nope, I didn't, and . . . that's why I'm running for treasurer," I added, wondering too late if that was actually a good line to deliver to what was clearly a table of menaces.

"Ah, so it's a distraction technique. Student accused of theft now runs for treasurer so no one focuses on the theft?" the cap guy said.

Why do they even care about the news on me?

And why are they even bringing up the stealing allegations to my face?

I tried to laugh again, but it just resulted in a weird sound emanating from a pained place within. "No, what I mean is that I'm confident in my ability to manage student funds, so much so that I'm willing to do it for the entire student body."

"Ballsy," said another person at the table. "To be so corrupt."

They all laughed and gave props to each other and turned their shoulders in, away from me, like I was dismissed. Like they were in middle school.

If it *had* been middle school, I would have smacked my clenched fist on the table so hard, it would have made their fries jump. Then I would have screamed a speech at them, and it would have been so fiery, the remaining fries in the container would have been scorched to a crisp.

But middle school didn't have Professor Mumford.

Who was now walking into the Commons from the hall that led to the law faculty offices. He had a serious face—just like his picture—and, under a head of gray hair and behind a gray mustache, he looked lost in thought. He clutched a handful of papers, and I wondered if one of them held a list of promising students for international human rights externships.

And a list of students who shouldn't get into the program itself, let alone be sent off into the world to get a coveted position at The Hague.

I moved away from the Table of Menaces in case they said something else foolish directed at me out loud as Professor Mumford walked by, and he turned around to notice.

He couldn't notice me until I got some positive press through the election.

Which was taking place the week after I got back from Hidden Bloom.

After grabbing a late lunch with Claire and Mariyah, I went home to sit on the front stoop of the building.

I was supposed to be studying at the library now so I could get back on my couch at my allocated time, but I needed to plan out how I was going to change Adam's mind.

I had to make a phone call.

Auntie Nandy, Mom's only sibling, lived in Doha and was

actually a spy of sorts for me. She was close to Adam—having been a good friend of his mother's before she passed away—and Auntie Nandy often visited him and his dad and Hanna.

If I wasn't sure of something with Adam and needed someone to feel him out, I'd just give Auntie Nandy a call and she'd deliver the goods on him. Almost like an FBI report, sometimes with timings, amusing redacted statements, and everything.

She went to bed at eleven thirty each night, so I had to call now to catch her on Doha time.

After making catch-up small talk, with our conversational pauses being filled by the old music Auntie Nandy liked to play in her condo, I took off my heavy backpack to ease some of the additional tension in my shoulders before I dove right into the topic I wanted this chat centered on. "So . . . Adam. You seen him lately?"

"Just last week. Hanna did a run to raise money for endangered species, and I went over afterward to help organize the collection. I had dinner there. Everything okay?"

"Yeah, great." I set the backpack on the step beside me and played with its zipper. "Did Adam seem—"

I hesitated. With Auntie Nandy, I had to be careful. She's one of my favorite people in the world, but she was a true empath, and she could unravel me in two seconds if she sniffed trouble in my voice.

Plus, while I searched for words, the worst soundtrack for my state of mind blasted into Auntie Nandy's space. It was one of those old songs she'd introduced me to before, "Leaving on a Jet Plane," a tragic ballad from the 1960s about someone boarding a flight and leaving their loved one behind.

I immediately stopped talking.

Instead of finding the right way to broach the topic of Adam's change in behavior, I let my throat clog right up on hearing the song.

Adam was flying off on a jet plane without me.

He *wanted* to fly off without me.

Did Adam feel even a fraction of the sadness the singer was wringing out of his voice in the background as Auntie Nandy patiently waited for me to speak?

I closed my eyes.

"I know what you're going to ask, Zoodles. Did Adam seem okay?" She paused, her tone softening as she posed the question, and I could envision her stop moving around in her room, stop getting ready for bed. I'd stayed with her for two weeks in Doha a few years ago (which was when and where Adam and I fell in love, sob), and whenever we talk on the phone, I'm constantly visualizing what Auntie Nandy's doing in her fancy all-white apartment like it's a movie playing in my head. Gauging by the sigh she just gave, she'd probably taken a seat on her bed to prepare to give me some facts. "No, he didn't seem okay. I was going to file a report to you, actually."

She lowered the volume on her music and then shut it off.

And, in the blessed silence, I regained my words. But, to make sure my voice wouldn't reveal even a tinge of my heartache, I cleared my throat hard before asking, "What did you see, Auntie Nandy?"

If Auntie Nandy visited him last week, it was before he was so vehement about going to Umrah, so whatever was going on with him didn't have to do with the latest turn of events.

"He was very quiet."

"But he's always quiet."

"No, not like Adam quiet, which is an observational quiet, his *oh, I saw you needed more gravy for your mashed potatoes so I'm passing it over* quiet. Not that kind of quiet. It was a listless quiet."

"Like he wasn't there?"

"Yes. Did you guys fight? Did you say something, Zayneb?"

"Auntie Nandy, I know you think I'm fierce, but do you actually think I'm unleashing my temper on Adam?"

"Zayneb, he looks like someone poked him with something sharp, and some of the life-giving air leaked out of him." Auntie Nandy was moving again. I heard drawers opening and closing. "Is he worried about the pilgrimage you guys are doing? The Hajj?"

"Who told you about that?" I didn't correct Auntie Nandy's erroneous use of the word "Hajj" to describe Umrah. Auntie Nandy wasn't Muslim and clearly didn't know Hajj was the greater pilgrimage done at a special, fixed time of the year, the one you must do once in your life as a Muslim—if you're capable financially and physically, that is.

Umrah was a pilgrimage to Mecca done at any other time. The lesser pilgrimage, without so many rites, and not as strenuous.

But maybe still hard for Adam.

"David told me this evening. He said it was his nikah gift for you two, and Adam wanted to do it earlier than later. That you switched England for Mecca. And that Adam is over the moon excited. I can't wait to see the pictures, Zoodles."

I swallowed. "Yeah."

Forget trying to convince him to change his mind. An Adam who was "over the moon excited" was beyond my plotting powers. His default setting is laid-back and mellow.

And, besides, I want him to be happy.

For some reason, my favorite Sesame Street song from when I was a kid, a sad song, drifted into my brain: "I Don't Want to Live on the Moon."

Adam was now rocketing over the moon on his jet plane and I

was left behind on earth all alone, my face turned to the dark sky, my eyes searching in vain for the whereabouts of my heart.

Wow. This thing with Adam was really exposing the mush inside me.

My beetle shell was breaking.

I cleared my throat again. "Yeah. Mecca."

"Is Adam worried about doing the pilgrimage? Is it physically demanding?"

"No, he's not, actually." How could I tell her *I* didn't want to go on Umrah?

That I'd actually been looking forward to curling up with Adam for a week, not hanging out with a bunch of people I didn't know at a place I wanted to visit while in the best state of mind, not while walking around with the opposite of that, a scrambled mind?

The election, The Hague externship, needing an apartment, Murie's bangs, and Professor Mumford's mustache would all jostle for a place in my mind's eye, completely clouding it, as I walked around the Kaaba.

There it was.

Across the street.

A solitary rose on a bush in front of a brownstone.

I carried on the rest of the conversation—reassuring Auntie Nandy it wasn't "Hajj" that was affecting Adam, that it was counting down the days until he saw me (ha, right, he wanted to go on separate trips), that I was aching for him, too (sob, so true, I needed those arms to hold me and keep me from falling apart), that we were going through a tough spell due to our distance but it was okay, *love you, Auntie Nandy, can't wait to see you at Christmas with Mansoor and Hodan's baby!*—all while staring at that rose.

I hung up and left my backpack on the stoop behind me and did something Adam would do.

Whenever he caught sight of a marvel he wanted to examine, he left whatever he was occupied with at that moment and went right up to it to look at it in fine detail. Silently, reverently.

I crossed the street and leaned forward on the black gate skirting the small patch of lawn housing the rosebush and looked at the single rose that had beckoned me.

Really looked at it.

Then I went back to my backpack and walked to the library to study.

I couldn't study and, instead, found myself drawing roses, ugly ones, on my arms.

Sadia's voice—"Zayneb! You're poisoning yourself with that ink!"—wouldn't leave my mind space, so I put the ballpoint pen down and decided to take a study break and watch some videos.

My favorite YouTuber and recent friend, Sausun, aka the Niqabi Ninja, had a new video up, but I bypassed it to search "Umrah" in her video uploads.

There were seven videos on Umrah. Each of them a vlog of her pilgrimages.

She's half-Saudi, her dad's side, so she probably went on Umrah on her visits back to Saudi Arabia.

I clicked the most current Umrah video. It was soundless, with no voice-over, no music or nasheeds, just scenes from Mecca and Medina.

I fell asleep watching it.

ARTIFACT ELEVEN:
ADAM'S R2-D2 ACTION FIGURE
INTERPRETIVE LABEL: *THE FRIENDS YOU'RE DEALT IN LIFE OFTEN MAKE THE MOST SENSE*

As soon as I began packing for London to meet the Umrah group, I thought of my friends from Doha International School, Connor, Jacob, and the Emmas (three girls all named Emma), friends who'd gone their separate ways after we all graduated high school but who continued to keep in touch.

They'd pitched in to get me a present when Zayneb and I got our nikah done in the summer: an automated carry-on that followed me as I moved through the airport, even onto the flight itself, without a single touch from me. It was the coolest gift and captured our deep friendship based on growing up as third-culture kids in Doha.

We knew life was never going to be without travel.

With my check-in luggage ready and zipped, I called Connor while finishing up packing the carry-on with essentials. He lived in California currently and was studying for the state exam to become a real estate agent. He was constantly showing me places for rent in attempts to entice me to move there. I told him trading one hot location for another wasn't in the cards for me.

"Mecca, huh. Isn't it hot *there*?" He twirled a pencil in his hand and then stuck it behind his ear into his big hair, still as shaggy and floppy as he'd worn it in high school. Somehow the most stereo-typically surfer-looking dude in our class ended up in California.

"I'm not moving there. Just going to . . . pray there." And we were also going to Medina to see the Prophet's masjid. Which I was really eager to visit. Hanna and Dad had agreed that there was a peaceful air in Medina that they'd never felt anywhere else, that every famous Muslim singer who'd sung about Medina (and each and every one of them did) was right.

"I thought you prayed all the time. Half the time you visited here, you and Zayneb and her brother were praying. Remember I ended up buying you a prayer rug because you were always sharing one with her brother?"

I laughed at his recollection of our visit to California the year before. "That's daily prayers. This is like special rites, like circulat-ing around the Kaaba. You know that black cube building you've probably seen pictures of? That's the Kaaba." I began folding the ihram I'd be wearing for Umrah—two pieces of white cloth, one that went around my waist and the other that draped across my chest and left shoulder, leaving the right shoulder bare. I didn't tell Connor about the one Umrah rite I was trying hard not to think too much about: Sa'i.

When I thought about Sa'i, my mind immediately went to Zayneb.

Because Zayneb being there would be Allah-sent.

But I can't think about Zayneb and Mecca. Ever since our last conversation about Umrah, we'd only had quick daily chats that hadn't gone close to the subject of our respective Thanksgiv-ing trips.

I hadn't canceled my deposit on Hidden Bloom because Zayneb was going to take it for her own vacation.

Dad had been surprised at the turn of events, but he'd taken one look at my resolute face and stayed quiet.

I'd pretty much been rescued from my previous sad state by this trip to Mecca.

It gave me a goal: land in Saudi Arabia, go to the Kaaba, and literally pray for a steady, secure job. And, if I got the opportunity, learn more about the Hijrah while in the lands where it actually happened.

I glanced at Connor, who'd gone quiet on my laptop screen. He was staring down at the phone in his palm. "Bro, that's a lot of moving. Seven times around the Kuby . . . Kabu—I mean, the cube-shaped thing, and then you have to run between two hills seven times too? You sure you can do this? This video I'm watching of it all looks intense."

"Hey, thanks for the encouragement, coach."

He'd brought up Sa'i.

Which is over two miles of walking—and, at some parts, running—without stopping, except on each hill to make dua. Dad had told me there were assistive devices I could use, including wheelchairs and scooters, but I'd told him I felt strong right now, alhamdulillah.

But maybe Hanna's physical training idea for me—which she'd brought up again—had been a good one.

Will everyone in the group run ahead and leave me behind? Alone?

Or will some feel obliged to go slow to ensure I'm okay, thus not focusing on their own Sa'i?

Zayneb would focus on her own Sa'i *and* ensure I was okay. She's a multitasker like no other.

"No, I'm serious, Adam. That's a lot to do in the heat."

"Again, love your vote of confidence. And it's not as hot at the time we're going. And that part, the hills part, is air-conditioned."

"All right, I guess it'll be okay with Zayneb there. Tell her I said hi. And that when you guys come down next, I want to go riding with her again. If she'll slow down a bit."

"She doesn't have a bike anymore. The last time, it was her brother's bike." I wasn't sure she'd even ridden a motorcycle since that visit to California. Her brother Mansoor had spent a couple of years teaching her, and she'd gotten her license two summers ago but then never mentioned it again.

The way Zayneb put it, riding had been a sibling bonding thing. The way Mansoor put it, it had been an "if Mansoor can do it, I can do it too" thing. He was always ribbing her.

I saw her in my head now as she pulled up her motorcycle at Joshua Tree National Park. She smiled at me after taking off her helmet, the startlingly blue sky behind her. I'd been riding with Connor, with Mansoor on another bike he'd rented following behind us.

"She can borrow my bike. We can take turns." Connor watched me shove my toiletries bag into the carry-on and zip it. "I hope she becomes a criminal lawyer. And shows up to court on a motorcycle." He smiled.

"Nope, she's studying human rights law."

"Are you okay?"

"Yeah." I pulled the carry-on off the bed and set it on the floor. "I'm excited."

"You just became weird suddenly."

Should I tell Connor that Zayneb isn't coming to Mecca? "I'd better let you study. Let me know how you do on the exam. I'll pray for you in Mecca. And I'll call you when I get back to Doha."

"Yeah, yeah, you say that and then forget. As soon as you got the girl, you disappeared on me."

"I got loads of time when I get back, remember?" Connor was the only person who knew about my gig-less situation—because he was unemployed too.

But he didn't consider it to be as stressful as I did.

He didn't have Zayneb's parents to think about. Or Zayneb.

"Hey, send me pictures of you and Mecca? I want to see you in the white monk robes. They look cool." He looked down at his phone again. "And the Kabu looks out of this world."

"Kaaba."

"It took me a year to learn Zayneb's name. Give me time for Kuba."

I laughed and ended our call.

The flight to London was, after the first hour, me sleeping the entire way.

It was the only method to get over two harsh things that would pop into my head whenever I started to get excited about doing this Umrah trip:

1. The first place I'd spoken to Zayneb was on a plane. From London to Doha. And I've never forgotten the way her eyes lit up when I said salaam to her. Before I actually spoke to her on the flight, Zayneb hadn't known I was Muslim when we'd first laid eyes on each other at Heathrow, she on her layover, me flying back to Doha from school in London.

Visions of her smile and those eyes kept invading my headspace.

2. Though we'd met at the airport, and first spoken on a flight, I'd never ever flown anywhere *with* her. As in, with her sitting beside me. We'd connected *in* Istanbul this summer and, in previous years, traveled with our respective families separately to meet up in places.

I just wanted to have her beside me on this flight.

Any flight, actually.

Instead, there was a man who slept with his mouth open and drooled, who kept flopping from one side to another, from my shoulder to another passenger's shoulder.

In the grand scheme of things, these were small problems.

But like little gnats that wouldn't leave me alone, the two thoughts about missing Zayneb kept buzzing in and out of my brain until I forced myself to fall asleep.

I had to be in a calm, peaceful state of mind for what was to come next.

I was meeting Shaykh Murtaza at the airport, after which he'd take me to meet the entire Umrah group at the masjid.

And then we were to fly to Jeddah tomorrow, the closest major city to Mecca, from which we'd drive to Mecca itself, insha'Allah.

Shaykh Murtaza held a sign that said ADAM CHEN, MY SON, like I was some stranger, but I instantly recognized his crinkly-eyed smile and wholesome full beard that had been more gray than white the last time I'd seen him. Which was over four years ago.

He also had on the same fez-type kufi he usually wore, brown today.

He wrapped me in a bear hug and then tried to take my carry-on along with my other luggage, but I showed him the niftiness of the automation.

"Ah, it's like R2-D2!"

I laughed. "Dad told me you'd become a *Star Wars* fan recently."

"Well, guess who got me into it all? That number one fan himself. Your dad and I debated Ewoks and Jar Jar Binks the whole day he visited me last. *Which one was more annoying?* was the question of the day." Shaykh Murtaza led me to the exits, rolling my big suitcase behind him. "I won because I proved Jar Jar Binks had more detractors in the world and that teddy bears were cute."

The ride to the masjid was filled with *Star Wars* opinions, including Shaykh Murtaza's insistence that the best way to watch the movies was in chronological order. "Your dad says *by release date*! Can you imagine? How does it make sense then?"

I didn't reveal that I'd tried to watch them in chronological order with Zayneb, and she couldn't get through *Episode 1: The Phantom Menace*. The only part she loved was Queen Amidala's speech in the senate, which Zayneb memorized and would spontaneously recite whenever she wanted to dramatically disrupt something with family or friends.

She appeared in my head now, with pursed lips like Queen Amidala. "I move for a vote of *no* confidence!"

And then, before disappearing from my mindscape, she broke out in a huge Zayneb laugh.

Was I going to think about her the entire Umrah trip?

Was it because she wasn't here, or because everything reminded me of her?

I knew it was neither. It was because I was utterly in love with her.

Most of the Umrah group was already gathered in the prayer hall when I got to the masjid. Well, the men were.

The women were in their prayer space. Shaykh Murtaza said they'd be joining us after salat, and then we'd do introductions.

The first one to enter our hall when the women convened with us made me blink twice.

Sarina.

Before Zayneb, Sarina was the only person I'd ever felt serious about relationship-wise, who I'd met at the Muslim student group on campus when I lived in the UK. She'd gone on to get hitched, but then I saw on my London friends' group chat that she'd gotten divorced a year ago.

In a long, flowy dusty-pink hijab that, because it had arms, actually became her abaya—like the prayer dress Zayneb wore at home—she smiled when she saw me, the corners of her hazel eyes crinkling with genuine happiness. "Adam! Assalamu alaikum!"

"Walaikum musalam." I said. And then, I don't know why, I added the extra benediction, "Wa rahmatullahi wabarakatha hu."

"I was so happy when my uncle said you'd be joining us. Alhamdulillah."

"Alhamdulillah." I nodded, suddenly remembering Shaykh Murtaza was her paternal uncle. "Rabbil alameen." *Why was I making everything coming out of my mouth extra pious suddenly?*

Maybe it was because I'd met her at the Muslim Student Union welcome dinner as a freshman. And all our initial conversations were always about Islam or being Muslim or MSU activities.

But then we'd veered off into talking about other things, including our goals and dreams.

When I'd been *this* close to asking her if we could explore each other as a potential couple, she'd left to visit Lebanon and come back engaged. And I'd met Zayneb a couple of months later.

The weird thing was that a few years ago, a friend on our London chat mentioned to me that Sarina had confided that if her relatives hadn't pressured her into that disastrous marriage, she'd be with "someone like Adam now."

That we'd had a good thing going back then.

Standing in front of her now, I looked at the carpet under my feet when I remembered that part.

"Don't worry about anything; we've got the whole trip all organized. And I'm setting up an Umrah chat group so everyone can stay connected. Because we're a small group, we only have one women's and one men's group, just eight each, including leaders. So you'll be well taken care of." She lifted an arm billowy with abaya fabric and indicated Shaykh Murtaza preparing the laptop and projector. "You'll get all the details now. Welcome."

"Jazakhillah." I nodded again and smiled at the ground.

Before joining the circle that was forming on the carpet around Shaykh Murtaza, I glanced behind me.

My breath caught in my chest.

Coming up at the rear of the rest of the women entering the prayer hall, wearing a trim bright blue hijab with a big brown knit scarf wound around her neck, was the answer to my unspoken prayer.

I guess it was still ringing plaintive and clear from my heart to be heard—and answered—by Allah.

ARTIFACT TWELVE:
ZAYNEB'S PHOTO OF BERTHA FATIMA
INTERPRETIVE LABEL: CHILDREN NEED STRONG NAMES TO LIVE UP TO

I FLASHED ADAM A SMILE BUT COULDN'T SAY MORE BECAUSE THE shaykh had started speaking.

But, sitting near the end of the women's semicircle, close to where Adam bookended the men's semicircle, I was able to continue smiling at him.

Then I stopped.

Because he was looking at me more than listening to the shaykh, who was now talking about our hotels and how logistics would go.

I tipped my head toward the shaykh. *Listen,* I mouthed to Adam.

He nodded. But kept looking at me.

All righty then. I'd have to listen doubly carefully for the both of us.

I turned away from Adam and pulled out my phone and started taking notes.

Thanks for being here

    Please pay attention

When did you get in?

    Adam, they're talking about changing into ihram. We have

to do it before we land in Jeddah. I think even before we leave London

    WE?

        Yes, I changed my mind two weeks ago. About the cottage. Your dad and the shaykh arranged it all. SURPRISE

To avoid seeing how that landed on an already-giddy Adam, I looked up at the shaykh, who was now prepping a video. From his presentation style, I could already tell he was awesome in more ways than just being super organized. He'd pulled strings for me with the Ministry of Hajj and Umrah, which he had a "special relationship with," to get me onboarded within a couple of weeks for the Umrah trip. My parents had been impressed and asked for his contact information for their next visit to Mecca.

I'd made sure to mention how it was all Adam's doing: this trip, the connections, the making-everything-happen. Which was technically true—Shaykh Murtaza *was* Adam's family friend—but also not true because Adam didn't even know I was joining the Umrah.

I would never miss an opportunity to sing Adam's praises to my parents—because, sometimes, what Mom said when she'd first met him in Qatar rings in my ears: *He's a very mature and respectful young man with a peaceful, kind aura, but he's still at the very beginnings of figuring his life out. He's not steady on his feet yet, which you should consider before making any kind of commitment.*

There was always the looming danger of my parents thinking we'd gotten together too early in our lives, that we were foolishly in love.

That it might not last and that they'd been dumb to give it their blessing.

So I bigged-up my Adam all the time. How he was bringing something new to the art scene with his creative reinterpretation of traditional craftsmanship from various Muslim heritages. That he was carving a career for himself.

I risked a look at Adam. Oh God, he was still staring at me.

It was good the shaykh knew we had our nikah done, otherwise he'd wonder why Leering Adam was going on Umrah.

Wait, you're staying with me tonight right?

At the shaykh's house, yup. I couldn't help insert a sad-face emoji. Way to kill the mood, staying at an Islamic scholar's house with his family, which included six young kids and, gauging from her hearty smile on the Internet, a very friendly (and probably very busybody-in-a-kindly-way) wife.

I would have to lie still the whole night next to Adam, with my hands crossed at the wrists on top of my stomach, lest the bed creak, alerting the entire house, should we make one move toward each other.

RIP Hidden Bloom Cottage.

RIP tiny purchases from Macy's.

After the presentation, when it was time to mix and mingle and get to know the others in our group, Adam did something uncharacteristic.

He, who wasn't into public displays of affection, actually held out his hand to me *in the masjid prayer hall, in front of everyone gathered.* "Let's go. Talk?"

Then he smiled mischievously, which, because he never does it, made him look like he was walking me into a torture chamber.

I grabbed his hand and rescued him from humiliation by quickly leading him out into the masjid foyer. "Are you okay?" I couldn't help adding a laugh after asking. He still had a mischievous gleam in his eyes. And his eyebrows were rising up and down suggestively.

My happy Adam was back.

"Let's go, um, talk, out there?" I motioned vaguely at the front entrance of the masjid, where I was sure there was some spot "around the corner" we could find.

He followed me out.

But so did Shaykh Murtaza. "Assalamu alaikum, Zayneb!"

I hoped my reply salaam didn't sound as bleak as I imagined it. I wanted me-and-Adam time.

It's been months.

"I'm so glad to finally meet you," Shaykh Murtaza said, his gray-streaked white beard a perfect match for his gray kufi. "Adam is like a son to me. I was the one who worked on him slowly over the years until he agreed to go to university in the UK."

I smiled at this, and he beamed back. He was actually pretty fashionable for an Islamic scholar. As discreetly as I could, I took in his pristine white kicks and tailored pants, again gray, peeking out from under his white thawb. Everything was pleasingly white and gray. "So happy to meet you . . . " Would I call him Uncle or Shaykh? Since he didn't look too old? But still needed some sort of respect? "Uncle. Oops, I mean, Shaykh."

"You can call me Shaykh. Or Uncle. Whatever works for you." He smiled again, this time at Adam. "I hope everything wasn't too overwhelming with the meeting today. Especially right after you both just landed in England. The presentation is actually all the information already e-mailed to you, so you can look it over on the flight should you forget." He looked at both of us in turn now. "And you'll get to rest at my home, which we'll leave for in just a few minutes, after I finish up one more task."

"Thank you, Shaykh." I nodded at him while still holding on to Adam's hand.

When the shaykh went back into the masjid, I again began looking for a good place for Adam and me to at least get a hug in.

A whole crowd of our Umrah group spilled out of the masjid.

Adam turned around when he heard their murmurs and laughter, and nodded and waved at them. Then he tugged my hand—toward them. "I want you to meet some people."

They were all people I'd already seen at the masjid but hadn't *actually* seen—even the women in the prayer hall upstairs. From the moment I'd stepped into the masjid, I'd been overwhelmed with thoughts of reuniting with Adam and the resultant glee had taken over all my senses.

And then after, I'd only had eyes for Adam in between paying attention to the shaykh.

I did my *hi, how are you* friendly face to five people I couldn't catch the names of but labeled in my head as a super-tall desi guy with a shaved head who watched everyone more than he talked; an older white woman with a tie-dyed purple headband in her short bobbed blond hair, her hijab around her neck now that she was out of the masjid; a cute couple—the guy looked Arab and the girl was Black, both wearing matching Moroccan thawbs, the kind with the pointy hoods attached, not on their heads but hanging long behind them; and a jovial man I guessed was Palestinian because his tween son had green, black, and red braces on his teeth, was wearing a keffiyeh around his neck, and a PALESTINE FOREVER T-shirt. His hair was abundant and curly and clustered in front of his forehead, the sides of his head short.

The boy was making jokes that I could tell only those of us who were on TikTok got, but everyone laughed along because he was so cute. His dad acted like his personal announcer. "He makes

TikToks. Funny ones about school and fried chicken sandwiches. And serious ones about Palestine."

I wanted to bump fists with the kid, but he was in the middle of another act, his arms already in action.

Then the masjid door opened, and a girl came out in a dusty-pink jilbab, the all-in-one hijab-and-dress type that's kind of cool when you consider the fact that you just have to wear one layer head to toe. Perfect when paired with comfortable shoes. And a nice purse or mini backpack, like the girl had on.

Maybe I'd get a jilbab in that style in Mecca or Medina. It would be handy for those days—those rare days, I admit—I wanted to walk around the world whatevering everything and everyone who tried to convince me I had to look a certain way to be sorted into the "stylishly approved" portion of world.

The all-in-one jilbab is a great *whatever* to all that—which is truly something I had to remember, because personally, I loved belonging in the stylishly approved club.

I typically spent a lot of time carefully choosing my outfit of the day. Like today I was wearing flared jeans with a short white mohair top and an oversized pink blazer. And Scarfy. And the same blue hijab Adam had seen me in when our paths first crossed—which didn't exactly match what I was wearing but I'd wanted to see Adam's eyes light up and, yes, I'd been duly rewarded.

But then there were days I just longed to sink into outfit oblivion.

The dusty-pink-jilbab girl smiled at me, and I realized I must have been staring at her the whole time I was writing an essay in my head titled "Big Hijabs Flick Off Society's Style Expectations." Then she came right up to our group and smiled some more, the freckles on her face scrunching together as she listened to the latest joke by the TikTok boy.

From far away, I could have sworn she'd been wearing makeup, that's how much her skin glowed. Like she was superbly, expertly highlighted. But now that she was close, I saw that . . . that . . . she just *glowed*.

She turned to me again and wrinkled her nose cutely as she laughed at the punchline of the boy's joke about erasers and pencils and their babies.

"Assalamu alaikum. You must be Zayneb?" the girl asked. "You left the prayer hall while everyone was making introductions. I'm Sarina."

I nodded and shook her hand. "Nice to meet you, Sarina. This is Adam."

Her freckles squeezed together again, like the corners of her green eyes, this time at Adam. "Yes, Adam, I know. Assalamu alaikum, again."

He salaamed her back.

"For some reason, your name sounds familiar," I said. "But not in a someone-I-know way."

"Maybe you saw it in your e-mail? I'm your group leader," Sarina said. "For the trip."

I nodded. "Yes! That's it."

"I'll be sending you a little spiritual pick-me-up each morning, and we'll meet in the morning to go over rites and expectations and do dhikr to get into the right state of mind for the day's plans." She tucked back a nonexistent strand of hair into the oval face opening of her jilbab, her wooden tasbih bracelet falling back onto her cuff as she did so. "I really hope it's the trip of a lifetime for you, sis."

"Have you gone before? To Umrah?"

"Oh yes, I've been leading groups for two years now. We do three a year." Sarina smiled at the masjid behind her. "I work with an organization my uncle, Shaykh Murtaza, founded years ago. It looks at ways to make Umrah and Hajj more accessible for all people."

"That's amazing." I wonder what she studied. To be doing this job. And be so at peace like she was. "By the way, I love your jilbab. Such a beautiful color."

"Jazakhillah." Sarina leaned forward to look over at Adam, who was standing strangely quiet at my side. "Adam, Shaykh Murtaza told me about the Hijrah map you made. I'd love to see photos of it."

I turned to see his face light up.

Okay, that was much better. I was wondering why he'd suddenly become so quiet, almost withdrawn—again.

I didn't realize until our disagreement about the Umrah trip how much I needed Adam to be happy or at least quietly content in order for me to even contemplate contentment for myself. It's like a prerequisite for me to just even breathe.

"Happy to share pics. I can ask my sister to take some and send them over." He nodded at Sarina and then immediately put his hands in the pockets of his hoodie.

"Great! I'll leave you two. I have to go over room assignments with the hotels in Mecca and Medina."

"Oh, about that, can Adam and I have our own room?" I looped my arm through the V of Adam's right arm. "I don't know if the shaykh put it in his notes, but we're nikahed. Just this summer."

"Ah, really?" She looked at our linked arms. "That's wonderful. Mabrook to both of you."

"So can that be arranged? For us to share a room?"

"No, I'm sorry. Didn't Shaykh Murtaza mention it?" Sarina smoothed a non-wrinkle in the arm of her jilbab. "The rooms are only quads, so we're split into groups of four to share rooms together."

"Can we pay extra or something?" I hoped my voice wasn't becoming whiny.

"No, the hotel only has quads available." She started walking backward, still smiling, but then suddenly came back swiftly to lean in and whisper, "Besides, you know the requirements of Umrah mean that you aren't allowed to be together *like that* as a couple, right?"

"But that's just in a state of ihram. Which is brief. Once—" I stopped, realizing I sounded super whiny. And super cringe.

"Zayneb, it's okay." Adam finally broke in, his face reddening. "We'll make sure to get our own room for Medina."

"Oh yes, Medina," I said to Sarina, who had started backing away again. "We'll be out of ihram then!"

OMG, I almost yelled that, that's how loud I was.

"Medina is quads too." She nodded and then opened the door to go back into the masjid. "So are the flight seating arrangements. Just working on that as well."

Then she smiled one last time before disappearing. And Adam sighed heavily beside me.

We left soon after with Shaykh Murtaza. As the bustling city scenes outside the car windows made way for the tidy monotony of English suburbs, I fell asleep in the back seat, only waking up when my phone beeped a few times in a row just as the car parked.

Layth, asking to FaceTime from Chicago.

"Bertha Fatima!" I chirped, apparently scaring the shaykh, who jolted while opening his door. "Sorry, Shaykh."

He laughed. "One minute you're snoring, and then you're yelling a strange name."

Before getting out of the car, Adam chuckled himself and said,

"It's our cat, named after my mother's old cat, Bertha, and Fatima al-Fihri."

"The founder of the first university?" The shaykh was out of the car but popped his head back in to ask me this.

"Yes, and look at her. Besides being brilliant, isn't she beautiful?" I held up my phone to display a photo of Bertha Fatima bint Muhammad al-Fihriya Al-Qurashiya Chen-Malik, gray and perfect—Adam's cat before she'd become mine, so *our* child—and then swiped to accept the video call from Layth. I motioned for Adam to get in the back with me. "Uncle, I mean, Shaykh, we'll get our luggage out. We're just talking to the friend who's taking care of Bertha Fatima."

"Nonsense, my kids will help with your luggage. They're home from school already." And with that, the Shaykh was hollering, "Musa, Mariam, Aasiyah, Maleeha, Nusaybah, and Yusuf, run out to help!"

Adam put his arm around me, and we snuggled closer to talk to our baby one last time before we went on pilgrimage to Mecca.

BERTHA FATIMA SPEAKS TO HER PARENTS

LET US TAKE A PAUSE FROM BERTHA FATIMA CONTINUING TO LEARN Adam and Zayneb's story to come back to the alcove room in Chicago, the one with that beautiful deep teal bookshelf wrapping around the place.

In addition to the interesting collection of items from the owner that provided hours of cat entertainment, the bookshelves also held items the catsitter Layth had either brought with him from Ecuador, where he lived most of the year, or things he'd bought in Chicago for his stay here to visit family. Like mandarin oranges. Which he loved, but which Bertha Fatima hated the smell of.

He'd *just* had a mandarin orange and was now, with those citrusy fingers, trying to hold Bertha up to the phone propped against a ceramic plant pot on the desk.

Bertha made her body uncooperative as he attempted to settle her into his lanky lap. But then she heard, "Bertha Fatima!" spoken in the voices she loved most in the world—Adam's and Zayneb's—and she tightened her nostrils to work with the fumes emanating from Layth's hands, just so she could stare into the tiny faces of her parents on the screen.

How wondrous, how tragic, to see their cooing faces but not smell them.

Adam smelled like wood shavings and a crisp day by the ocean, with a hint of cloves trod under the foot of mountain goats that had played in a fir forest briefly. (Though Bertha Fatima had never emerged from any of the apartments and houses she'd lived in in North America, she'd met many, many visitors from many, many far-off Muslim lands that did indeed have frolicking goats.)

Zayneb smelled like cocoa and coffee and the lavender soap she often bathed with at night to try to go to sleep like a baby, which she did, snoring as soon as her head hit the pillow.

Now Zayneb was telling Bertha Fatima things about a trip she and Adam were taking. How they wouldn't be able to talk to Bertha Fatima for a while but what they were doing was important, as it was visiting the house of Allah, and that there would be lots of things to do and different time zones. "But as soon as we get to a standstill for a bit of time, and *that* time makes sense for Layth, we'll make sure to call, okay, baby?"

In response, Bertha Fatima pawed at the screen and then tried to squirm away when another whiff of mandarin oranges attacked her as Layth caught hold of her to prevent her from knocking over a glass of water beside the phone. She jumped off his lap as soon as he loosened his grip for a moment.

"Have a safe trip and don't worry about Bertha; she's doing fine," Layth said, after wagging his finger at Bertha Fatima, who was now sitting under the desk, right paw raised in readiness to lick-wash all citrus traces off her face. "Will you guys get a chance to connect with Janna there?"

"She's going to try to come by before we leave for the airport tomorrow afternoon," Zayneb said, leaning against Adam in the back seat of the car she was in. "Are you going to see her before you go back to Ecuador?"

"I don't think so. Her London term ends in December, and she can't afford to come back to Chicago for a visit before that. And I can't afford to come up here again. Until the summer." He paused and looked at the sticky note attached to the base of the burnt-orange lamp on the night table, that he'd dashed his mother's flight information on. She was flying in from the UK and renting this room after he left for Ecuador, while she visited his uncle, her brother.

Who was married to Janna's mom.

"So, about that, are you guys . . . um . . ." Zayneb looked up at Adam, like he had the right words plastered on his forehead.

Adam cut in. "Are you guys official? That's what Z wants to know."

Layth smiled, and it was the kind of smile that answered questions instantaneously. "'Official' is a huge word. Let's just say, if I had Wi-Fi at the animal sanctuary, we'd talk every day instead of the once a week we were doing on Fridays when I went into town. Now that I'm up here, yeah, we talk every day."

"Once a week from the rain forest is already huge. Officially huge," Zayneb said, an amused smile on her face. "To use sacred Wi-Fi access on Janna like that? Huge."

"And okay, she did go visit my mom when she first got to London in August. But I don't know if that's because of me or because *her* mom told her to." Layth raked his fingers through his long hair, and some of it fell into his eyes, the ends skimming his cheeks. Which was a great cover for the flush spreading across his face.

His mom had called Janna "pyaari," had loved her, had gushed in a way that was embarrassing, actually.

"Aw, that's so cute. Listen, Janna is precious, so don't break her heart. She helped get me through final year of undergrad with her texts about life."

"She got me through last year too." Layth's voice became quiet, the sadness he sometimes pulled on like a hoodie settling into his features.

Zayneb noticed and thought about his past, what she knew of it, how he'd lost his only sibling in a car accident. "We're going to pray for you, singular, *and* you two as a couple, in Mecca. Right, Adam?"

Adam nodded. "For you two to be as happy as Zayneb and I are." He put his arm over Zayneb's right shoulder and reached across to the other and pulled her back tight into him. She closed her eyes, savoring this first hug in a long time.

Layth said ameen and thanks and bent to bring the phone down to Bertha Fatima to say bye.

She meowed at Adam and Zayneb and went back to cleaning her face.

It was the last time she'd see her parents across the waters this happy together.

PART TWO

And proclaim unto all people the pilgrimage; they will
come on foot and on every [kind of] fast mount, coming from every
far-away point [on earth], so that they might experience much that
shall be of benefit to them. . . .
—*Surah 22:27–28*

ARTIFACT THIRTEEN:
ADAM'S MINIATURE (FAKE) SNAKE PLANT
INTERPRETIVE LABEL: ABSORB LIGHT WHEREVER IT MAY COME FROM

THE NEXT MORNING, BEFORE OUR FLIGHT, SHAYKH MURTAZA held a brief meeting via Zoom with our group to prepare us to get into the sacred state of ihram, the first stage of Umrah.

We were in his study, a large, bright sunroom with white walls and even white plank flooring, but dark furnishings and a deep red Persian carpet on the floor. There were twelve various-sized snake plants littered around the stacks of books on the floor—gifts from his wife to clean the air.

She was also in the room with us, sitting beside Shaykh Murtaza in front of his desktop computer. Everyone called her Ustaadah Ramlah because, even though she wasn't a trained teacher or scholar, she often sat with Shaykh Murtaza while he taught and explained what he said using more colloquial, sometimes humorous, sometimes confusing, terms. She also knew French and Urdu, being of mixed heritage, and translated some of his lectures into those languages. I'd seen her in many of his YouTube videos before I joined the Umrah group.

She was now reminding us about not using scented products after we entered ihram. "Scent is like adding ketchup and mustard and sriracha and secret sauce to the burger, and then you don't taste the burger. Even the vegetarian burger." She nodded at Zayneb after saying this. "We want to be present in our natural states on pilgrimage. One hundred percent natural beef, as they say. Or ground veggie." She smiled at Zayneb.

Zayneb shook her head and mouthed, *Not vegetarian*, but it was in vain.

Somehow, last night's dinner had been a strange comedy of manners, with Ustaadah Ramlah thinking Zayneb was pregnant with our second child, studying to become a police officer, and vegetarian. No matter how many times Zayneb tried to explain herself, Ustaadah Ramlah deepened the plot.

We couldn't tell if it was because of Zayneb's midwestern American accent falling on British-French-Urdu ears or it was because of Ustaadah Ramlah's I-already-know-you demeanor.

Or even if it was due to the many folds of Ustaadah Ramlah's hijab, wrapped in several layers over her head and ears.

"Is she coming with us?" Zayneb whispered, sitting beside me on the carved wooden settee by the window. "On Umrah?"

"I actually don't know," I said, reaching for her hand and intertwining our fingers.

"She has so many kids. Who would stay with them if she did?"

"Do you not want her to come?" I looked down at Zayneb, amused.

"No, I'm not saying that." Zayneb gripped my hand tighter. With her other hand, she ran her fingers on the arms of the settee, exploring the little nooks of its carvings. "Change subject. Maybe they can read lips from across the room. This is a nice wooden sofa thingy."

"I'm pretty sure it's walnut." I discreetly examined the wood under the square cushion we were sitting on. "And from the workmanship, it's modern, made to look like an antique Moghul piece."

"Love traditional furniture. And I like the way it fits just us two," Zayneb murmured, leaning her head on my shoulder before glancing at the desk across from us where the meeting was still going on. "Uh-oh, she's looking over."

"And once you take that ghusl shower today, no more hanky-panky—do they still use that word nowadays?" Ustaadah Ramlah raised her voice and chuckled at the screen and then peered at us again. "No more relations between partners after ghusl. Though we only have Adam and Zayneb and Sahaan and Fatima going as couples, we should all be aware of this condition of ihram."

Shaykh Murtaza turned to her. "You're forgetting another couple going."

"Oh yes, us." She laughed and wagged her finger at him. "Stay away, Murtaza."

Zayneb let go of my hand.

As soon as we got back into the guest bedroom, I took Zayneb's hand again and led her to the bed. Last night, we'd both been exhausted and had fallen asleep mid-conversation, with our clothes on, after just one kiss. And then this morning, we'd woken up late and scrambled to get to the meeting.

She unpinned her hijab and sat down on the side of the bed, but she did it limply, like she was tired again. I sat next to her and lifted her chin. "Kiss?"

"Adam, why am I incredibly exhausted? Like we've already finished a huge trip?"

"Jet lag. It's two thirty a.m. in Chicago right now." I wrapped my arms around her waist and lay on my side, pulling her down with me, and she joined, almost reluctantly, her eyes on the ceiling.

I held her snug, awaiting her readiness to kiss. "Doha time is eleven thirty in the morning, so that's why I'm not doing too bad."

"No, it's different. I feel tired in my soul. Already." She turned her entire self to look at me, hijab still on but falling back, its ends splayed across opposite shoulders. A few curls immediately sprung loose from her scarf band.

"You've got so many things going on. You have a right to feel tired." I traced the edge of her jawline from where it met her hairline to her chin and then up the other way. "When were you going to tell me about running for treasurer?"

Her eyes widened for a second, and then she sighed. "I'm not actually running."

"What do you mean? I saw it on your campus news site."

"I'm just doing it to throw someone off. There's no way I'm going to win." She flipped on her back again. "My roommate was talking about me to campus media. This guy who works for one of the news sites confirmed it. That's how they were making everything up about me, Adam. So I'm running against her."

"Huh, revenge? Is it me, or does that sound weird—and not like you, Zayby." I put my hand on her waist and tried to tug her gently to me again, but she was still. And stiff. "Anyway, let's not talk about that. We have just half an hour or so before we do ghusl for ihram. Enough time for some *hanky-panky*."

She sighed again, a really deep sigh, and then touched the edge of her right eyelid, stroking it. "I thought once I joined the trip and got here, I'd get into the Umrah mood, but it's not happening. I'm actually wondering how I'm going to do this when I'm so exhausted. And then as soon as I get home next week, I have to prepare for exams."

I flipped on my back too, my legs dangling over the side of

the bed like Zayneb's, the worry I'd held at bay since making the Umrah decision creeping in at the edges of my mind.

No, it wasn't worry. It was guilt.

Zayneb, who had balked at this trip, was now on this trip. When she should be resting and recuperating—like I had done for almost three full weeks in the lead-up to this day.

Instead, on the heels of so much, she was going to be adding to her stress.

How much of that was my fault? Because I'd been so adamant I was going to go to Mecca regardless of what she said?

What kind of a partner was I?

I closed my eyes but not before they started filling up and a tear started rolling down without my express approval.

Zayneb sat up. "Adam."

I wiped my face and opened my eyes, and—just perfect—all the tears dammed by my lids ran down my cheeks gleefully, intent on embarrassing me. I made a sound between a chuckle and a groan, without looking at Zayneb. "I'm sorry, Z. I just added to your load. By insisting on changing the trip."

"No, Adam. I didn't mean it that way." She stroked away the trails of wetness on my face and then bent her head and kissed their paths, ending at my lips.

When we finally fully kissed, my mouth tearstained, it was salty but sweet, and held all the emotions I hadn't been able to share with her.

I pulled the whole of her to me, and she fell on top, her hands going behind my head to pull us even closer, my arms already so tight around her. I'd just started kissing down her neck when there was a loud thumping noise on the door.

We both drew away and froze, breathless. "Did you lock the

door?" Zayneb whispered with lips flushed from the way I'd kissed them so hard.

I wanted to kiss them even harder but instead answered her query by shaking my head.

We broke apart and sat up, adjusting our clothing, Zayneb buttoning up her shirt.

The thumping became harder, and then the voice of one of Shaykh Murtaza's kids broke through. "Adam, someone's here to see you and Zayneb. Someone called Janna. And Mama said you lot can you use the bathrooms downstairs to get ready because there are two loos with showers. And Mama says you only have an hour and a half left before you leave."

"I feel like she's going to add *and Mama says no hanky-panky, because she heard the bloody bed creaking*," Zayneb mumbled in a British accent before getting up to go to the mirror on top of the dresser to redo her hijab.

I laughed. "As soon as we're out of ihram, we're going to find some place of our own."

"In Mecca?" Zayneb said. "I feel weird about hanky-panky in Mecca. It's such a sacred place."

"But I can't go so long with you beside me."

"Trust me, I can't either." Zayneb turned to me. "That's one of the other reasons I feel like I'm not going to have a good Umrah. I'm going to be thinking of you the whole time."

"No, insha'Allah, you won't. Once we get into ihram, spirituality will kick in. I just know it will happen. Let's go see Janna and then get ready. We'll make dua together."

"Ya Allah, make my Umrah real," Zayneb said, and then we went to meet with Janna.

ARTIFACT FOURTEEN: ZAYNEB'S DRIED ROSE
INTERPRETIVE LABEL: EVEN WHEN THEY FADE, MEMORIES ARE USEFUL TEACHERS

EVEN THOUGH ADAM WAS RIGHT BESIDE ME AS WE WENT DOWN THE stairs to see Janna, even though I'd wanted to be with him for this holiday break and agreed to his choice of a trip because the idea of being apart was too unbearable, I couldn't stop the rise of several unhappy thoughts:

I don't want to go to Mecca right now.

I'm not in the mood for Umrah.

I thought it would automatically appear within, the mood, once I saw Adam and met the group and met the shaykh.

But no.

I was more exhausted. And cranky. And the opposite of in the mood.

And I had only half an hour to get in the mood.

Before I took on the responsibility of ihram, before I entered the sacred state, I had to become ready to renounce the world.

Ihram meant that we were entering another state of consciousness.

Doing so, focusing on the spiritual, had always been a struggle for me . . . and so now, when I had to plunge deeply into such a state, it was the greatest struggle ever.

Especially when I had a million and one things going on in my life.

The image of the rose growing across the street from "my" apartment building in Chicago came to me. It had reminded me of how Adam saw the world: He focused on one thing, zooming in on it.

Now it reminded me that the biggest thing going on in my life right now was my relationship with Adam.

I wanted to preserve it. That was my goal.

So you have, like, twenty minutes to get spiritual, Zayneb.

WE MET JANNA TWO SUMMERS AGO WHEN A GOOD FRIEND OF Zayneb's got married to Janna's brother. Since then, and after Janna started college in Chicago, Zayneb had become closer with her. Now Janna was in London for a semester abroad as part of her History of Literature program.

I stood aside as Zayneb and Janna hugged and watched as Zayneb immediately perked up from her former sluggish state to lead Janna back to the sofa she'd been sitting on when we entered the living room.

While they chatted away happily, something dawned on me: I hadn't really had the chance to hang out with Zayneb's friends. Whereas she'd met and even traveled to see some of mine.

It was neat to see Zayneb so comfortable yet energized and animated—different from the way she was around my friends, where there was some reserve still.

When we eventually got to live with each other, would there be a merging of my friends and her friends? Or would we somehow miraculously make new ones? Or would it be a combination of all three that would be invited to the weekly game nights Zayneb had already mentioned a few times as part of "our future"?

The only game I wanted to play was chess with Zayneb, just me and her.

Another question ran underneath everything for me: Would Zayneb's friends even accept me, want to be around me, eventually *like* me? Once they knew the real me, that is?

Because I'm not outgoing. At all.

Socializing is absolutely not my idea of a good time.

And all these years, even though people have encouraged me to change, I just haven't cared enough to try to. It's too draining to pay constant attention to and remember everyone else's personalities and preferences and care about them as much as I do about the people who are already in my circle. So I just keep things surface-level with most people I meet and make sure to stay far, far away from social events.

Zayneb's games night sounds excruciating.

Like right now, I hadn't said a word to Janna except "salaam" and "how's it going?" And I knew a big part of that was because I was afraid that she—and all of Zayneb's friends—would think I was boring.

That spectacular Zayneb was out of my league.

But then, if somehow my prayer came true, and I joined Zayneb in Chicago, I was pretty sure Janna would be part of our lives.

So instead of sitting here relaxed, just observing them from this chair I was in, another carved walnut faux-antique number, I figured I'd better start being friendly now.

I'd better make a chess move to secure my endgame.

I leaned forward and waited for a pause in their conversation.

There was no pause in their conversation. It was as if I was watching a well-rehearsed, fast-paced skit or the longest, friendliest volleyball rally in the world. *Your turn now,* they telepathically communicated a millisecond after verbally sharing something.

I was about to settle back in my chair, content at being ignored, when the image of Zayneb tapping her chin while looking out of her apartment window at a wintery Chicago, contemplating the possibility of us living together, entered my mind. If she couldn't fit me into her social life, she'd be reluctant to hasten the entire idea of "Adam and Zayneb Season Three: Together in Chicago."

Do it, Adam. Be social!

I burst into the midst of their words. "We talked to Layth yesterday. You know he's taking care of our cat, right?"

Finally, a pause. Both of them turned my way, but, from my vantage point, it appeared to be weirdly in slow motion.

And then Janna's face, framed in a black hijab with a dark green beanie pulled on top, crumpled.

She whipped her head down, in tears.

I got up and walked over closer to Zayneb and then walked back to my chair, unsure of what to do. "I'm sorry. Did I just say something stupid?"

"No, you didn't," Janna said, drawing a breath. "It's okay."

"*Are* you okay, though?" Zayneb asked. She moved closer to Janna on the sofa to place a hand on her arm.

"Yeah, completely." Janna looked up at me and smiled. "Agh, Adam, now you're going to feel weirded out about trying to talk to me ever again. Because I cry for no reason." She ended with a laugh, and immediately my shoulders stopped tensing.

I joined my laugh, tentative, to hers. "No." I hesitated for a second and then chose to ignore each voice of caution rearing itself to make themselves collectively known in my head as a loud blare and, instead, went full steam ahead with my real thoughts. "Actually, I just said all that because I was worried *you* were thinking, does this guy ever talk to anyone? Is he really that rude? And *then* I thought you'd think, forget getting to know Zayneb's dude, because he doesn't make sense."

Janna shook her head. "I'd never think that. Because I'm usually you. Exactly like you, happy to just be sitting back listening."

"She's telling the truth," Zayneb said, turning to me, a reassuring smile on her face. "Janna's only this talkative when it's just us two."

Janna laughed again. "So I totally get you, Adam. Don't stress about not making sense."

Such a bolt of happiness shot through me that the contentment I'd experienced before just sitting there unnoticed felt like I'd been standing outside in winter without a jacket.

Now I was bundled in a coat—with a mug of hot chocolate in my hands.

I finally laughed for real. "Okay, that was awkward. But good, too, I guess. Sorry I brought up Layth."

"I got emotional because we're trying to figure things out, Layth and me. My dad's not happy about the idea of us. Okay, he's adamantly against it. And I'm kind of surprised that my mom is too. She's usually a little more open to hearing my take." She smiled, but it was like the ends of her lips weren't strong enough to push against the sadness weighing in her mind. "My mom even thinks I got my septum piercing because of him. As if he's some kind of influence. And it's not even like I'm spending so much time with him or that he's my focus. Not at all. I have a million essays to write."

"That sucks, I'm sorry." I thought about Layth. And the way he'd been *for sure, I can take care of Bertha Fatima* without a moment's hesitation. Even though he spent every day taking care of animals at the sanctuary he worked at in South America, and even though he was now on vacation, he'd been game. He was the only guy I knew who worried about the state of the natural world enough to make it his full-time job. "From the little I know of him, I think he's a pretty good influence."

"I just want my parents to be open to the possibility of him." Janna pulled on the edges of her sweater sleeves. Like she wanted to shrink into its oversize depths. "Of him and me. But they keep asking, what's he studying? What's his career?"

"My mom wasn't happy about the idea of me and Adam, either. She was like, no way. And she talked my dad into thinking the same. Because they also thought he didn't have a career," Zayneb said. Then she caught sight of my face. "That was at first. But now my mom loves Adam," she added quickly. "A lot. More than she loves me, actually." A weak laugh ended this.

I sat back in the settee, quiet again.

Well, I'd never known *that*.

That Zayneb's mom didn't like me when she met me.

I mean, my first impression had been *exactly* that, but I'd chosen to focus on other signs in her mom and, back then, had refused to dwell on the nagging voices that said, *You don't cut it for Zayneb, buddy. You don't offer a future for her.*

I'd never known with actual certainty that her parents had balked at me. I'd just thought I was imagining things.

The feelings of inadequacy that this Umrah trip was supposed to squash roared inside me.

Change the subject. "Hey, they have another one. Your fave, Zayby." I gestured at the carved chair I was in.

Zayneb nodded, her face stricken. She was probably reacting to my face, which was probably flushing a bit.

Or a lot.

"You guys like those?" Janna looked at neither of us, choosing to focus on my chair instead. "My dad has them all over his house. He has a connection in Pakistan who can get you guys 'export quality' traditional furniture."

She winked at us.

But Zayneb didn't respond.

I knew her inside and out, and I knew she was beating herself up for blurting that part about her parents, that she was burning within for making me feel bad.

So I pushed on with the worst small talk on the planet. "Yeah, Z likes the two-seater kind. The mini sofa, you know?"

"Dark or light wood?" Janna kept the stupid conversation going.

As if we were going to buy furniture tomorrow or something.

"Walnut, so dark wood."

"Cushioned or just wood?"

"Cushioned, for sure. Otherwise it's like a bench."

"Yup." Janna got more animated. "There are some styles with beautiful mother-of-pearl inlay work. Would you guys like that?"

"I think plain is better. Goes with more stuff. And I'm sure it would be less expensive."

"Yeah, but remember, my father will get you the *ultimate best price*." She said the last words like she was in an ad.

"We're not buying a sofa, Janna," Zayneb cut in quietly.

An awkward silence descended.

"Oh, I almost forgot: Sausun is in Saudi!" Janna burst out, sliding forth her phone from where it was tucked into the wrist of her sweater. She started tapping on it, occasionally looking up at Zayneb. "She told me to give you guys her Saudi details in case you can catch up with her after Umrah, insha'Allah. I'm just messaging you her number there."

I didn't know what she was talking about. "Who?"

"Sausun. The Niqabi Ninja? YouTuber?"

"The Niqabi Ninja herself?" I sat up, still on my Zayneb-please-don't-feel-bad train. "Zayby, we have to meet up with her. She's your fave." Was I trying too hard?

Everything—the settee, Sausun—was Zayneb's fave.

Except this conversation.

"Cool, yeah, Adam, we're friends. We hung out through Janna. Thanks for her info, Janna. Yikes, look at the time." Zayneb stood up. "We have to do ghusl for ihram still. You wanna hang here while we get ready, Janna? Then we can say goodbye right before we leave for the airport."

"I actually have to get going, my Uber to the train station's almost here. I prearranged so I don't get in the way of your trip." Janna stood up and leaned in for a hug with Zayneb. "Have the best Umrah experience ever, guys. And, Adam, next time you come to Chicago, I'll take you and Zayneb to this makerspace studio that's close to Layth's rental. He showed it to me because I sew things but have no space in my dorm. It's amazing."

I nodded. At least one worry was abating: Maybe Zayneb's friends weren't going to hate me after all. Well, at least the one in front of us right now. "Hey, we told Layth we'll make dua for him in Mecca. And of course we'll make dua for you, too, insha'Allah."

"And for the idea of *the both of you*, too. If it's good for you," Zayneb added. "Thanks so much for coming by, girl. Absolutely love you so much."

Janna hugged Zayneb again and waved at me.

We walked her to the door and watched her get into an Uber, and then Zayneb turned to me.

ARTIFACT SIXTEEN:
ZAYNEB'S SAGE-GREEN CHIFFON HIJAB
INTERPRETIVE LABEL: *A GIFT YOU DIDN'T WANT STILL INVOLVES THE GIVER'S HEART*

SPIRITUALITY STARTS NOW. I TOOK A DEEP BREATH. "I'M SO SORRY, Squish. I never thought about how that would sound to you, what I said about my parents."

"Hey, come on, don't worry about it. You were just trying to make Janna feel better." He reached for my hand.

"I never think things through. Sometimes I think I'm changing, getting better at not just going with my first impulse, but then—" I picked up his other hand, and we turned to face each other in the enclosed vestibule between the front door and the foyer, a space that was essentially a landfill for kids' shoes. It smelled like it too. "Please forgive me? I'm trying to get ready for ihram but feel like I'm going to fail the first minute in."

"There's nothing to forgive, but yeah, sure, since we both have to clear our consciences before Umrah, you're completely forgiven. And forgive me, too?"

I leaned against him and nodded. "But there isn't anything you've ever done to me, Adam."

"I feel the same about you." His body relaxed even more, and I felt a chuckle rising in his chest before I heard it. "Except when you screamed at me that time at the museum in Doha. And then ignored all my messages after."

"If we're talking about ignoring messages, what about when *you* ignored mine even before that fight in the museum? When we first met? But yeah, I forgive you."

"And I forgive you for all those secrets you kept from me too," he said. "When you were surprising me with Bertha Fatima."

I'd frozen when I heard the word "secrets"—afraid he knew about the things I wasn't telling him, especially that I didn't have a place to stay right now in Chicago—but calmed down, sharing Adam's laugh.

Mental note: Follow up with all the landlords I'd contacted previously.

Who'd never gotten back to me ever about any availabilities.

Where was I going to stay during exam week? Maybe I'd have to splurge on a hotel.

Until that confrontation with Murie, I thought she'd back me up in convincing the others to let me stay on with them until I secured a new place, even if it was into January.

Also, right up until I flew to London, Ava still wasn't at the apartment much.

She was staying barely one day a week currently, if even that.

We were friends now, via texting and online, but I could never just outright ask her, *Could I use your room when you're not at home?*

My eye, the left one this time, started twitching.

Spirituality starts now, I told myself, breathing in and out slowly, my face against Adam's chest.

For weeks, this was exactly where I'd wanted to be. With Adam, wherever he was, in his arms.

So I had to be happy.

. . .

I sat quietly with myself in the guest bedroom while Adam was showering downstairs, doing his ghusl.

I was supposed to go to the other bathroom, but I was still gathering my strength to enter ihram happily.

From prepping for this trip by reading the group e-mails on the flight over, and listening to the shaykh yesterday, I knew I had to make the intention solely for the pilgrimage before I purified myself to enter the state of higher consciousness.

A renunciation of this world to enter into a state that's just between me and Allah.

I raised my hands to make dua.

A knock, followed by "Can I open?" followed by the door opening a crack. "I know Adam's downstairs, so it would just be you."

I lowered my hands, ignoring the voice that said, *She just opened the door before I said yes, which is a major pet peeve of every human being.* "Yes, come in."

Ustaadah Ramlah bustled in with various pieces of clothing draped on her outstretched arms. "What are you wearing for ihram?"

"Jilbab." I indicated my carry-on standing upright by the dresser. I'd chosen a simple khaki jilbab, nothing fancy like Sarina's.

Seeing Scarfy draped over the bedpost, I realized the jilbab was a lighter shade of the color of my cashmere scarf.

Which was nice, I think? If Umrah was done in the fall in the UK?

I shook my head free of images of me giddily tripping around Sussex in a chunky knit sweater and Scarfy, hanging off Adam's arm.

Get with the program, Zayneb.

"Jeans? Not a good idea." Ustaadah Ramlah shook her head at

the jeans I had on right now. "You want to be in a state of rejection of this life, so it's best to be fashion-less, if that's a word."

"No, I'm wearing an abaya, but the kind with no opening." I went to my carry-on to show her.

"I brought some gowns for you to try on. You can take any of these or all of them too, and buy one extra in Saudi, because we have five days there." She spread four on the bed. "I already have mine selected, but if you wanted my colors, I can give you mine instead. Black, gray, brown, and navy. I left the young colors for you."

Jilbabs that were pale pink, bright fuchsia, baby-blue, and sage-green were spread-eagled on the bed, each with ugly embroidery in garish contrasting colors at the neck. They were paired with scarves in the exact same shades—the unbelievably huge square kind of hijabs that Ustaadah Ramlah wore draped in sort of a medieval way, the folds woven and falling accordion style under her chin, and hooked up on either side of her head.

"Fashion-less" was a word, definitely.

Astaghfirullah.

And I was leaving for Umrah in an hour?

"I have one already." I turned around from unzipping the carry-on and pronounced my words carefully and slowly. "A *gown*. Two, actually." I also had a black abaya folded in my check-in luggage, the kind I could pull on over the few sleeveless cotton dresses I'd packed. "Then I'll be buying more in Mecca, insha'Allah." Again, I slowed down my speech and enunciated purposefully.

"You can't wear jeans to Mecca and then buy your Umrah clothes there. We change into ihram here, remember?" Ustaadah Ramlah held up the bright fuchsia jilbab for me. "This one is very nice."

I stopped unzipping the carry-on. I can't remember the last time I felt this frustrated talking to someone.

There was only one thing to do to ensure a smooth Umrah: just give in.

Surrender.

Make peace with the situation.

As I chose the pale pink and sage-green jilbabs to get her to leave, I couldn't help but wonder why being spiritual was so damn hard.

I decided I had five minutes to not be spiritual, so I went on social media and scrolled and responded to people and looked at my best friend Kavi's latest touches to her apartment in Paris, where she was doing further studies in art. She was supposed to come back to our hometown for winter break, and I couldn't wait.

A new message popped up from Ava as I was about to check out what Murie was up to. **Lars came by again last night. I know you're on pilgrimage so just ignore until you get back. Just wanted to record it here. It's not just a hookup. He's going to be around ALL THE TIME.**

I went to Ava's Twitter profile and read her header again. I'd found it inspirational when we first followed each other on all our socials, and I wanted a dose of that now.

It was made up of two empowering statements, and the first just spoke directly to my activist heart:

> **You are not obligated to complete the work, but neither are you free to abandon it.**
> **—Pirkei Avot**

It reminded me of something Dad always says: *Allah looks at our intentions and efforts, so start from a good place and just try your honest best. That is enough.*

The second one on Ava's profile brought to mind Mom and

how she used to remind me to seize the moment, that *the good you can do at this very moment is the most powerful good of all*:

Do justly now. Love mercy now. Walk humbly now.
—Book of Micah

It also reminded me of Sadia, who was forever quoting from her favorite series, *Ertugrul*. I actually had an *Ertugrul* quote she sent me once as my phone's wallpaper: *There is a door of hope in every moment of life that remains*.

Maybe I was feeling all sorts of things because of everything happening all at once, but thinking of Mom and Dad and Sadia just made me cry.

Do justly now. Love mercy now. Walk humbly now.

I phoned Mom and Dad, and Sadia and her husband, Jamil, and then Mansoor and Hodan, and said salaam to all of them for the third time since I started on this trip from Chicago, which was just yesterday. I even insisted on speaking to the baby through Hodan's belly. She called me silly in Somali like she always does when I fixate on funny things, and *that* made me cry with nostalgia, and Mansoor asked me if I was PMSing and Hodan punched him in the arm and I just missed them all suddenly.

Then I repacked everything I'd taken out for our brief stay here and made dua with the intention of Umrah, and went downstairs to make ghusl.

I asked for strength to fill my heart as the water flowed over me. And serenity to walk calmly for the next few days.

Then I dried off and changed into the sage-green jilbab and sage-green hijab and prayed two rakahs carefully in the sitting room, which was spread with prayer mats now, and went to meet everyone in the foyer, where the kids had already brought all the luggage.

Apparently their grandparents were coming over to stay with them while the shaykh and Ustaadah Ramlah led us on Umrah.

Adam came down the stairs slowly in his ihram, two large unstitched white cloths—one secured around his waist with a belt, reaching down to just above his ankle and another cloth wrapped around his torso with one end flipped over his left shoulder. He held his coat in one hand, and the way his face was beaming, my heart immediately filled with beautiful peace.

I helped him into his sandals, open-toed footwear revealing heels and ankles being part of ihram for men, and then slipped into my shoes.

I was going to Mecca, the house of Allah, with Adam.

On the ride to the airport, sitting between Ustaadah Ramlah and Adam in the back of a van being driven by one of the shaykh's assistants, I didn't dwell on a solution to a math problem that had entered my head unbidden: If there were eight of us women, and we were in quad rooms with one leader in each room, then there was a 50 percent chance that Ustaadah Ramlah would be my leader.

That hit me so hard, I physically flinched.

Spirituality starts now, Zayneb.

ARTIFACT SEVENTEEN: ADAM'S BOARDING PASS
INTERPRETIVE LABEL: *EN ROUTE TO CHANGE*

AFTER PASSING THROUGH SECURITY, WE RECONVENED AS A GROUP AT our gate.

Walking through the airport to get to this point was the first time I opened my eyes to what Zayneb must go through each day wearing hijab. It felt like everyone whispered to themselves, did a double take, or stared politely or impolitely at my ihram.

I think I was the only one who noticed, because Shaykh Murtaza just moved through the crowds like the Umrah pro he was to get settled at our gate. He looked like he'd worn two pieces of cloth with no underwear all his life.

I wasn't embarrassed. Not at all. It felt noble to be wearing ihram.

Though "noble" comes off wrong, as it connotes a tiny bit of arrogance that feels intrinsic to the word, and I didn't want any of that invading my heart after I'd entered this spiritual state for Umrah.

It was more like confidence of purpose. Like I had a destination to reach, and that destination was beyond all the stares or curiosities or contempt of other humans.

It was like I was moving toward entering another realm.

I was going to a place first built thousands of years ago by Abraham. And from that time until now, countless people from all walks of life, from all corners of the globe had assembled in that space to remember the sacred. And I was privileged enough to be part of a flow of humanity that stretched across time and space, a flow that will continue even after I leave this earth.

I smiled again at Zayneb walking beside me, my carry-on keeping pace on the other side.

What Shaykh Murtaza had said about the automated case came to my head: R2-D2.

Wearing ihram and walking with others similarly clothed, it truly felt as if I was in a *Star Wars* world, as though I'd left my old life behind on another planet.

I don't know if it was the serotonin flowing through me, but my body hadn't felt so energized in a long time.

We greeted everyone in our Umrah group gathered at the gate with salaams, and when we drew away from Sarina, Zayneb pointed out how no-nonsense and cool her outfit was. "I need to get one of those in Mecca. Remind me, Squish."

Again, Sarina was wearing a one-piece head-to-toe jilbab, this time in mauve, with thick white sneakers and a white backpack.

"Masha'Allah, everyone looks well rested and ready!" Shaykh Murtaza beamed at the group. "Stay around this area and maintain your state of Umrah readiness by doing dhikr and focusing on the purpose of this trip."

"And take a moment to come see me to learn your hotel room group—you'll be seated together in that group on the flight to get acquainted a bit as well," Sarina said. "Insha'Allah, you'll be feeling comfortable with each other by the time we check in, after which we'll immediately go to the Haram, to start our tawaf."

"Make sure you've got everything ready to go the minute we reach Mecca, insha'Allah," Ustaadah Ramlah said. "The flight is about six hours, so you'll have time, but still be prepared. And it's easier to organize your belongings here."

"That sure is a lot of instructions," Zayneb said quietly, before catching my eye. "But in a good way, I mean."

"Alhamdulillah, they've got everything organized." I began moving toward the group members gathering around Sarina but paused to turn back to Zayneb. "You coming? To check your room group?"

"I'll wait until it clears up a bit." She pointed at some empty seats a few aisles over. "I'll be sitting there. Doing dhikr."

I nodded and waited by Sarina.

"Adam, you're with Sahaan, Shaykh Murtaza, and Isa." Sarina checked her list. "And, Zayneb, you're with . . ."

"She's over there." I indicated Zayneb's direction with my head. "You can tell me, and I'll pass it on."

"Sure, she's with Mila, Fatima, and me."

I thanked her and went over to Zayneb.

The smile that lit her face on hearing her roommates was wondrous, and I knew more than ever, this Umrah was going to be the second best thing to happen to us this year.

The best thing being getting our nikah done, of course.

Four years after we first caught sight of each other at this same airport.

And now we were going to Mecca together?

"Subhanallah," I said, pulling the upper ihram cloth, the rida, taut after I removed my arm from it so I could put it around Zayneb. "We're like half a day away from seeing the Kaaba. I can't believe it."

She leaned her head against me and whispered, "Alhamdulillah," and closed her eyes.

"Sleep," I whispered into the top of her hijab, arm still around her, before using my other hand to open the flagged e-mail from Shaykh Murtaza on my phone.

I was going to go through the attached PDFs again. I wanted the rites to come naturally, so I'd been reading over the process repeatedly, like I was studying for an exam.

As soon as we landed in Jeddah around midnight, and cleared customs, we'd be getting on a minibus for the hour-long drive to Mecca. Then we'd check into the hotel, deposit our luggage in our rooms, and immediately meet in the lobby to head over to the Haram to do tawaf, the first rite of Umrah.

Then we'd pray two rakahs and drink Zamzam and then do Sa'i.

Sa'i. Walking seven times between two hills.

After doing seven circuits around the Kaaba.

I'd better rest like Zayneb was doing right now.

ARTIFACT EIGHTEEN: ZAYNEB'S BOARDING PASS
INTERPRETIVE LABEL: *EN ROUTE TO DISCOVERY*

ALHAMDULILLAH, I KEPT REPEATING.

Adam was in the row of four seats right in front of me, and since he was sitting next to the aisle and I was sitting next to Sarina, who was in the aisle seat behind him, I got a little glimpse of Adam through the space in between seats. If I tilted my head. And stuck it out a little.

Alhamdulillah.

And the airline was Saudia, so they welcomed all pilgrims via a special Umrah announcement—and there were quite a few of us pilgrims sprinkled throughout the plane. The pilot said they'd announce miqat, which was the point at which we crossed over into sacred territory for Umrah, and we pilgrims could take turns praying in the space provided.

Alhamdulillah.

On the other side of me was the blond woman named Mila, maybe in her early thirties, now in black hijab. After a welcoming smile to myself and Fatima on the other side of her, she took out her prayer beads and started making dhikr right away. Which was really nice. To have such a peaceful seatmate.

Alhamdulillah.

And Sarina was my leader, not Ustaad—well, let's just say I was going to have a better experience with communications on this trip.

I guess it was easy being good if you focused on seeing the positives around you. Which was something I'd always loved about Adam—how he consistently saw the marvels of life, even the simple ones, whereas I noticed the things that needed to be fixed.

Like that Sarina kept getting out of her seat to check on the four rows of our Umrah group, all behind one another in the middle set of seats on the aircraft, like she was a flight attendant or something. And when she sat back down, she had to adjust herself a lot so she didn't sit on the billowy arms of her jilbab, which meant I had to lean over almost into Mila's space while Sarina settled into her seat. I apologized each time to Mila, but Sarina didn't apologize to anyone.

But anyway, *alhamdulillah.*

"Do you feel ready?" Sarina asked after she came back to her seat for the fourth time. "For your first Umrah?"

"I do," I said, snuggling into Scarfy, which I'd brought along as a blanket and/or pillow. It wouldn't fit into my luggage, but I'd wanted to bring it on the trip—maybe in some strange homage to our canceled Hidden Bloom trip? Or maybe it was to remember Sadia, because it was her gift to me. "Thanks for all the prep. It's all so well organized."

"Of course, and, really, no worries." Sarina buckled in, took her iPad out of the seat pocket, and put her tray down to use as a surface to prop it on. "So are you done with school or still studying?"

"I'm in first-year law school."

"Wow, masha'Allah. And you made time for Umrah. Impressive."

"It's a gift from Adam's father, for our nikah."

"That's generous. But still, you had to make time in your hectic schedule to do this, so again, masha'Allah."

"Yeah, I doubled down on the studying to get ready. Which is kind of easy as that's the only thing I'm doing right now anyway. Adam and I don't live together, so I have plenty of time to focus."

"Yeah, he told me he didn't end up finishing school. I remember he'd been so excited about first year."

"First year?" *What does she mean, "remember"?*

"We went to school together. In London." She scrolled through a bunch of e-mails and then opened one and, before reading it, peered at me quickly. "Didn't he tell you?"

He didn't.

Oh wait, he did. A while ago.

That's why the name Sarina was familiar.

Not because of an e-mail.

Because of Adam.

"Okay, your turn." We were lying on the grass in Gulhane Park in Istanbul this past August. I'd just told Adam about all the crushes I'd had, ending with the most serious one: Yasin—a family friend of one of my best friends, Ayaan.

I'd met him at her house one day. And it had almost resulted in coupledom as Yasin had liked me back. A lot.

But then I discovered he was into writing things about Muslim girls and their hijabs online in true haram-police fashion.

After Ayaan's cousin Hodan married my brother Mansoor, Yasin actually even approached Mansoor after their wedding to be the go-between for us, to see if "we could try again," and my brother told him that my heart was elsewhere. He didn't reveal the exact location of my heart—Doha, Qatar—but Mansoor made sure Yasin knew it was a no-go.

Ayaan started dropping hints that Yasin had actually reformed, had moved on to "refine" (her word) himself, but by then, I was too far gone for Adam.

By then, I was sure that if Adam and I didn't end up together, I wouldn't want anyone else.

No one even came close in my heart.

The last I heard, Yasin was studying political science. And single.

In Gulhane Park, I showed Adam a picture of Yasin, and he raised his eyebrows. "You gave *him* up for me?"

"Yup. May he meet the right someone for him. Ameen." I'd actually first fallen for Yasin's looks. *WHO'S THAT?* had been the first thing out of my mouth at Ayaan's when I'd spotted him coming up from the basement with her brothers.

I flipped my head to face Adam, realizing my shallow self had first fallen for *his* looks too—which were kissably perfect in the waning light of approaching Maghrib. We'd chosen a hidden spot near the mini masjid in the park and would soon have to leave for prayer when we heard the adhan. So I needed to know about Adam's crushes fast. "Again, your turn."

"Emma Watson. Yara Shahidi. But both when I was young"

"They don't count; they're both famous actresses. And you were a baby."

"You know about the girl in fourth grade."

"Again: You were a baby."

"Then I guess I only had crushes when I was a baby. On older women."

"That sounds really gross." I turned on my back and stared at the Istanbul sky. "Like really no one else?"

"After my mom died, I spent five years just trying to figure life out, remember? I don't think I focused on too many things intensely at the time." He played with my fingers in his hand. "And in high school, there weren't that many Muslim girls who knew English well at Doha International School. And I'd decided I was only into Muslim girls at that point."

"What about after high school?" I kept prodding because I wanted to know if I was really truly the first person he'd fallen in love with. I already felt the glow starting inside at knowing that I was, but I needed Adam to state the fact plainly as it really was: *Zayneb, you're the first girl I ever fell for.*

But he'd become quiet.

I turned to him again, propping myself up on an elbow to get a good look at his entire face.

Oh my God, he was flushing.

Instead of saying, *Aha! So there was someone before me!* as was my first impulse, I waited. Not because I was trying to be patient, but because the glow inside me was extinguishing slowly . . . and by the look on his face, I wished I hadn't asked.

It was something serious.

He hadn't opened his mouth still, even after all this time of me staring at him waiting.

That's how serious it was?

"Who was it in college, then?" Great, my voice was low and solemn and the complete opposite of how we'd started this conversation, which was fun and light and joking around.

"Just this girl named Sarina. In first year."

"Sarina. What a pretty name."

"You think so? I personally prefer the name *Zayneb*." He smiled at me and then reached up to trace my lips.

"Sarina, it sounds so serene. Was she?" I couldn't stop the urgency in my voice. I didn't recognize the feelings in me—the glow seemed to have erupted into a flame, and it needed stoking for some scary reason.

"I guess so? In a way?" He dropped his finger from my lips and looked at the sky again. "Anyway, that was, like, years ago."

"Four years ago."

"No, five, because when I met you, I'd moved on. Completely."

"So was it before you left school?"

"Yeah, around the beginning of freshman year. First half. Do we have to talk about this?" He suddenly whipped his head to look at my eyes, and I immediately looked down, afraid he'd see the hurt in them.

Why was I hurt?

He'd met this Sarina before he met me.

And then he'd fallen hard for me. *Me*, who was now lying beside him, who got to kiss him and make out with him and make love to him all the time—well, not all the time, but whenever we were together—and there was nothing that was going to change that. Insha'Allah.

But I knew why I was hurt.

In his more than usual reticence, I saw a truth: Sarina had made a huge impact on him.

And that just thrust me into a place I'd always grappled with in relationships, even friendships, before: jealousy.

"Zayneb? Are you upset?" He turned on his side and propped himself on an elbow too. "You told me about Yasin. And it's not even the same. Sarina and I had never come close to an agreement or anything."

"But were you going to ask her? If you guys could get to know each other for coupledom?"

Again, he went silent. Then gazed at the grass that he was stroking absentmindedly—as my hand was out of reach for him because it was fiddling nervously with my hijab. "Yes, okay, I was."

"Then what happened?"

"Then I learned I had MS and that's all I cared about." He lifted his eyes to mine. "You know I'm not a great multitasker. Except when it has to do with my love for you and everything else in my life. No other girl made me want to juggle things like you, Zayneb. For you, anything."

And then he moved in for a kiss right at that moment and the adhan for Maghrib went off and the flames extinguished and the glow took over and I forgot all about Sarina.

Until now.

She was sitting right beside me, making notes with her Apple Pencil on her iPad.

I noticed how her fingers were smooth, with short but cute nails. How she had only one thin silver ring that held a cut-out heart in the center. She wore it on the ring finger of her right hand.

Did the cut-out heart mean she missed someone?

Stop, Zayneb.

"So what about you? Are you with someone or talking to anyone or already married?" I asked. "Or just not into that?"

"I *was* married—got engaged, actually, in the middle of first year, married the next year. Family—well, relatives in the home country—arrangement." She smiled at me and went back to underlining something on the iPad. "But it didn't work out. We ended things last year."

"Ah, okay. Anyone new now?"

"No, but I *am* looking, if you know anyone. And I'm pretty upfront and particular about what I want," she said, setting down her pencil. "Shaykh Murtaza is helping look for me."

"Hey, if I know someone, I'll help." I added an enthusiastic nod to this. "Are you looking for someone who's finished school and started their career or—"

"No, those things don't matter to me. As long as his deen is really important to him, and he works hard at whatever he does, I'm willing to talk to him."

"Oh, I just brought that up because you said you're particular, so I thought you had, like, career expectations."

"No, I'm insistent on deen, and, Zayneb, you may not know it, but these days that's hard to find." She sighed. "You're blessed. You got one of the few remaining good ones."

I knew that was supposed to make me feel better, but it actually made me feel worse.

Like a tiny lick of jealousy fire was getting fanned due to some oxygen I was sending it.

"Alhamdulillah," I said to Sarina. "Alhamdulillah."

Sarina patted my arm and unbuckled and put her tray up and tucked her iPad and pencil in the seat pocket. Then she got up and moved in the aisle to the seat in front of her.

"You guys doing good here?" She nodded at Adam and Shaykh Murtaza beside him and then the other two guys from our Umrah group adjacent to them. "Shaykh, they're going to announce miqat soon, so if you want to help Adam get to the bathroom and prayer area, that would be great. He can get comfortable there before it gets busy."

I sat up straighter to try to catch Sarina's eyes.

Adam didn't need help—he was feeling good, his MS was in remission.

And, anyway, if he did need anything, *I* could help him.

She moved back a bit so Adam could get out of his seat. I half stood and reached over and touched her arm. "I can help Adam with things. And take him to the prayer area."

"It's okay, insha'Allah. Shaykh Murtaza will help. He promised Adam's dad. And I'm always here," she added as Shaykh Murtaza and Adam walked forward. "I'll follow them right now to make sure all is well. So not to worry. You can concentrate on your own ibadat, alhamdulillah."

I sat back down, but it was against my instinct, my impulse, my inner voice, which was roaring, *Go be with your Adam.*

But I knew that was my nafs, my lower ego, saying, *Adam is yours, and no one else has a right to be with him.*

That's your pride, Zayneb. Squash it—you're on Umrah.

I had to tame the lion within that was always ready to fight everything and everyone, even serene spiritual leaders who had a weird undercurrent you couldn't put your finger on.

How much had Sarina liked Adam back, when he'd liked her five years ago?

Before my mind could go down that hole, I received a text over Wi-Fi.

Assalamu alaikum, this is Sausun-in-Saudi. As soon as you're done with Umrah, text me. Our home is on the way to Medina and my father is big on treating pilgrims so we'd like to host your entire group. Just tell me the date. We're out near the water so you'll get a bit of a different experience here than the busy city life insha'Allah. Umrah mubarak.

I closed my eyes and imagined myself with Adam near the water, under the starry sky, away from the rest of the group for a bit, Sarina—and Ustaadah Ramlah—nowhere near us.

Insha'Allah it will be okay.

Insha'Allah.

ARTIFACT NINETEEN: ADAM'S MOM'S BEE BRACELET CHARM
INTERPRETIVE LABEL: BEELIEVE IN CHANGE

AFTER LANDING, IT WAS ALL A BLUR OF QUIET, SOLEMN WAITING PERIods in between bouts of activity: lining up in Umrah processing queues; getting our passports looked at; picking out our luggage, after which porters took charge of our bags; going through customs; being ushered toward exits by airport officials Shaykh Murtaza knew; bursting out of automated double doors to the awaiting lineups of taxis, buses, vans, and minibuses, one of them ours; then finally being seated next to Zayneb and on our way to Mecca.

As soon I took my spot on the vinyl bus bench, I felt like breaking down in tears of happy relief.

The weather was perfect, I'd had a great sleep on the flight, Zayneb had come by my seat after using the bathroom and stood chatting for a while—until a flight attendant asked her to move—and I was excited to see she'd looked more like herself, more fired up.

"We're here!" I said, nudging Zayneb with my shoulder, pointing out the window as the bus pulled out of the lineup.

"Almost. We still have to get to Mecca."

"Why do you have that blanket with you?" I touched the brown blanket she held folded in her lap. "I don't think you'll need it. You want me to shove it in my carry-on?"

Shaykh Murtaza had requested that R2-D2 not be put in the back with the rest of the luggage as it had my medicine in it. It was now in a space beside the driver's seat, just one row up from us.

"I'll hold on to it. It's the scarf I was wearing before. I actually bought it for our cottage trip," Zayneb said. "You feeling okay? Or tired?"

"No, I slept a lot, remember? I'm ready. And really excited. You?"

"I didn't sleep at all, but it's okay. I'm going to use my stay-up-all-night-cramming-for-exams energy for this."

Sarina came by our seat as she moved to the front of the bus. She turned to all of us when she got beside R2-D2. "We've started Umrah, so stay in a state of patience and forbearance, focusing on your connection with Allah. Shaykh Murtaza will now share some duas we can say as we approach Mecca."

Sarina went back, and Shaykh Murtaza got up from his seat behind the driver. Ustaadah Ramlah began to rise too, but Shaykh Murtaza said, "I'll be okay, dear," and she sat back down.

"Alhamdulillah," Zayneb said aloud.

"Yes, that's the spirit, Zayneb!" Shaykh Murtaza exclaimed with joy, his face seeming even more animated without his kufi on top of his head. "Gratitude, patience, trust, opening ourselves up to Allah."

He led us in several Arabic duas, with English translations. We kept repeating the Talbiyah, which we'd started on the flight as the plane approached the miqat, one of the geographic points that encompass the sacred territory of pilgrimage, *Labbayka llāhumma labbayk, labbayka lā sharīka laka labbayk, inna l-ḥamda wa n-niʿmata, laka wa l-mulk, lā sharīka lak.*

At Your service, Allah, at Your service. At Your service, You have no partner, at Your service. Truly all praise, favor, and sovereignty are Yours. You have no partner.

"Focus on your inner landscape. On all that is going on internally," Shaykh Murtaza reminded us. "A clear landscape within, where you can see and reflect on your motivations and inclinations and intentions, is a gift. It can help us survive the harsh conditions of life here on earth. It can lead us to refine ourselves. And to a state of surrender to God's will, trusting He will take us where we need to be if we rely on Him only—which is a state that comprises the greatest happiness in the world. Truly. Being at utter peace within our own soul because it is connected to the Sustainer of all souls."

Zayneb nodded beside me and bowed her head in reflection. Again, I was struck by how serious and focused she'd become since we entered ihram.

There was so much of her to get to know still. And I had a lifetime, however short or long it was willed to be by Allah, to do that.

For that, I was grateful.

I looked out the window as the bus moved through the busy streets, changing lanes back and forth abruptly, onto a highway that began with blocks of commercial plazas on either side and gradually transformed to being surrounded by rocky, dusty terrain—much the same as what I saw when we drove out of Doha.

My gaze was on the scenery outside, but I was really trying to concentrate on the landscape within, like Shaykh Murtaza reminded us to.

Which meant thinking about being braver and more honest and open with everyone in my life. The way Mom had been with me.

Dad had discovered Islam a year after Mom passed away when I was nine. And then, a year after that, when I was eleven, I became Muslim like him.

Mom hadn't been Muslim, she'd been Christian, but she encompassed so much of what I loved about my faith. She was principled and gutsy and the sort of truthful that stood out and was sometimes embarrassing. And she was caring, so caring that when I was little, I thought everyone spent their birthdays volunteering and giving charity like she did and like she took me to do on my birthdays. Like dropping food off and volunteering at the food bank or spending time at an animal shelter or serving at a soup kitchen.

And then after, we'd spend the rest of the day at an amusement park. Each year, we went to the same park in Ottawa, because my birthday was during the summer when I visited Canada from Doha during school breaks.

We always saved the bumblebee ride for last because it was my favorite. It was so low-key and completely uneventful, but I remember that if I closed my eyes, it felt like I was the bee itself.

Mom loved watching me and always paid to let me go on the ride as many times as I wanted.

Bees were also her special thing. She had bee necklaces and charms and sometimes even found funny bee pajamas and slippers.

She told me she'd been afraid of bees until I was born. "I knew they were good for the world, so I didn't hurt them or, God forbid, kill them, but I couldn't stand to even see them," she told me one day as we watched a bee buzzing around the sedums in grandma and grandpa's yard in Ottawa when I was seven. "But when you were born, someone gave you a huge stuffed bumblebee as a gift."

"And that made you not afraid of them anymore?" I leaned against her carefully while my eyes followed a bee that had just landed on one of the sedum flower bunches.

Mom had begun using a walker more frequently for her MS,

and I was aware that, even with my small size, I could maybe topple her if I was too rough.

"No, I just saw that you loved that bee toy so much, that you saw something in it that I didn't." She wrapped her arms around me from the back, and I chanced tucking my head under her chin. But gently. She responded by nuzzling the top of my head. "And I thought, what could you see in that bee that I don't? Why were you as a baby not afraid of something that I'd learned to fear?"

"And that made you not afraid? When you thought that?"

"No. Thinking that made me want to learn about bees. And I spent years learning."

"Learning made you not afraid?"

"No. Unlearning did." She turned me around and kissed the top of my head. "You taught me to unlearn. That means take everything I'd learned about something and look at it again and see the things that I'd gotten wrong. Like before, I'd thought that every time a bee buzzed around me, it was planning to attack me."

I laughed at that, at the imagery of bees having a meeting to prepare to attack Mom. "They don't want to attack humans, Mom."

She laughed with me. "I know. Even then, when I was scared of them, I knew it, but I couldn't stop thinking they were out to get me. Until I unlearned about them, and relearned that they have certain dances that they do to communicate with each other, to tell each other what kind of flower is nearby and where it is and other information. I didn't understand that dance language, and so I interpreted it wrong. I thought it was all about me . . . when really, they had their own lives and worries and things to think about." She looked behind me at the sedums. "Through bees, I learned to take myself out of the center of things. Out of the middle, like I was the most important thing in this world."

"But you're important too," I said, a reoccurring fear beckoning me to consider it again. It was what I'd held quietly inside when I found out Mom had gotten sicker recently.

The fear was that she'd go to the hospital forever. Because whenever she went there, Dad kept reassuring me that the hospital was doing a good job taking care of Mom, better than we could at home. *What if she thought she wasn't important at home anymore and then went to the hospital?* That's what my seven-year-old brain asked me. "You're important, right, Mom?"

"I'm important. Just like you are and Dad is and the bees and the flowers they love. Just like everyone is important." She turned me back around and pointed at the bees. "When you know that and believe it and act upon it, everything and everyone around you will feel at peace with you."

I nodded and finally allowed myself to fully relax against her. She seemed so strong in that moment.

It was only years later, when I thought about that experience with Mom, that I understood why she had seemed so strong then: because she was frank, her heart open, her mind as well, and she spoke without pretenses and with utter honesty.

Like every time I tried to confirm something about what she told me in that moment, she simply opened herself up more.

No, I just saw that you loved that bee toy so much, that you saw something in it that I didn't.

No. Thinking that made me want to learn about bees.

No. Unlearning did.

She was up-front about her process, how she'd been wrong. She didn't jail her vulnerabilities.

Recently, I'd realized I wasn't like that.

I had Mom's sense of principles, but I didn't have her bravery and her unfiltered heart.

I had to break down the sense of protectiveness—or maybe it was shame?—I felt whenever I thought about revealing my setbacks.

Like how I'd failed at securing a livelihood.

How I was pretending to be okay on my own.

When I actually needed someone there for me every day. *Maybe to even help support me.*

I turned my head slightly, leaning it against the window, and took a quick look at Zayneb.

She had her chin resting on her clavicle, eyes closed, her shoulders moving gently up and down.

Finally asleep.

I carefully loosened my rida cloth and eased my right arm out slow and steady and then put it around her and held her in case she fell forward when the bus driver changed lanes roughly again.

As she snored quietly against me, I gazed at the dark sky and thanked Allah that Zayneb was in my life. Just as I finished whispering a dua that she would be okay with my current circumstances and truths, whenever I felt strong enough to tell her, the tall clock tower showed up on the horizon, the one abutting the Masjid al-Haram.

I held on to Zayneb, so she wouldn't shift, and sat up.

There were more trees and greenery now, dividing the opposing lanes of traffic as we neared the birthplace of the faith I'd embraced after Mom's passing.

We went through a tunnel and came out to buildings growing closer and closer together, and then, suddenly, we were confronted with the rock faces of mountains that had been standing by, stalwart, watching pilgrims for thousands of years.

I gazed at those mountains, visible even in the dark due to all the lights around them, and thought about one of the reasons I'd chosen to be Muslim.

It was for the same reason we were all wearing identical clothes on this bus: two simple pieces of cloth for the men, no way to distinguish ourselves by the cut and style and quality of our garments, and basic, unembellished clothing for the women.

It was for the idea inherent in Islam's ideals that there is no difference, no elevated status, no clergy structure, no lines of nobility to distinguish any of us humans, except by the good we do, measured only by Allah, not humans.

As the blinding white light of the masjid surrounding the Kaaba came into view and my eyes teared up instantly, what Mom said so long ago spoke to my heart: *Everyone is important. When you know that and believe it and act upon it, everything and everyone around you will feel at peace with you.*

I woke up my Zayneb and she opened her eyes to the light of our destination.

ARTIFACT TWENTY:
ZAYNEB'S BOTTLE OF ZAMZAM
INTERPRETIVE LABEL: CONSIDER THE SOURCE

As soon as we deposited our luggage in our hotel rooms and used the bathrooms, I was raring to go.

I thought I'd crash, I thought I'd want to take a shower to refresh myself, I thought I'd need a break, but nope, that one glimpse of the masjid was enough to wake and shake me.

It was exciting. To be in the same spot that I'd read and learned about in Sunday school classes at the masjid, at Islamic conferences, from my parents, from Muslim spaces, for all these years. To see it come alive in real time, in real life.

Also, all the pictures I'd seen of Masjid al-Haram, whether the many artistic renderings that hung in people's homes, including my parents' home, or real photos, didn't do the place justice.

A lot of them were *ugly* compared to the real thing.

I knew there were lots of artificial lights around the place—from the masjid, from the streets, from the hotel complexes close by, including the one we were staying in that was located inside the clock tower itself—but there also appeared to be an out-of-this-world glow permeating the entire site.

A scientific person would have said that the glow had perhaps something to do with all the lights bouncing off one another, but I saw the glow as being atmospheric. Like it came from the sky and rose from the ground and bulged out to secure the whole place in a luminescent bubble.

Like we were inside an orb anchored between the earth and sky.

And in a little while I would finally be seeing the Kaaba! My body and mind tingled as it hit me that I was approximately five minutes away from one of the most historic and spiritual sites in the world.

Upon meeting up with some of the others in the hotel lobby, I could see I wasn't the only one who felt this way. A palpable energy flowed through all of us as we waited for the shaykh and his group to come down so we could all walk over.

I texted Adam. **You good? We're in the lobby. Next to the yummy spiced coffee.**

As if in reply, one of the elevators opened, and Adam stepped out with his group and several pilgrims, his roommates as well as others.

I'd never seen his face so bright. Even on our nikah day.

Without any conscious thoughts sending the command, my feet immediately began moving toward him like I was a moth drawn to the glow.

But from out of nowhere, Sarina and Ustaadah Ramlah appeared in front of me and were already meeting Adam and Shaykh Murtaza in the space in front of the bank of elevators.

Then they headed to the side to confer among themselves— Shaykh Murtaza, Ustaadah Ramlah, Adam, and Sarina.

I watched from a distance, from between them and the group I'd just left, hesitant about whether I should burst into their huddle. Would I be interrupting?

Someone came to my side. Fatima. "What's going on? I thought we were supposed to leave for tawaf?"

"Don't know." I shrugged. "Let's go check?"

If Fatima came with me, I wouldn't be just feeding the irk beginning to reveal itself again: Why did it feel like Sarina was constantly trying to interfere with Adam?

"Everything okay, insha'Allah?" I called out as we approached them.

"Yes, no worries," Sarina answered, her right hand making a *shoo, go back* motion.

The irritation roared inside me, and I quickened the remaining steps to close the gap so I was right with them.

What is wrong with her?

Ugh, we weren't supposed to get angry or upset or agitated in any way during Umrah. Astaghfirullah.

Adam turned to me and nodded. "Zayneb, you're just the one we need."

"I'm here." I moved closer to him but couldn't stop myself from staring at Sarina. "Yeah?"

"They're checking if I'm going to need a wheelchair for tawaf," Adam said. "But I think I can do it. If we're not too much on the outskirts, and closer to the Kaaba, insha'Allah."

"If we need a wheelchair, we have to get it from the accessibility offices—there are two separate ones depending on the kind we're interested in. Ones with an attendant assigned to push or ones without, where we'll be pushing ourselves, or even fully motorized ones," Sarina said, looking at Fatima instead of me for some reason. "And so we'd need to head there first, as a whole group or just a few of us, and then we'll meet you guys."

"You just heard him. He said he doesn't need one." I tilted my head to try to get Sarina's eyes on me. "Besides, I'll be with him the whole time we're doing tawaf, and if we should need one, I'll go get one."

"That will disrupt his tawaf," Sarina protested, now looking at the shaykh, whose eyes were ping-ponging from Adam to me to Sarina, confused. "We should decide things before we start. It's too far to go get a chair in the middle of things."

"He decided already." I spoke slowly. "And there's no one better to advocate for himself than Adam."

"He said he doesn't need one, Sarina." Ustaadah Ramlah put a hand on Sarina's arm. "I know you care a lot, subhanallah, but the one you care about has expressed himself."

Wow, I guess I spoke so clearly that even Ustaadah Ramlah understood me.

Sarina shrugged and raised her eyebrows and ran a finger under her chin where her jilbab's headcover met her face and started walking to the rest of our group, some of whom were still sampling the delicious cardamon-laced lobby coffee.

I turned to Adam and held out my hand. "I don't think holding hands as we do tawaf is considered hanky-panky," I whispered, and he laughed before taking my hand in his.

"Just to let you know, I said it a few times. That I didn't need a wheelchair," Adam confided. "I've been feeling really good. That's why I wanted to do Umrah in the first place."

"And you have your cane on standby. And if we need to, we'll go slower than everyone else."

He looked down at me with such love in his eyes that I could feel my whole self flushing.

Which was subhanallah because it just put a stop to me pondering Sarina again.

I didn't want to think about her during my first Umrah rite. I wanted to be thinking of my inner landscape, of Allah, of why I was here.

• • •

After stepping out of the hotel and walking the marble-floored space outside, under the middle-of-the-night sky, we got to the entrance to Masjid al-Haram. We took off our shoes and placed them in bags provided and entered the masjid with our right feet, repeating a dua after the shaykh. Then, after padding quietly in awe through the masjid for a while, we moved toward the archway of one of the entrances to the courtyard, and all of a sudden I glimpsed it: the Kaaba.

The structure two billion of us around the world faced when we prayed.

Tears rolled down my cheeks as we all paused to repeat the special first-sighting-of-the-Kabaa dua after the shaykh.

It was shrouded in black velvet like in all the pictures I'd seen but stood taller than I'd envisioned it. Again, the lighting was otherworldly and made it seem like we'd stepped into another realm of existence.

Here, at the Kaaba, it felt like we were in the very middle of the luminescent orb.

The pull I felt was like nothing I'd ever felt before—a magnetic connection.

We followed the groups of people heading toward the majestic cube, keeping an eye on the back of the shaykh's head and Usta-adah Ramlah's white hijab. As soon as we got to the corner of the Kaaba that housed the Black Stone, we would turn so that the Kaaba was on our left side and start circulating around it seven times counterclockwise.

The shaykh had told us he was going to do his best to get us as close to the Kaaba as safely possible, into a flow that wasn't too crowded, so, as I held on to Adam's hand, I forced myself to tear my eyes away from the Kaaba and put them to work following our group leaders. We needed to get near in order to shorten the circumference Adam would be walking.

I was also ready to elbow anyone out of the way if I thought they were getting too close to us. I knew from having read accounts of Umrah that some people push as they do tawaf—perhaps absentmindedly, perhaps in their zealousness—but I wouldn't let that happen to Adam.

We pulled through, and suddenly we were facing the corner of the Kaaba with the Black Stone, a stone we Muslims believed came from heaven, but we were still on the outer edges of the circulating crowds. A safer space.

The shaykh turned to all of us. "I think that the best thing to do is for a few of us to try to get closer with Adam, and then the rest of you who are able to, do tawaf from here, which is less busy but may take a bit longer with more walking. Sarina you can lead the outer group in the duas. We'll meet right by the pole over there to make our prayers after tawaf."

He looked at Adam and me. "You two come with us. Insha'Allah, we'll find a good spot. But don't think about getting close to the Black Stone. It's too dangerous, with all the people pushing. Just hold up a hand in salute and repeat the dua after me."

I nodded and held on to Adam's hand tighter. He tapped my calf with his cane. "I don't want my fingers broken while doing tawaf," he said with a laugh.

I loosened my hold and said bismillah and let Adam go ahead, behind Ustaadah Ramlah as she followed the shaykh.

"Be careful," someone called out from behind me.

I didn't need to turn around to check who it was. "Labbayka llāhumma labbayk," I whispered to ground myself in the task at hand, to attempt to smother the ember still burning inside that sparked and was prepared to roar whenever I heard her voice.

A miracle occurred, solely, I was sure, due to Adam's pure intention to visit Mecca: By speaking to one of the guards near the Kaaba, and indicating Adam's mobility cane, midway while we were making our tawaf, the shaykh was able to get us a little clearing of space, aided by the guard who'd taken note of us.

We were part of the flow of humanity from all parts of the globe, circulating like the earth herself. I wanted to close my eyes to feel how I wasn't just myself anymore, how I was part of all those around me as we wore the same clothing, said the same words, and moved the same way, but that would be foolishly dangerous, so I tried to fix my eyes on the black fabric of the Kaaba, to reflect and concentrate.

But that was short-lived. My eyes were constantly moving around, checking for obstructions in Adam's way. Even though the guard had taken mercy on us, I couldn't be assured that he'd continuously keep clearing a space for us.

I wanted to feel like I was part of the blur of people, that we were all one, but I couldn't.

Right as we turned on our sixth rotation, a break in the crowd appeared near the Black Stone. I could literally take a few steps, and I'd be able to touch it!

I tapped Ustaadah Ramlah. "We're so close to the Black Stone now. Can we try?"

She shook her head. "It's not necessary. Just do your duas, do Talbiyah."

"But there's an opening. And it looks safe, Ustaadah." I slowed down to point at it, and Adam let go of my hand as his other arm was looped through shaykh's, who was leading him and holding Adam's unused cane for him.

I wanted to touch it—the Black Stone, a gift from heaven.

I knew it wasn't necessary, but I just wanted to.

To think, the Prophet had touched it many times so long ago and had actually helped restore it to its rightful place with a brilliant plan.

After a fire almost destroyed the Kaaba, when it was being rebuilt, the clans begin arguing as to who should be granted the privilege of placing the Black Stone back in its spot. They finally agreed on a solution of sorts: The next person who came through the gate would decide which clan it would be.

The next person who came through was thirty-five-year-old Muhammad, five years before he became a prophet. The clan leaders asked him to settle their argument, and he asked that a cloth be brought. He set the stone in the middle of the cloth, and each leader held a side of the fabric and, working together, brought it to the Kaaba. Muhammad then set the stone in place.

By virtue of his idea, he also set peace in place.

I teared up now just thinking about the story we were told as children.

"No, Zayneb, we can't touch the Black Stone." Ustaadah Ramlah put her arm on my back and pressed. "Look, Adam and Murtaza are already way up ahead. *Labbayka llāhumma labbayk . . . ,*" she started chanting for me to repeat, like I was a child.

I looked ahead, and yes, Adam and the shaykh were rounding the next corner.

I joined in chanting and picked up my pace, but suddenly a crowd of people moved in between us and Adam and the shaykh, and Ustaadah Ramlah and I were swept farther away from where we wanted, *needed*, to be.

I had to get back to Adam.

But we couldn't, as additional pilgrims merged in and we found ourselves more on the outskirts of the crowd.

We completed the last tawaf, now a longer circumference, on our own, and as Ustaadah Ramlah and I made our way back to our designated group meeting pole, and as I started making dua that Adam and the shaykh would be there, I realized I'd repeated Arabic duas after the shaykh and Ustaadah Ramlah but made none of my own personal ones. None at all.

I'd been too busy following along or looking out for Adam.

"This is why Murtaza said not to fixate on the Black Stone," Ustaadah Ramlah said, shaking her head at me. Again, like I was a child. "You can't think only of your particular wants, Zayneb."

I was on the verge of replying—especially when the truth was I'd been thinking of Adam's comfort the whole time—but then I saw a beautiful sight that replaced the irritation of being scolded with the feeling of relief: Adam and the shaykh were back with the rest of our group.

I whispered my regular refrain, alhamdulillah, and then turned back to glance at the Kaaba again.

Had I really just concentrated on taking care of Adam and mindlessly repeating people's duas, while not reflecting and praying for my own self? Was this Umrah going to be all about Adam for me?

I joined the group and did the two rakah prayers beside Adam, and then sat, preoccupied with my own thoughts. As Fatima and her husband Sahaan brought us Zamzam water to drink, I noticed that Sarina was nowhere to be found.

"Tastes amazing," Adam said, finishing his cup with a satisfied look on his face. "Subhanallah for such precious water."

"But a tiny bit salty, don't you think?" Sahaan said, with us on the carpet now, sitting cross-legged.

"Like actual spring water, you mean?" Adam took another cup offered by Suhaib, the thirteen-year-old with his dad in our Umrah group. Someone else approached with another cup of water for Adam. "Oh wow, everyone's trying to heal me with the blessed waters." He laughed.

The shaykh sat with us too and raised his hands, palms up. "Let's say some duas of shifaa while you drink. I promised your dad."

We all raised our hands, and the shaykh led us in duas for Adam's healing and all our healing, and then we drank some more. Sarina was the only one not there.

"Where's Sarina?" I asked.

"She went to arrange the wheelchair for Sa'i," the shaykh said. "For Adam."

Adam nodded. "I asked her to, Zayneb. I wanted to make sure I could do it in peace, while concentrating on my prayers between Safa and Marwa."

"Oh. I thought you'd been okay while doing tawaf?"

"Nearing the end I felt really tired, like I needed a good rest. So the wheelchair will be perfect."

I nodded. "I'll push you, then."

"No, it's okay, Zayby—she's arranging a motorized scooter." He took another drink of Zamzam. "We just have to meet her there. She'll have it all ready, alhamdulillah."

"That girl, subhanallah," Ustaadah Ramlah pronounced. "I've never met a more caring, selfless soul than Sarina. I pray all the best for her in this life and the next."

"Ameen," Adam, and everyone else, said.

ARTIFACT TWENTY-ONE: ADAM'S PAKOL
INTERPRETIVE LABEL:
VULNERABILITY IS UNDERRATED

THIS IS THE WAY THE STORY WENT, AND THE STORY WAS IMPORTANT to me, especially at this point in my life:

Abraham's second wife, Hajar, on her own in a barren desert with an infant son, ran seven times between two hills, stopping at each to climb atop it and peer into the distance, looking for a source of water.

She'd traveled to the valley of Bakka with Abraham, and when he'd left her and the baby behind as he traveled on, she said, "With God, surely we will not be lost."

But this trust was tested when they ran out of water.

Thus, she'd laid her son down and searched, certain she would find what she needed if she just looked.

Thus, where she'd laid her son, a spring gushed forth.

And that water, Zamzam, gushes forth still to this day.

A reminder for all to put in consistent effort and continue to seek their provisions, with hope born from utter trust.

Walking between the hills of Safa and Marwa, or wheeling between them as I was doing right now, entailed reflecting on Hajar's story. Though the marbled surroundings today—the hills, enclosed in glass, and the paths between them were now part of the Masjid al-Haram building—resembled nothing like what she'd looked out upon, the aim of the pilgrim was to physically and mentally and spiritually experience Hajar's *searching*, which was the literal translation of Sa'i, by focusing inward.

To keep on seeking even when what lay around you looked barren and unpromising.

Believing that the to-and-fro between the hills wasn't futile, that pacing was productive, went against everything we'd been taught in school, everything we were, in fact, taught everywhere.

We were always taught that there's a path forward to reach our goals and to stay on that path, and pass through each milestone, to reach a destination.

Like how I saw Chicago with Zayneb. How I'd been hoping for a way to open up to take me there.

But instead, here on pilgrimage, we were told to believe that there was inherent benefit in the searching and waiting for things to unfold.

Which was hard.

As I wheeled in the center lanes designated for assistive devices, between pilgrims walking in opposing directions in separate lanes, I tried to feel trustful that I'd get what I needed. That it wasn't the sense of *arriving* I should treasure but also this very scary time of wondering and hoping and praying.

I couldn't do it.

Maybe I'd fixated on the physical part of Sa'i because I was afraid to unearth what was going on inside me: that I was losing trust and hope in my abilities—that I'd put more stock in those than in Allah. That I'd switched to thinking that what happens to me in the future was ultimately in my hands.

When it wasn't, as Hajar showed us so long ago.

I glanced to my right side, where, beyond the balustrades

dividing our lanes, Zayneb walked, sometimes quicker than every-one else, sometimes slower, always in an attempt to stay with me as much as possible.

After she'd balked at going on Umrah, I'd wished for her to be with me here in case I needed her assistance for Sa'i, but now I didn't need it; I had the assistance of this scooter. But she was still by my side.

I wondered how tired *she* was; after traveling all the way from Chicago to London to Jeddah to Mecca, and then doing tawaf, here she was now doing Sa'i at four a.m. Mecca time.

As I watched her, several thoughts struck me at once: *Zayneb is like Hajar.*

She keeps on trying—with everything—even when things are hard for her. Even if she doesn't know if things will turn out.

She's a striver, always on the go.

She finds her purpose in movement.

Whereas I find comfort in stillness.

Maybe Zayneb needed to reflect on the stops we did when we got to each hill during Sa'i.

Maybe she needed to remember that pausing to take in your surroundings was good once in a while.

Maybe for me, I needed to focus on the motion.

That there was value in moving even if it didn't take you any-where.

Again, hard to do.

So, between Safa and Marwa, I prayed for a destination: to be with Zayneb.

I prayed to live in a location that wouldn't be hard on my MS.

I prayed for a cure for all MS patients, or at least for us to live with ease and energy.

I prayed for a job. Really hard. Like tearfully hard.

I prayed for everyone I knew by name.

I prayed for Zayneb, to find rest and peace and joy in the midst of her busyness.

And then I prayed for me to have the strength to tell her everything, even the thing that scared me the most: that I was afraid she would leave me because I needed her too much.

We finished Sa'i at Marwa and made our last duas. When we exited Masjid al-Haram, the sky was still dark, but it was nearing Fajr.

To end our Umrah, and leave our state of ihram, the men and boys who were going to shave our entire heads went with Shaykh Murtaza, while those who were trimming a bit of their hair went back to the hotel to do so. Then we were going to meet up to have a meal—which now, at this time, was breakfast—at the hotel before we crashed.

I said salaam to Zayneb before joining Shaykh Murtaza, Sahaan, Alim, and Suhaib and his dad, Khaled. My other hotel roommate, Isa, had taken one of the older men in our group earlier to shave his head, and they were now resting at the hotel.

Alim, who'd always had a shorn head, even before Umrah, joked that he was going for the closest shave ever in his life.

Shaving our heads would be a reminder of this renewal we'd committed to as pilgrims, that we were leaving ihram and entering a new state: back to our lives, but, insha'Allah, more mindfully.

"With this act, we end our state of ihram," Shaykh Murtaza reminded us as we set off to a licensed barber he knew well. "We don't stay in a state of complete renunciation of this world as we are to rejoin it, to continue our purposes here on earth."

"While focusing inward, too. Which is the hardest, Shaykh,"

Sahaan said, putting a hand to my shoulder to help me walk across the cobblestoned sidewalks.

"After we get our sleep and meet again, remind me to tell everyone the story of the fork," Shaykh Murtaza said. "It's a personal story, but I hope it helps us as we continue on to Medina during this trip."

I was tired, but I perked up on hearing Medina mentioned.

Medina al Munawwara—variously translated into English as the City of Light, the Enlightened City, the Luminous City—was once known as Yathrib, the first place that welcomed the Prophet, peace be upon him, when he was being persecuted in Mecca. After his death, in addition to the City of Light, it was called Medina-un-Nabi, the City of the Prophet, because of how he transformed it.

My capturing of his migration to Medina via the Hijrah map was what got me going on *this* trip today.

And now I'd get to trace the path to Medina myself. With Zayneb.

Some of our group prayed Fajr at Masjid al-Haram before our breakfast meetup at the hotel, but I chose to pray in the hotel room—following the imam in the masjid from our rooms, that's how close to the Kaaba we were—after which Sahaan took a picture of me in ihram to share with Connor.

Before heading down to the restaurant, I took a shower and changed into the white thawb I'd bought in one of the shops on my way back from the barbershop.

I couldn't stop staring at my bald head in the mirror after I changed. I felt more exposed without all that hair.

Vulnerable.

Like I was all face, and so every emotion was more easily readable.

Maybe I should have bought a shemagh like Sahaan did to cover his head. Maybe we could go quickly right now to the mall attached to our hotel complex and get one.

I stuck my head out of the bathroom. "You okay with stopping at the mall before we head to breakfast?"

"We're already running late." Sahaan was sitting on his bed eating dates from the bag he'd bought from a date stand outside the barbershop. His shemagh was already on his head. He'd said it was going to take a while to get used to not having his curls, that the air on his scalp would feel cold. "What do you need to get?"

I stroked my head. "I feel naked, bro. So a kufi or a scarf?"

He laughed. "I got you." He removed his shemagh and got off the bed, holding it out.

"Oh no you don't." I started closing the bathroom door so he wouldn't be able to hand the traditional red-and-white-checkered scarf to me. "It's okay. I'll go bald."

"I got a cap in my luggage. I'll just wear that."

"Let me wear that, then. You wear the new one."

"All right, deprive me of my ajr, then." Sahaan went to the luggage standing upright beside his bed and set it down. After unzipping it and rummaging around for a while, he held up the kind of kufi men wear in Afghanistan and parts of Pakistan. "Here ya go. My pakol, passed down from many ancestors going far, far back, to our Ottoman roots."

"Really?" I hesitated from taking it.

"Really? You think us Afghans were part of the Ottoman empire? That was a test of your historical and geographical knowledge. You failed." He shook his head before wrapping it in his shemagh again.

I laughed and accepted his pakol.

When I glanced in the mirror this time, I not only felt like a different person from the one who'd left Doha and London, I looked it too.

Zayneb wasn't at the restaurant when Sahaan and I got there. After we piled our plates from the breakfast buffet and set them down at an empty table near a window, I texted her and told her I'd saved her a seat.

Just as I put the phone by my plate and picked up my napkin to place it on my lap, I felt a touch on my back.

Shaykh Murtaza, back in his kufi, bent down. "We're sitting over there if you two want to join us?"

"Is there space for Zayneb?"

"And Fatima?" Sahaan added.

"Fatima just got to the table," Shaykh Murtaza said. "And Zayneb was exhausted, so she decided to sleep now and eat later. Sarina already put together some food to take to her as well."

I got up and picked up my plate, and Sahaan followed suit.

They were at a big round table that, along with Shaykh Murtaza and Ustaadah Ramlah, had Sarina, Fatima, a woman whose name I didn't know, Alim, Suhaib, and Khaled. Sahaan and I got the last two seats.

We talked a bit about the Umrah we'd just done, but mostly we just ate in grateful, tired silence.

I was actually looking forward to the bed I'd left behind in the room. I couldn't wait to succumb to it.

Thinking of Zayneb in deep sleep in her room just made me smile.

I didn't care that I was grinning strangely into my plate, at my second boiled egg, before taking a bite of it.

"Adam," Sarina said from across the table. "I have news."

I looked up at her. "Good news?"

"I hope you think so!" She beamed and picked up her phone to type into it. "Those photos you sent me in London of the Hijrah map? I shared them with my brother who works for a major UK retailer and he shared them with his boss and she loved them."

"Ah, that's great to hear." I nodded, happy. "It's the first time they've been shared, so it's amazing to get the feedback."

"The news part is that they wanted to know if you'd be open for a commission. To make scaled models for different departments for the flagship store. Whimsical stuff."

"Ah, that sounds like a great idea!" Shaykh Murtaza was already excited.

Almost as excited as I was. Though another feeling surpassed the excitement: astonishment. "Really? That would be cool. I'm in between projects, so, insha'Allah, this might work out."

"My brother Waleed is actually in Saudi for meetings to open a store here. I was going to meet him in Medina. . . ." She scrolled her phone, searching. "Oh yay, he said yes, that he was able to set up a meeting when we get to Medina, if you're open to talking shop on the trip."

"You're out of ihram, so you can conduct business with no worries," Shaykh Murtaza assured me, passing Ustaadah Ramlah a small plate of pita triangles for her hummus.

Ustaadah Ramlah took two pieces and nodded at me. "You can dress your burger self now. Add the ketchup, even sriracha." She laughed before biting into the pita she'd swiped over her hummus. "You're a fully loaded burger."

I groaned.

"And I'm excited that if you get this job, you'll be spending time in England again!" Shaykh Murtaza grinned at me, rubbing his hands together like he had thought this idea all up. "Adam, coming back to me!"

Sarina crinkled her nose and laughed with us before adding, "Waleed leaves before we do from Medina, so it will have to be right when we arrive on Tuesday, insha'Allah."

"Sure, that could work." I let the gratitude spreading inside reach my face. I'd just made dua exactly two hours ago, and it was already happening? The answer to my prayers?

I asked for a job, and I'm literally being handed one.

My smile must have looked really kooky spreading even wider on a flushed face, but I wasn't ashamed to share it with Sarina. "Jazakhillah for passing the pics on to your brother. Really grateful."

"Of course, don't even mention it, Adam."

Something behind Sarina caught my eye, a flash of light green, like the jilbab and hijab Zayneb had been wearing on Umrah.

Wait, *was* that Zayneb who'd just walked into the restaurant? I rose a little to check, but no, I must have been imagining it.

Maybe I was seeing things I wanted to materialize.

PART THREE

*He is the One Who has made the sun a [source of] radiant light and
the moon a light [reflected], and has determined for it phases so that
you might know how to compute the years and to measure [time]. . . .*
—Surah 10:5

ARTIFACT TWENTY-TWO:
ZAYNEB'S HOTEL ROOM KEY CARD
INTERPRETIVE LABEL:
A SPACE OF YOUR OWN IS UNDERRATED

I'D BEEN HUNGRY, BUT I LEFT THE RESTAURANT A SECOND AFTER setting foot in it.

I returned to the hotel room and got back into bed, the bed I'd lain awake in since returning after completing the Umrah, angry at myself.

During Sa'i, every time I thought I was getting to a spiritual space within, where I was concentrating and reflecting on what it must have been like for Hajar to not lose faith and to patiently persevere, two things would pop into my head, both things Ustaadah Ramlah said:

You can't think only of your particular wants, Zayneb.

I've never met a more caring, selfless soul than Sarina.

And then I just became a mess. Between Safa and Marwa. On Umrah.

In the midst of losing it, while walking the seven circuits, I'd consoled myself with the fact that I *was* being there for Adam, that I wasn't selfish.

And then I had to remind myself that I wasn't a terrible person for letting something Ustaadah Ramlah said in passing almost destroy my Umrah.

But now, ten floors below this bed, Adam was in the restaurant smiling at Sarina, at a table with no space for me—even though he'd said he'd saved me a spot.

His text message letting me know he was waiting for me was why I'd come down in the first place, instead of staying sulking in the room.

Something was wrong with me.

The Zayneb pre-Umrah would have just galloped up to the table and joked, *All righty, thanks a lot, Adam, for saving a spot for your one and only.*

This me was shocking.

It was demure. It was wrapped up in a terrible sense of self.

And all because of Sarina?

And all because of Sarina.

Because she was different. She was calm and confident but not in a *Hello, I'm here!* way; more like, *Let me think ten steps ahead to make way for everyone else to have a perfect time.* She was effortless at efforting.

And a lot of her efforts were going into Adam.

She *was* selfless. She *was* spiritual.

She was not me.

Because though I also liked to think ten steps ahead and I was all about effort, these were all reserved for big problems out there in the world.

And for me.

Which was of course okay—except that Adam had liked Sarina a lot once upon a time, and, yes, it was apparent she'd liked him back a lot too.

I removed the brown blanket scarf I'd been clutching to my chin and sat up in bed to stare at my still-packed luggage. Was it too late to change rooms?

I think I could take Ustaadah Ramlah over being exposed to Sarina's spiritual superiority—even with Ustaadah Ramlah's apparent ability to easily destroy my soul.

But Sarina's aura would end up destroying the whole of me.

And there was still the entire trip to bear. Which entailed more Mecca, then travel, then Medina.

After spending most of today resting, we were going to meet in the lobby at four p.m. to go see Cave Hira and then have dinner. Tomorrow, whoever wanted to partake in a second Umrah was going to travel by our minibus to a nearby miqat location and change into ihram again.

Those of us who weren't doing another one, like me and Adam—because we'd agreed one Umrah was enough for us due to his MS fatigue and my mental fatigue—were going to spend the next day visiting the Masjid al-Haram as much as possible. Then we were to leave for Medina to spend three days, after which only I was going to fly back to London on Friday so I could get back to Chicago by Sunday morning.

Sausun. She'd said for all of us to stop by her place on the way to Medina. The whole group.

I hadn't told Shaykh Murtaza about the invite, and now I thought about that for a minute.

What if *only* Adam and I stopped there? For a bit of time to ourselves? While the others went on to Medina—after which we could all meet up at the hotel?

The more I thought about this idea, the more I felt like it was the right course.

Time for old me to come back. Make decisions, do things, take charge.

I found Sausun's message again.

Assalamu alaikum, this is Sausun-in-Saudi. As soon as you're done with Umrah, text me. Our home is on the way to Medina and my father is big on treating pilgrims so we'd like to host your entire group. Just tell me the date. We're out near the water so you'll get a bit of a different experience here than the busy city life insha'Allah. Umrah mubarak.

I typed fast so I wouldn't rethink things. Hey salaam Sausun! Thanks for getting in touch. Wow, it would be awesome to come see you. One thing though, it would just be Adam and me as the group has their itinerary set in stone. Adam and I will be able to wiggle away no problem to see a friend. :)

Then I followed that up with a promise that I'd let her know when we'd be coming by the end of today, latest tomorrow.

I felt so much better after shooting that off that I was able to finally close my eyes and sleep.

I woke up to the sound of the Dhuhr adhan from the masjid reaching into our rooms. It was beautiful, and I lay listening for the entirety of it with my eyes closed before lifting my head to check on what the others were doing.

The room was dark, drapes drawn shut, and everyone else was sleeping.

Mila, the woman in her thirties, had the bed closest to the window. She'd told us her story of recently finding out that she'd come from a Slavic Muslim background and how she'd reverted to her ancestral faith. We'd all agreed she should get the best spot, being the eldest of all of us. She was now lying on her side snoring lightly, her short blond hair held back with a yellow fabric headband, her hands tucked under her pillow.

I was next to her, and then it was Fatima. She slept like my sister Sadia, shrouded in her bedcovers.

Sarina was in the bed closest to the door.

I couldn't see her from where I was, but I imagined her in an old-fashioned white nightgown, her hair rippling artfully around her face, spread across her pillows, her hands evenly spaced apart and gripping her bedcovers while she lay on her back. Fairy-tale like.

Like an uppity princess waiting to be kissed.

I decided to go to Dhuhr prayers—as I'd heard the call and *I was right next to the Kaaba.*

But I'd do it by myself.

As noiselessly as I could, I slid myself out of my blankets, tucked the brown scarf I'd been using like a teddy bear under my pillow, and unzipped the carry-on at the foot of the bed to get out my khaki jilbab, fresh underclothes, and toiletry bag. I tiptoed to the bathroom with these items, wondering if a quick shower would wake anyone up.

I turned the shower head on and then opened the bathroom door quietly to peek out.

No one had stirred from their beds.

I knew that I had fifteen minutes to get to the masjid, as that was the duration between the adhan and the iqama, so I took a five-minute shower, dried off, and changed into my own jilbab and black scarf.

I opened the door to Sarina. She was wearing a raggedy T-shirt and track pants and holding a toiletry bag. Her brown hair was in a ponytail. "Going to Dhuhr? Wait for me—I'll just be two minutes."

"The prayer will start in five minutes so I have to leave. You know the elevators. They take forever." I moved fast to place my stuff on top of my carry-on.

"Okay, then, forget brushing my teeth." She laughed and grabbed her mauve all-in-one number and stuck it over her head, on top of her T-shirt and track pants. "Voila, I'm ready."

I rose from kneeling by my carry-on and nodded.

I led the way to the elevators quietly.

Sarina was also quiet, her fingers moving the wooden tasbih beads she always wore on her wrist as she made dhikr. Then, as soon as we stepped into the elevator, she turned to me. "Adam won't be coming to Dhuhr. He's going to rest until Asr and pray them together. Then some of us were thinking of meeting to get some shopping done." She wound her tasbih back around her wrist. "And I brought food for you for breakfast, well, now lunch, so if you're hungry, it's there waiting for you in the room."

I looked straight ahead but nodded.

Why was she telling me all these things about Adam? Like he was her partner?

I took the reins back. "Adam and I are invited to a friend's place that's on the way to Medina. So we'll meet you guys at the hotel in Medina later, maybe even a day later. We're going to be arranging our own transportation, so not to worry."

"Does Adam know about this?" Sarina asked. "Because he wants to get to Medina as soon as possible, to meet my brother Waleed. Because Waleed has a new commission for him, insha'Allah, at the company he works for. A very lucrative commission, alhamdulillah. So I don't think Adam would want to miss the opportunity."

The elevator doors opened and she stepped out, but I stayed

behind, waiting until people exiting other elevators had filled in the space between us before I left. Then I took another route to the masjid.

Unfortunately, it was longer, and by the time I heard the imam say the first takbir to start Dhuhr, I had to join the prayer lines being made outside the masjid itself.

I cried silently in prayer because I couldn't recognize the fiery feelings reaching for all parts of my soul, mind, heart.

Then I went back to the hotel room, and, before shrouding myself in bed like Fatima, I swiped wistfully through photos of Hidden Bloom Cottage, a vacation where it would have been just me and Adam.

As "You Are My Sunshine" drifted out faintly from the website, I now understood why Adam had previously found the song melancholy.

ARTIFACT TWENTY-THREE: ADAM'S ZAMZAM WATER BOTTLE, EMPTY
INTERPRETIVE LABEL: NOURISHING YOUR HEART STARTS WITH PAYING ATTENTION

I'D JUST FINISHED PRAYING ASR WITHIN SIGHT OF THE KAABA.

I still couldn't get over it.

Sarina took a picture of me and Sahaan with the Kaaba behind us, and I sent it to everyone I knew, including Connor. He got a special message with his photo.

Today I'm wearing a thawb and pakol (hat). Look them up and practice pronouncing them before we meet again. :)

Sarina took more pictures of Fatima and Sahaan as a couple, and I felt that pang again, the one I'd felt earlier when the four of us had walked over from the hotel for prayers.

I wished Zayneb was here with us.

But Fatima told me she'd tried to gently wake her a few times to no avail. She'd been out cold.

I felt horrible that she'd come all the way to Mecca only to stay in her hotel room.

Maybe Sarina saw my face, because she quickly mentioned that Zayneb had been to Dhuhr at the masjid earlier, which made me feel better.

At least she'd gotten an opportunity to pray with the jamaat here—*in Mecca*, the one spot all Muslims faced when we prayed, wherever we were in the world.

Of course, I absolutely wanted her to get all the sleep she needed. It just felt weird that the last time we'd connected—sort of—was on the bus ride from the airport. Contemplating the lush red carpeting under my feet now, I savored the memory of her sleeping against me. And then I smiled, remembering her wide-eyed first gaze at the splendor of the masjid when I woke her.

"All four of us?" Fatima asked, bringing my gaze back to my surroundings. She rifled in her bag, looking for something. "I have a selfie stick."

Sarina nodded and got on the other side of Fatima, and I joined Sahaan. We smiled for a few shots, our backs to the crowds circulating around the Kaaba just meters behind us.

Sarina promptly added the pics to our Umrah chat group.

"Now we can do your shopping." Sahaan collapsed the selfie stick and stuck it in Fatima's bag before looking up at me. "You can get your own headgear."

"Ah, so much for your good deed. You want your pakol back?" I lifted it off my head. "Here you go. I'll let the world say hello to my bald head for the first time."

"Nah, that's yours to keep for good, a gift. I just wanted to check out the mall here," he whispered, nodding at the backs of Fatima and Sarina, who'd started walking to the exits already. "And I'm using you as an excuse. Fatima has me on a strict no-purchases-allowed plan until we get to Medina. Apparently the shopping's better there. Better deals, better stuff. She brought an empty suitcase for gifts for everyone back home."

"I'm on a tight budget, so I'm all for waiting too. But we can go check it out." Dad had given me some extra money as he'd said it was hard to not get at least a beautiful prayer mat or dhikr beads or the special perfumed oils Mecca and Medina are known for.

What he'd given me was all I had, so I wanted to be careful with spending on this trip.

"You guys coming?" Fatima turned around. "The mall's quieter at this time."

"And we're meeting soon for Cave Hira," Sarina reminded us. "I want to get back to the hotel earlier to make sure everyone's able to come, which means waking people up."

She looked at me and I knew she meant Zayneb, and for that I was grateful.

I couldn't imagine visiting Cave Hira without Zayneb.

After weaving in and out of several identical stores stocking expensive religious items, all next to each other exactly like in the souks in Doha, we came upon the section in the mall designated for clothing.

Sahaan quickly found me the best-priced shemaghs. He haggled on the one I wanted—a black-and-brown-checkered one—until he got the price down by almost 30 percent.

I was just about to hand over the money I'd taken out of my wallet when I saw Sarina across from us, at a shop selling women's clothing.

Fatima and she were rifling through the hijabs, and I put my money away. "Let me just go check something out?" I motioned vaguely outside the shop we were in. "Shukran," I said kindly to the shopkeeper, aware that he was not happy with my change of plans after he'd finally agreed to our price for the shemagh.

But I'd just remembered something I needed more.

Sahaan followed me over to Sarina and Fatima. "What was that about? That was an excellent price I got you."

"Sorry, I gotta get something else." I paused to get Sarina's attention. And then I told her what I wanted.

Ten minutes later, I had spent almost all the money Dad had given me.

We still had some time before Sarina had to head back to organize everyone for the Cave Hira trip, so Sahaan suggested we get some fruit juices from the street stand he'd noticed right outside the shopping complex and chill for a bit.

In the lineup of juicing choices, I was happy to see guava. It had quickly become my favorite fruit, introduced to me by an unlikely friend I'd made in Doha, Zahid, an older man with a family of his own that included a daughter my age.

Zahid was with me when I had my first major MS attack as he drove me home from a mall in his taxi. He'd stayed around and come back when I needed him. And then we'd become friends who visited each other's homes every few months for dinner.

I'd kept my promise to make dua for him at the Kaaba. His dua request: to retire to the house he was building in his native country, India. Currently he lived in a single room in an apartment he shared with other families—which he was content with as he had his wife, daughter, and young son with him. And in my meals with them, I knew there was a lot of happiness in that small place.

But I'd also seen the lushness of the land on which he was building his house in south India, and I knew his heart's desire lay in deeply green, open spaces promising freedom to roam.

With the rest of the money I had remaining, when Sahaan, Fatima, and Sarina had turned away with their drinks, I tipped the juice stand owner, another worker from South Asia, and made dua that this sadaqa so close to the Kaaba be accepted on behalf of Zahid—who'd shown me extraordinary generosity from the very moment he'd met me.

He'd shown me the soul of all goodness, of all faith traditions, the answer to all problems in the world: truly want for others, even others you have no connection to, what you want for yourself.

I caught up with the others, guava drink in hand, and we sat leaning against the giant columns outside the hotel watching crowds move around the tiled courtyard, most heading toward Masjid-al-Haram.

It was getting to that time in the day when the temperature was lowering, and with our cold drinks, it was very comfortable.

I was so happy Dad had suggested Umrah.

From the way a job opportunity opened up so quickly to the sense of belonging I felt here, it was apparent I just needed to get things moving in my life instead of solely sitting around—in Hanna's shaggy pink chair—worrying.

"Wow, I didn't even realize this exhibit was yours, Adam. I went to the museum in September and saw it." Sarina paused to take a long sip on her straw while scrolling on her phone. "I'm on your website now, to pass it on to my brother. Were you in London for it? For the exhibit?"

"*Fixed Stars?*" I shook my head. "A friend of mine set it up. I'd shown it in other cities, and he ended up arranging the London show. That's neat you saw it."

"Yeah, the artist's name was listed as A. Chen, and I never connected the dots," she said, laughing. "I loved it. What are you working on now?"

"Besides the Hijrah map, nothing much." I looked at the minarets rising from the masjid that wrapped around the Kaaba and thought about Mom and honesty, and not jailing vulnerabilities. "The truth is I've been waiting for a commission for a while now. That's why the possibility of your brother's company having something for me is literally a dua come true."

"I'm so happy." Sarina beamed. "With this portfolio on your website, I can't see them saying anything but yes."

Fatima leaned over to see what Sarina was looking at. She raised her eyebrows. "Wow. You're talented, Adam. Masha'Allah."

"A lot of it is just artistic reinterpretations of traditional Islamic art. It's already all there—the wow. I'm just translating it, sort of."

"Still, you need to know the language to translate it," Sarina said. "More than one language."

"That's deep." Sahaan looked at me, impressed. "So if you weren't commissioned to do something, what would you be focusing on?"

"Something that turns this all back in time." I waved my free hand around the complex housing the Kaaba. It was the largest structure in the world by surface area, able to hold four million people at once, but at one time it had been a totally barren land with a crying baby and woman searching for hope.

The mountains that overlook the place had seen all the changes, just like Jabal Al-Noor, the mountain we were going to visit soon, just like all the mountains in the world.

I told them about my *Grains of Sand* exhibit idea.

And until we had to leave, they listened raptly, with eyes that seemed to completely understand everything I said.

I finally had an audience that was captivated by and sold on my pitch.

• • •

The taxi deposited us near the foot of Jabal Al-Noor, by the steps that led to Cave Hira.

The driver then parked the taxi farther down the street. Shaykh Murtaza made sure to tell each taxi driver taking our group in sets of four that they had to go as far up to the mountain as possible, as taxis often brought visitors only to the closest intersection, adding to the distance people had to walk.

He also wanted to make sure I got a good view of it, as I wouldn't be going up.

It was strenuous for most people and, anyhow, visiting it wasn't a part of Umrah and there weren't any extra blessings to go see the cave. It was more a matter of witnessing the location where Islam first began with the command "Iqra!"—"Read!"—revealed to an illiterate man, who then became the beloved Prophet, peace be upon him, to generations and billions of people all around the world.

I got out of the taxi and looked at the mountain finally without the barrier of a car window between us.

It was rocky terrain all the way up. There were steps made of cement with cobblestoned sides that snaked their way up to the cave. We were told these would take around half an hour to climb.

I wanted Zayneb to climb. I knew she wanted to—in London, she'd mentioned being excited about the possibility of seeing the cave.

But in the back of my mind, I was worried she'd want to stay behind with me.

I didn't get a chance to confirm anything with her because even though I'd texted her and waited as long as I could in the lobby, we hadn't connected before the taxis arrived.

She hadn't come down. Hadn't replied to my texts.

Shaykh Murtaza ended up telling each hotel room group to

meet the taxis he'd ordered on their own and that we'd reconvene at the base of Jabal Al-Noor.

I took a swig of my still-cold bottled Zamzam water and turned to check if the other taxis had arrived. The road, with decrepit adobe houses on either side, was empty.

While we waited, Shaykh Murtaza told Sahaan, Isa, and me some facts about the mountain. I half listened because half my brain was praying there was nothing going on with Zayneb.

The last time I'd seen her was after Umrah, in the hotel elevator going up to our separate rooms.

ARTIFACT TWENTY-FOUR:
ZAYNEB'S TRAVEL PRAYER MAT
INTERPRETIVE LABEL:
THE ABILITY TO RESET IS ALWAYS PRESENT

I'D WOKEN UP REFRESHED TO A BLESSEDLY QUIET, EMPTY HOTEL room, and, in the light, actually, *in the noor* of the Meccan afternoon sun streaming onto my face from the drapes open wide, I'd made the intention to start anew.

To seal this intent, I'd taken a second shower, prayed Asr, and, sitting on my travel prayer mat, made dhikr.

Then the door had opened, and Mila walked in just as I was contemplating the soggy remains of the breakfast Sarina had brought up for me. In addition to being hungry, I'd also been ready to eat it in a small gesture of reconciliation—yielded from an attempted commitment to thinking positively. And kindly.

Sarina had thought of me lying tired and hungry in the hotel room while she was laughing it up with Ad— No, restart.

Sarina, thinking of me lying tired and hungry in the hotel room, had extended some care to me. I will thus eat her offerings of goodness and grace.

The last time I'd eaten was in the Jeddah airport when I'd gotten an ice cream bar from a freezer vending machine while waiting for our luggage to come through, so I was ready to pounce on those rubbery scrambled eggs.

But then Mila, bless her heart, brought back some fried chicken for me.

The best fried chicken in the entire world.

And not just because it was still crispy and hot and fresh in its foil container—so crispy and hot and fresh that when I removed the cardboard top, a waft of deliciousness immediately entered my nose, met my brain, and activated the release of serotonin.

No, it was also because of what Mila told me.

As I fell upon the chicken and fries and sesame-seed-covered bun like a prisoner being fed for the first time, Mila told me her friends in London had mentioned that she had to try this place called Albaik, as the owners gave charity on each and every sale made.

This was blessed chicken right here.

"It was crowded, but the wait was worth it." Her own meal box in her lap, Mila daintily ripped chicken apart with her fingers before bringing small pieces to her lips.

Aw, she'd waited to eat with me.

"Thanks for bringing some back for me," I said in between wolfing down the flesh I sucked from a chicken wing with the force of the strongest vacuum, maybe the latest Dyson my mom was always wanting to buy.

"Of course. You poor thing, so tired. I knew the other two girls were probably going to eat together as they were out already." Mila nodded to herself. "And yes, I saw them on my way back to the hotel. They were having some drinks just outside."

I tore through a drumstick, wondering how I'd never been a huge fan of fried chicken before. This must be something served in jannah.

"Just to confirm, Adam is your partner, yes?" Mila asked. "You're together? Married?"

I nodded. "We got our nikah done right before the summer. We're having the official wedding a few years down the road, though."

"Oh, yes, I thought so." Mila ate a fry thoughtfully, loosening her black hijab. She'd opted for the thin black shayla with black abaya outfit that many women wear in Mecca. But she looked distinct because on top of her shayla she wore a bright pink fabric headband to keep the hijab from slipping back. It was endearing.

"Why were you asking about Adam?"

"No reason."

I was working on my third piece of chicken when I thought about Fatima and Sarina hanging around together. "Was Fatima with her husband—I think Sahaan is his name? Outside the hotel just now?"

"Yes." Mila ate another piece of chicken, again in a measured way I couldn't understand, given the taste of what we were eating.

I wanted to ask if Adam was out there with them but didn't want to bring attention to my discomfort should the answer be yes. "Who else was with them? Was it most of the Umrah group?"

"No, just the four of them. Sahaan, Fatima, Sarina, and Adam." After saying that, Mila dropped her eyes to her meal box.

I paused chomping on the juicy chicken breast, wiped my mouth with the back of my hand, and lowered it back into the box.

As my smile fell, the hotel room door opened, and Sarina and Fatima walked in holding shopping bags, drinks—delicious-looking ones—in hand.

"Zayneb!" Fatima looked genuinely happy to see me awake eating fried chicken in bed.

"So happy to see you're rested and eating, alhamdulillah." Sarina smiled flaccidly. "We're leaving for Cave Hira in five minutes, insha'Allah. Taxis will be here soon, so anyone wanting to use the loo, do so now."

She went into the bathroom.

I sealed my chicken box, pressing down on the foil edges to secure the cardboard top, set it on my nightstand, and stood up to dust the crumbs off myself with a napkin.

"We missed you," Fatima said, setting her bags on her bed. She sorted through them and selected one, which she held out to me. "Here's something for you. From Adam. He thought you might want to wear it now."

I smiled and reached for the thick paper bag with crisp folds, fancy gold Arabic font on the front, and gold tassels hanging from the handles. "Thanks."

He'd thought of me.

Of course he would.

He's mine.

Why wouldn't he think of me?

I didn't want to open the bag, the present, in front of anyone, so as soon as Sarina came out of the bathroom, I went inside and locked it.

I took out the clear plastic package in the bag and unsealed it to pull out a folded dress, made of soft, dusty-pink fabric.

I held it up by the shoulders and shook it so that it would open down to reveal itself.

It was a jilbab exactly like the ones Sarina always wore.

In the same exact color as the first one I'd seen her in, the first one Adam had seen her in too—well, since the first time he'd seen her five years ago.

"Do you like it?" Sarina's voice at the door. "Adam loves them and thought you'd want one, so he asked me to help him buy the jilbab for you. I chose the color. If you don't like it, they said you can exchange it. But Adam loves the color too. It's exactly like one of mine, remember?"

I didn't answer and instead flushed the toilet.

"I'm sorry, I didn't hear," I lied. "I'm just using the bathroom. Stomach upset. Do you mind? Leaving me alone in the bathroom?"

I said that last part sarcastically.

"Sure," she responded, again not apologizing, as was her modus operandi. "Fatima's up next, so if you can hurry, please, as we need to get down to the lobby."

I didn't hurry but stayed until I'd stilled the rage enough for it to not show up on my face.

Which meant we were late going down to meet our taxi.

I didn't care, because all I could envision was Adam expecting me to emerge from our taxi looking identical to Sarina.

At the foot of Jabal Al-Noor, the shaykh gave us a quick overview of the significance of the mountain in our deen and then reminded everyone that we didn't need to go up to see it, that there were no religious obligations to do so. He also warned us that it was narrow to get into the cave itself, that there would be a big lineup, and that if we couldn't get down in adequate time to meet the taxis he'd ordered to pick us up, we were to forgo attempting to see the cave.

According to him, there was a high likelihood we wouldn't be able to get in anyhow.

The shaykh would be staying with Adam as he'd climbed Jabal Al-Noor several times, so he encouraged me to go up if I wanted to.

I briefly glanced at Adam, who'd been staring intently at me since I arrived, while I studiously avoided him in case he saw the awful thoughts roiling in my brain.

Why didn't he send one of those delicious drinks that he'd been enjoying with Sarina up for me? Along with that jilbab attempt at making me into a clone of her?

And, while he was having fun with Sarina and the other young couple on the trip, why didn't he think, Zayneb hasn't eaten for a while now, so let me go see her in the room with some food, and not just text her a million times?

Why did I always have to be the one to look out for him?

"I want you to go see the cave, Zayneb," he said, smiling encouragingly. "Don't worry about me. Shaykh Murtaza is giving me so much behind-the-scenes info that I'll feel like I've experienced it all myself."

The shaykh laughed. "That's my Adam, always looking on the bright side."

I decided to keep my response short. "Sure, I'm going up."

Adam's smile became bigger, and he leaned back on the railing behind him, relaxed. The shaykh had assured me that the taxi Adam had come in was parked down the street, on standby so he could sit inside it should it get too hot outside, so I knew he wouldn't be uncomfortable.

For that reason and for the reason that I just needed to get away from things on the ground, I'd decided to go see the cave.

Sarina was going too, but she'd already started at the head of the group, so I wasn't too worried about being around her. And Ustaadah Ramlah wasn't even here with us at Jabal Al-Noor.

She'd stayed back with an elderly woman in her room who felt dizzy. One of the girls in their room had severe asthma, so she'd stayed too.

So of the girls it was just Sarina, Fatima, Batul from the other room, and Mila and me. Other than Shaykh Murtaza and an elderly man who also sat against the railing beside Adam, all the other guys had followed Sarina.

Suhaib and his dad, Khaled, took a bunch of videos at the foot of the mountain, presumably for another TikTok. Mila told me Suhaib had been tracking the entire trip, except the Umrah itself, that way. She said she'd been sending his cute videos to all her family and friends as they were better than her recounting.

I tried to let everyone go ahead so I could be on my own trailing behind them, but Fatima and Mila waited for me.

Though the concrete steps were wide enough for the three of us, we trekked the mountain in single file.

It just felt more contemplative to walk alone in my thoughts, and maybe they felt the same way.

I was thinking of our Nabi, sallallahu alaihi wasallam, climbing up Jabal Al-Noor alone, without the aid of any human-made stairs, to go sit in a cave by himself for days and days, until the provisions he brought with him ran out.

I'll never forget the day I learned what he was doing in the cave.

Before, in all my previous Sunday school classes at the masjid, I'd been taught that he was praying. But one student had asked, "But he didn't know how to pray yet, because he hadn't learned about Islam yet, so how could he be praying?"

We'd learned that he was praying in the best ways he knew how, from the knowledge people had passed down from Abraham's time.

To the restless child I was, who was all about action, this seemed a little boring. To sit quietly praying without fully knowing how to pray.

But then I had Sister Layla as a teacher for Sunday school one year.

And she told us that the Muhammad, before he became the Prophet, sallallahu alaihi wasallam, used to also sit in the cave to reflect on the ways his society had gotten unjust and corrupt, the powerful preying on the weak, babies buried alive for being girls, women inherited like possessions.

Sister Layla said he didn't like this, the tyranny he saw around him. But he was softhearted and didn't know how to change things.

So he would get away from it all and sit in the cave to grieve and pray for change—yes, in the best ways he knew how.

And then change came via an injunction from an angel— "Iqra!"—telling him to do something he could not actually do: *read*.

I remember when sister Layla said that word, "iqra," her eyes had lit up, and a slow smile had taken over her face.

And in that moment, it had been possible for me to believe that change could come.

Because the Prophet, sallallahu alaihi wasallam, did something he thought he couldn't do. He received guidance and learned and taught others.

He led the change in his society by creating a revolution of knowledge. That knowledge spread and opened up the world. At a time when Europe was burning texts and Arabia was ignoring ethics and morality, Muslims went on to carefully preserve and translate Greek and Roman works, to make countless discoveries in science and math and sociology, sharing their discoveries and knowledge through universities and libraries from the very beginning.

I remember that story connecting "Iqra!" to a knowledge revolution so well because I heard it right when I was doing my fifth-grade project on Wilson Bentley's snowflakes.

I returned from that Sunday school class with a new rigor and focus.

I wrote about snowflakes like I was translating a precious text, suddenly aware that I came from a scholarly heritage that didn't want the world around us to descend into injustice and tyranny, but be uplifted by knowledge and science and growth.

It was the first of many As I received, but more importantly it was the first time I saw how valuable putting in effort was.

I just wanted to sit for a small reflective moment in the cave and pray for blessings upon blessings on my Nabi, sallallahu alaihi wasallam.

For some reason, when Mila, Fatima, and I reached the platform at the summit, we were all by ourselves.

Mila pointed out another set of steps leading down on the other side of the platform. "It's the way to the cave. The rest of them must have already gone down there."

Before we followed them, we surveyed the city of Mecca as it lay below us in small blocks of dune-colored buildings, with the sparkling clock tower housing our hotel in the distance blocking any view of the grand masjid encircling the Kaaba, and we wondered aloud about what the Prophet had seen when he'd looked out fourteen hundred years ago.

We debated the clock tower itself, one of the most expensive buildings in the world. I said it was distasteful, garish, Las Vegas-y, and exploitive to workers, that the Prophet would probably have wanted to use the billions spent on it to eradicate global poverty. Fatima brought up that it housed more pilgrims than ever had been housed before, that it had opened up pilgrimage to more people. "How many governments would be willing to spend their money like this? To house religious pilgrims? It's not the most expensive only for show, the entire thing also holds the most hotel guests anywhere in the world too. And it's engineered so that the adhan sound travels for miles from the top without deafening anyone below. I say those are all extraordinary feats."

Mila had a perspective somewhere between ours. "Yes, plan and build for pilgrims, but do so with the ethics Islam teaches us. I mean, before I came here, I read all the Qur'anic verses on pilgrimage, and Allah directly says it's not enough to care for pilgrims if you're not upholding the teachings of the faith. So workers should have rights, in a just society that doesn't discriminate, and instead upholds justice."

"Which is far from the reality here," I said, looking at the city the Prophet had wanted to transform. He ended up transforming it and the world, in the shortest amount of time of any revolutionary in existence, but now this country needed a reminder of its revolutionary roots.

Then again, so did a lot of the world.

I remembered Adam pointing this out when I'd brought up worker rights with him in Doha, when I'd learned of the exploitive employment conditions in the Gulf countries.

"Have you ever looked into how migrant workers are treated in North America? It's the exact same conditions," he'd said. "I'm not saying that it's right, but no one place has the monopoly on exploitation. It's a global problem led by greed."

And then he'd shown me articles about the conditions of migrant workers in his home country of Canada *today*, akin to modern-day slavery.

Besides being eye-opening for me, I'd also been taken aback by his passion—which was so different from his usual self. But then I realized he'd become comfortable in and, to a certain degree, loyal to his society, which was Doha, and I was also comfortable in my society, my life in the US, even though there was stuff I couldn't stand.

It all came down to how much of our comfort we were willing to give up to confront the injustices hiding among us.

It also came down to not being loyal *only* to our local societies but loyal to justice everywhere, for everyone.

Thinking about this inescapable truth, I followed Mila and Fatima down the steps and through a narrow crevice that opened in front of the entrance to Cave Hira, to the entrance of "Iqra!"

Sahaan and a couple of the other guys from our group were inside, while a few more waited outside.

I hung back until it was just me and Mila, once Fatima went down the rest of the way with Sahaan. There were other people not in our group waiting their turns, but I finally had a bit of alone time to sit inside the space my Nabi had, to reflect and pray.

I prayed for him, and I prayed for me to be dogged in my pursuit of equity and justice.

I tried to see the scene below as we came down the Mountain of Light as a happy thing: Adam still leaning on the railing between the shaykh and the elderly man, with everyone around them in groups, talking.

I didn't dwell on the fact that Adam's group included Sarina.

In the cave, I'd decided to rise above all that pettiness and remember my own soul—the one that was into fighting injustice, not fighting someone Adam had had a crush on a million years ago.

And then Adam turned around and saw me and his face . . . his face! The way his eyes widened and he grinned like he'd just seen the best thing in his life.

I smiled back at him and finished the last few steps and went right up to the huddle in front of him. "Assalamu alaikum."

"Walaikum musalam, my Zayby." He reached out his arm. The shaykh moved away to join another group, and I finally found myself by Adam's side, my body resting lightly against him. "How was it? Tell me you took a picture of you up there for me?"

"I didn't. Somehow that was far from my mind." I looked up at him, at his cute hat covering his shaved head, which I never got a good look at. "It was so peaceful and perfect for reflecting. And I'm glad I didn't get a pic. It seems such a touristy thing to do."

"Some people do it for memories or to share with loved ones who couldn't be there," Sarina said. "I just posted some in our chat."

I resisted the thought that presented itself to me: *Who asked you?* And the thing my brother Mansoor always used to say to me when I'd tried to eavesdrop on discussions he was having with Mom and Dad: *This is a conversation between* a *and* b, *so* c *yourself out.*

I resisted those trifling thoughts and just reached for Adam's hand.

We clasped hands, and, secure, I finally looked at Sarina. She was holding her right hand out, fingers curled protectively around something in her palm. "What's that?"

"Sand for the *Grains of Sand* project," she said. "Well, after the shaykh confirms with the authorities it's okay to take this tiny bit with us."

Okay, finally a topic that was safe. Sand. "*Grains of Sand* project? Is that something for the Hajj and Umrah group you work for?"

"No, it's Adam's next exhibit idea. The beauty of sand grains, and the memories they hold. And Sahaan, who has a master's in maths, was saying that there's also a mathematical formula that is artistically and geometrically and spiritually beautiful in sandpiles.

It's esoteric, but I don't doubt that Adam can connect and translate it all through his art." Sarina opened her palm to reveal the sand in it. "I got some for Adam from near Cave Hira. So he can magnify it for his project."

I knew I was squeezing Adam's hand really hard, but he didn't make any noise. "Right. It's like when we were talking about snowflakes, right, Adam? How they're so beautiful magnified?"

Adam nodded and wiggled his fingers in my hand.

I loosened my fingers but still kept his hand in my grip. "As most people know, no two snowflakes are alike. But most people may not know who proved that."

"Who?" Sarina asked, her forehead furrowed at me, her hand still a claw around the "sacred" sand.

"Wilson Bentley," I said, realizing I was talking a lot about something no one had asked about, and that I sounded drunk. "He lived in the early nineteen hundreds, and he took never-before-seen photographs of snowflakes. He called snowflakes ice flowers. Adam can be the Wilson Bentley of sand."

Sarina didn't say anything, just turned around to check if the taxis were here.

"Sand and snowflakes are really different, though. One disappears, but the other stays around forever." I knew I didn't sound sane any longer, but I also couldn't stop.

The taxis were here!

Before she led the way, Sarina turned back to me, her hand clutching her sand for Adam tight, like her life depended on it. "You're right. Sand stays around forever."

"But snowflakes become water. And water is life!" I said, all my resistance to pettiness breaking down. "Right, Adam?"

"Right." He turned to me as everyone went to the taxis. Even though no one was around with us, he bent down to whisper. "Zayneb, are you okay? What's wrong with you?"

"What's wrong with you, Adam?" I tried to whisper, but my words came out like a hiss. "Why didn't you tell me about your *Sands* project? Why didn't you send me juice? Why didn't you come see me with food?"

"What?" He looked taken aback.

"Why did you hang out without me? And then buy me the same clothes as that sand-holding homewrecker?" I immediately shut my mouth.

And clamped my eyelids shut, my eyes stinging with shame. *What was I even saying?*

I had just succumbed to pettiness after such a personal revelatory experience on Jabal Al-Noor.

After committing to rising above it all.

And remembering the piety of my beautiful Nabi, sitting alone in a cave, grieving for a society that did not rise, but descended.

Astaghfirullah.

I whipped past Adam and got into the taxi beside Mila.

ARTIFACT TWENTY-FIVE: ADAM'S PLASTIC FORK
INTERPRETIVE LABEL: WHAT'S BETWEEN ONLY YOU AND ALLAH IS THE MOST IMPORTANT THING

I STARED AT THE MENU FOR SO LONG, SHAYKH MURTAZA GOT UP AND came around to my side of the table to see me. "Adam, did you choose? We are waiting for you."

I nodded and lowered the menu slowly.

I'd been hiding behind the large plastic fold-out menu, afraid to see everyone's faces.

Zayneb was right beside me, but ever since we'd pulled in front of the restaurant and gotten out of our taxis, she'd been unnaturally quiet.

As we'd proceeded to take our seats, everyone else had gotten unnaturally quiet too.

In the midst of the din of a restaurant full of diners, we were a hushed oasis of calm. Apparently noticing this, the waiter approached our table reverently.

"I'll have the nasi goreng," I said.

"I'll just have a lemonade," Zayneb said.

"Why aren't you eating?" I asked, tipping toward her slightly so she could hear the question—which I'd asked like a ventriloquist, my mouth hardly moving.

It felt like the entire Umrah group was poised to hear our every word.

"I ate just before leaving the hotel," she murmured.

Her hotel roommate Mila nodded from across the table. "Albaik. We had Albaik. Has anyone else tried it? So good."

The table suddenly broke out in conversation, all talking about fried chicken.

Alim leaned over and whispered something to Shaykh Murtaza.

Shaykh Murtaza picked up a fork and his water glass and tapped it to get everyone's attention. "Alim just reminded me I was going to share a story about a fork. Yes, a lowly fork, this utensil we eat with."

Once everyone settled down again, Shaykh Murtaza leaned forward. "Ustaadah Ramlah is not here to help me, so I'll have to be as down-to-earth as possible. But that shouldn't be hard with what I'll be sharing." He paused and held up the fork. "In my kitchen drawer at home, there's a special fork, an expensive high-end one. But we only have one of them as it was a gift from my great-grandmother in France. As some of you know, I'm mostly Lebanese and a fraction French. So, anyhow, my great-grandmother had a beautiful set and she wanted everyone in her family to have some part of it, and she had a huge family. So, one item was passed down to me. The fork." He held up the fork again, having lowered it previously as he spoke. "But no one in my family—my wife, my kids—seems to know the difference between that special fork and the others in our kitchen drawer. To them, it's just something that helps you get food into your mouth."

We all hung on to his every word, but I couldn't tell if it was because of his delivery or because of the fact that this was better than talking about fried chicken or trying not to watch me and Zayneb.

"So that's where the crux of my story rests. No one knows the perfection of this fork, except me. No one knows how sturdy and strong it is, how it feels weighty in your hands, so much so that you automatically eat in a more polished way. Or at least I do. It's a beautiful fork, this one." He examined the fork in his hands now as though he were looking at his great-grandmother's fork. "But only I know its excellence. When I open the drawer and it's available there right on top, I get excited; I feel invigorated; I perk up!" He turned to me and Zayneb and Sahaan and Fatima and Suhaib, the youngest people in the group. "You will see when you get older that these little things will begin to excite you, too."

Suhaib laughed, his neon braces brighter in the dim restaurant light. "What happened with the fork? Did someone steal it?"

"What happened with the fork is that I began to hide it sometimes. Because I wanted to make sure that when dinnertime came, it would be available to me." Shaykh Murtaza said this solemnly, almost angrily, and I stopped grinning. "And I realized that the fork had become a litmus test of sorts for the state of my soul. When I wanted others to enjoy the fork, when I passed it to someone who casually asked for a fork, when I didn't pounce on it the moment I sighted it, I knew my soul was in a good state. When I cradled the fork like Gollum in *Lord of the Rings* does with the ring, *my precious*, I wasn't doing too well inside. And only I and Allah knew this. What's only between you and Allah is the most important thing of all to pay attention to—nothing else comes close to it. Because while everything has rights over you in Islam, your soul, the part of you no one knows, has the greatest right of all, because it's the part of us directly connected to the Greatest of all."

Everyone was quiet at the table.

"Did I convey that clearly enough?" Shaykh Murtaza asked. "Or should I let Ustaadah Ramlah translate it for me?"

"No, it was very clear." Zayneb spoke up. "You're just saying what you said before on our drive from the airport but in another way, using the coveting of a fork as an example. You're saying our inner landscape should be our most important focus."

"Yes, and that we should get in the habit of checking ourselves regularly, using our mundane everyday behavior as a guide to the state of our inner landscapes." Shaykh Murtaza nodded and smiled at Zayneb, and I felt warm inside. "Train ourselves to cultivate it, to refine it, to make it grow and, ultimately, soar."

From across Shaykh Murtaza at the other end of the table, Sarina asked, "May I add something, Amu?" When he replied in the affirmative, she went on. "Another way to check the pulse of your soul is to take stock of how you see another's soul. And if it's not in an uplifting way, then apply the balm I've discovered."

I wanted to ask what it was, because she paused for a long time, but I'd become aware that there was some bad energy between Zayneb and Sarina, and so I stayed quiet.

When Sarina finally spoke, it was with eyes clearly glittering with tears. "The best balm for our own souls—even in pain—is to soothe another's soul. It immediately heals us. I discovered this when it was too late for a friend, but I've been on a quest ever since to think of others before myself."

"Masha'Allah," I whispered, feeling the depth of her feelings, Zahid immediately coming to mind, how he'd acted toward me during my MS attack. I thought I'd said "masha'Allah" to myself, but apparently it came out into the air around us, from the way Zayneb whipped her head to look at me.

She turned back and coughed and became quiet.

Waiters showed up with our food just then, putting an end to the reflective stillness that had settled over our table.

When we got back, some of the group went to pray Isha at Masjid al-Haram, but I went to the hotel room, exhausted.

For me, dinner had not gone well, as Zayneb had stopped talking after that "masha'Allah" I uttered.

She was now at Isha with Mila.

While Shaykh Murtaza was making wudu so that he and I could pray the final prayer of the day together, I lay on my bed and FaceTimed with Dad and Hanna. I caught them up with everything and promised I'd continue making dua for them.

"Where's Zayneb?" Hanna asked. Zayneb was her biggest role model. She'd taught Hanna how to effectively start petitioning for better laws on animal welfare.

"She's in another room. It's split like that."

Shaykh Murtaza came out of the bathroom, and Dad glimpsed him. They said salaam to each other, and then Shaykh Murtaza told me to continue my conversation. "I'll talk to your dad after."

"About Zayneb, make sure you two get some time for yourselves," Dad said. "What about in Medina? Are you going to stay together?"

"It's the same. We're in quads, men and women separate."

"Are you able to meet up for some time with each other, or is everything regulated?"

"No, but Zayneb's tired, so she's been catching up on sleep. And I've been letting her."

"Okay, that's good. Insha'Allah."

After Dad spoke to Shaykh Murtaza for a bit, he hung up and we prayed Isha.

I realized I hadn't made it a point to see Zayneb during this trip. It was my fault why she was acting strange.

Z, let's meet in the lobby for Fajr? Just us two? We can walk around after prayer.

She didn't reply, like earlier, so before I went to sleep, I wrote, **I'll come by and pick you up from your room fifteen minutes before salat time.**

ARTIFACT TWENTY-SIX: ZAYNEB'S SKY-BLUE SUNDRESS
INTERPRETIVE LABEL: KEEP TRYING TO FLY, BUT ONLY IF IT'S POSSIBLE TO

AFTER PRAYING ISHA, I STARED AT THE KAABA. IT WAS SO CLOSE, and I was so lost.

I hated myself for the way I was lashing out.

Mila had said she was going to spend the night at the masjid, as near to the Kaaba as she could get, and I'd thought what a great idea, to spend the night praying and asking forgiveness sitting right at the center of our deen.

So I'd pulled a Sadia and, after checking in with family back home, I locked my phone in the hotel safe, only taking the Albaik chicken box in a bag with me, in case I got hungry later. The hotel room was freezing cold, so I knew the food was still okay.

Mila nudged me now as I sat making dua after salat. "Let's go find a little spot farther back, in the masjid itself. They don't like people staying here for too long." She indicated the guards who stood in the courtyard around the Kaaba like parking attendants, the women in khaki outfits with niqabs.

I followed her inside the masjid to a quieter spot but where we could still see the Kaaba, near a pillar with shelves containing Qur'ans in them. I took one of the mus'hafs and crossed my legs on the floor and read for a bit. Then, with the Qur'an still in my lap, I leaned against the pillar and thought about the strange fork story Shaykh Murtaza told us.

I knew he was trying to emphasize examining your own intentions and inclinations and motivations for things, but I was lost on why he'd focused on the fork.

So what if you wanted a nice fork for yourself once in a while? Didn't you deserve it?

It was just a fork.

Don't others deserve it too? I immediately heard Sadia and Adam, the two softest souls I knew, ask in my head.

Shaykh Murtaza told us to focus on the mundane.

I couldn't think of one mundane thing where I coveted something to the exclusion of others.

And wow, for Sarina to so quickly draw attention to her "selfless self" after Shaykh Murtaza's story—when he was trying to teach us to develop a quiet strength of character, one not shared with the world—was really something.

But then, here I was, sitting in the Haram so close to the Kaaba, thinking of how another person needed to examine themselves.

After making istighfar, as I was falling asleep beside the pillar with the beautiful lulling sounds of people praying all around me, and Mila curled up on her own prayer mat, Sausun's invitation came unbidden to my head.

I was the only one who knew she'd invited *everyone*.

But I hadn't told *anyone*.

Not even Adam, actually.

I made a note to tell this mundane thing to Shaykh Murtaza, to tell everyone to come.

Hunger from eating only once in the past twenty-four hours

gnawed at me. I briefly wondered if I should leave the Haram to eat my leftover Albaik, but then remembered Mom and Dad had broken their fasts right here during their Umrah trip in Ramadan, with the food handed out for iftaar.

I reached into the bag to open a corner of the Albaik box and took a strip of cold chicken. After eating a second piece, I felt so sluggish from fatigue again that it was too much effort to continue. I tied the bag closed and succumbed to sleep.

The sound of the Fajr adhan woke me, and I rubbed my eyes to the realization that instead of praying all night, I'd slept. Mila was also massaging her eyes and fixing her shayla, tightening it and adjusting the pink headband on top so her bangs tucked back in.

We made our way to the bathrooms, which were all located in a separate building outside the masjid itself.

A long escalator took us to the biggest lineup of toilet stalls perhaps in existence, or "So! Many! Loos!" as Mila exclaimed in excitement. It was rooms and rooms of bathrooms with another, delineated section for rooms of clustered wudu stations.

The best part was that all the toilets had water hoses next to them, like what I'd seen in Doha and Istanbul, so you could properly clean yourself after.

Mila and I made wudu, sitting down next to each other at one of the ablution spots, and something struck me as I stood up and saw the splatters of water on my jilbab.

I had not once thought of how I looked since arriving in Mecca.

Usually I spent a lot of time assessing myself in the mirror, adjusting my hijab perfectly, applying a bit of makeup before I emerged in public—like, at least fix my eyebrows, add a smidgen of lip gloss and eyeliner. But ever since I got here, I'd just been "whatever."

As we were going back up from the underground bathrooms palace, I saw the same "whatever" condition in others around me. No one looked polished or . . . touched up.

Everyone walked around plain.

And it just felt comfortable to be surrounded by such plain people who didn't seem to care that everyone else was #nofilter too.

I mean, I loved looking good. I think it's especially important when you identify as a Muslim so visibly to communicate a neat and well put-together image. I took a lot of care and had a lot of fun, actually, as I organized my outfits. It gave me life on blah days—to choose fun threads.

But it also felt amazing to leave that behind for a bit.

I stepped off the escalators and back onto the marbled floors outside the masjid. Mila had told me that the marble all over the Haram was a rare kind from Greece, and just as I was about to retort with *luxury!* she'd told me that it was actually the type of marble that kept the coolest under the heat of the sun's rays. "It's actually more environmental than using energy to cool floors."

I guess cool floors were important for worshippers because we all walked around the masjid under the blazing Meccan sun in bare feet.

As we joined all the other people heading to the Haram to pray Fajr, Mila and I discussed what we'd seen so far in Mecca. I brought up the fact that not one of the cleaners we saw in the bathrooms or in the Haram itself were Saudi. They were all from South Asian or African countries. "Is there a rule about that? Like, you're from *this* country so you're worthy of these jobs? But *we* can never stoop that low?"

"Yes, I noticed that too. It's creepy. There's also the humanitarian catastrophe in Yemen, over a quarter of a million people dead." Mila said the next part in a whisper like someone would overhear us.

"Because Saudi Arabia upheld a blockade and conducted a war strategized by your country and mine, the US and Britain. And France."

I understood her fear, why she was talking so quietly.

The repression of those who spoke the truth was swift and decisive.

Here—and at home, too, actually. Anywhere that people wanted to protect their interests and comforts.

Ya Allah, let me be of those who help free people from the tyranny of the powerful, I prayed as we approached the Haram. *Through ethical, nonviolent, and peaceful means.*

Wow. That was my first personal prayer in this sacred place. And it came spontaneously from my heart.

We removed our sandals as we got to the gate we usually entered through, Bab Abdul Aziz, which was the most crowded but also closest to our hotel.

"Zayneb!"

I turned.

Adam. *With Sarina right by his side.*

And Fatima, Sahaan and the shaykh, and some others from our Umrah group behind them.

I waved salaam and then proceeded to go in without waiting for them to catch up.

But Adam caught up with me, his breathing uneven from running. "Where were you?"

I gestured with my hand at the masjid.

"What's wrong?" He put out a hand to stop me from moving away. "Zayneb?"

"Nothing, Adam." I shook my head. "Just trying to focus on spirituality. Practicing spiritual silence."

He dropped his hand, and I got away. Mila, who had hung

back to wait, followed close behind. "Zayneb, I'm sorry, but I have to ask: What was that about?"

I walked through seated worshippers, carefully weaving around people praying, until I found us a small opening facing the courtyard, where we could still see the Kaaba. Which was, again, surreal.

It was right in front of us.

Mila set her backpack down. I had nothing in my hands, since I'd thrown away the bag of Albaik already, so I just stood to pray two rakahs before Fajr.

After sunnah prayer, I sat making dhikr while waiting for the iqamah. Mila waited until I'd finished counting my subhanallahs, alhamdulillahs, and allahu akbars on my fingers and then hit my shoulder with hers gently. "Again, what was that? *Spiritual silence?*"

"What?"

"I'm not trying to be nosy, just concerned." She pulled on her headband, and the movement caused some of her hair to peek out. "Like an older sister."

I laughed. "That's what nosy people say, you know. That they're concerned."

"Well, I have a right to be nosy. As someone who's been married happily for five years, to someone who's not even Muslim, I know how to give counsel on harmonizing your relationship."

"Oh, your husband's not Muslim?"

"No, I reverted after we got married." She tipped her head at me. "But nice try, getting away from my question. Why are you giving Adam the cold shoulder?"

I didn't reply, and, alhamdulillah, the iqamah started, and we all stood up for Fajr, raising our hands up to our ears to throw the world behind us.

. . .

But Mila was relentless. As we walked to the hotel after salat, she was back on the topic. "So I didn't ask you what happened before we went to the restaurant last night, but obviously something went wrong."

I kept my mouth shut. I barely knew Mila. She was way older than me. And I sensed flower-child vibes from her, like, if she wasn't wearing an abaya, she would be in a yellow dress with a floral wreath in her hair, holding a loaf of banana bread she'd just baked or something.

"You guys looked so happy when I met you at the masjid back in London. And I don't want to hear that something went wrong here of all places."

When she put it like that, I felt a twist in my gut. But still, I didn't want to talk about it.

Once we got inside the hotel, as we walked across the lobby, Mila said, "Still showering and getting ready for breakfast, right?"

Stepping into an elevator, I nodded, though I was wondering how I'd handle seeing Adam again. "Can we get a table just us two?"

We were now huddled in the back of an elevator full of people, but still Mila turned around to clutch at me. "Zayneb, no, please. Why?"

We exited on our floor, and because the room was empty, my guard within loosened.

I told Mila I found Sarina's behavior odd and wondered why Adam didn't put more distance between them when it was clearly obvious she was trying to connect with him. I also gave her the intel that Adam had seriously liked her before.

"Why don't you just talk to him?" Mila sat on her bed and shook her head. "Come on, it's a simple fix!"

"We just never have time." I took off my hijab and pulled off my jilbab, under which I had on thin cotton pants and a tank top.

I made a face. "We're in separate rooms! I seriously hate these quad rooms. No offense. I mean, I like being with you."

"None taken. If I was here with Jack, my husband, I would have wanted our own room too." Mila looked wistfully out the window. "I hope one day he can come back with me. On our own, without a group."

I nodded, but then remembered that Jack wasn't Muslim. Did she know that non-Muslims weren't allowed in Mecca because it was a city only for worship?

I decided not to bring that part up. "Insha'Allah, you guys get to come together."

"Well, if he somehow becomes Muslim, too."

"Ameen." I smiled at her and, with my toiletry bag and fresh clothes in hand, got up from kneeling beside my luggage. "You sure you're okay if I shower first?"

"Yeah, I just need a little shut-eye." She propped some pillows behind her on the headboard and, still sitting up, leaned back against them. "Hey, I got an idea. You and Adam sit together at a table for breakfast. I'll arrange it. Get you guys away from the group."

"But." I paused at the doorway to the bathroom. "I don't want to get into the whole thing with him in public, well, in front of the Umrah group."

I thought about seeing him just now outside the Haram. How excited he'd been to see me, whereas I'd just gotten irritated.

And I knew that irritation and anger and all the strong feelings that arose in me each time I saw him were just a cover for the real emotion I was hiding: sadness.

I looked at Mila, who was cushioned by pillows and considering me from her bed. She was kind. I decided to be vulnerable with her. "I'm afraid I might cry if I'm talking things over with him."

"Of course." She nodded sympathetically and drew her bed-cover up around her more snugly. "Then why don't you guys eat breakfast somewhere else? Just you two?"

I couldn't believe I'd never thought of that.

Today was a perfect day for an excursion of our own, actually. Today was the day that members of our group who wanted to do a second Umrah were leaving to do so—including Sarina, the shaykh, and Ustaadah Ramlah. Even Mila and Fatima and Sahaan were going.

Almost everyone was, except me and Adam and the two elderly people in our group.

Adam and I would finally be by ourselves.

We could have a real date at a restaurant. And even come back to one of our rooms to chat more comfortably. We could sit beside each other in Masjid al-Haram. And talk properly.

We could take a happy-couple picture in front of the Kaaba!

We could just be us on a trip—like we're on our own trip.

"I can tell you love that idea." Mila was smiling at me. "The way your face is in a dream state. I love it!"

I laughed and waved my hand in front of my face jokingly to "revive" myself. "No, I'm just thinking of when everyone goes for second Umrah. We could have our time then."

"Yes, I love it. Have a breakfast *and* a dinner date!"

I smiled at her and went into the bathroom and showered and got ready, changing into a sky-blue sleeveless sundress over which I wore the black abaya I'd brought. I topped that with a gray chiffon hijab.

While Mila was in the shower, I took my phone out of the safe, and, while it was charging, checked messages.

OMG, Adam had wanted to spend Fajr with me earlier.

He'd probably come to get me from the room and ended up running into Sarina and Fatima, heading to Fajr too.

I felt awful for jumping to conclusions.

That he'd met them, well . . . Sarina, on purpose.

Again.

I had to reach out to him like Mila said and just talk. . . .

Want to go for breakfast together? Outside the hotel? Just us two? I added a heart.

Luckily his reply came while Mila was still in the bathroom, so she didn't see the way my face performed a somersault of emotions— from hope to irritation to suspicion to hope to anger to sadness.

I'm heading back to eat breakfast in my room. Gotta finish something. I didn't get a chance to tell you because you're obviously avoiding me but I'm meeting someone in Medina for a commission. They want me to write up a proposal so Shaykh Murtaza is lending me his laptop.

The gig Sarina got him.

Can't you do it after breakfast?

No. We're leaving for Medina tomorrow.

And?

And Sarina has to look it over before she goes for second Umrah in the afternoon. It's going to take me a while to get it all together. And they need it tonight.

I wanted to shut down again, especially with a vague headache starting suddenly, but I had to plow through. **About Medina, wait, let me call you.**

"Assalamu alaikum. Remember Sausun? Niqabi Ninja? She wants us to stop by her place on our way to Medina. Can you adjust the timing of your meeting for the commission?"

"No, I don't think that's going to work. He's leaving to go back to the UK tomorrow. We're just doing a quick meet."

I was quiet.

"Are you there?" Adam asked.

"Yeah, it's okay. I'll tell Sausun no, then."

"Wait, what was that?" He drew away from the phone to listen to someone. "Oh, Sarina says that if you want to exchange the pink jilbab, you have to do it today because we're leaving early in the morning, insha'Allah."

"You're with Sarina?"

"I'm with the group that came to Fajr. Ustaadah Ramlah wanted to look at the shops."

"What about dinner, then? Can we go to dinner together, at least?" My voice was full of angst and I knew he felt it, and that just made me want to hang up. But Mila's statement, *Come on, it's a simple fix!* just kept popping up whenever the shutdown reflex flared in me.

I, too, believed that. Adam and I just needed time to ourselves, and everything would get better instantly.

"Yes. As soon as I send the proposal off. Is that okay?"

"Yes."

"And, Zayneb." He paused, and I could hear the sounds in the background fading. "You know I love you, right? A lot?"

I nodded but didn't say anything to him except salaam because Mila was fixing her hijab by the mirror outside the bathroom. And I knew my voice would betray me the moment I opened my mouth—by revealing the sadness within.

Because my stupid brain, starting to pound now for some reason, was saying, *Why did you have to move away from Sarina to say you loved me, Adam?*

ARTIFACT TWENTY-SEVEN: ADAM'S HOTEL PEN
INTERPRETIVE LABEL: GET YOUR PURPOSE SORTED FIRST

I STARED AT THE BLANK SCREEN OF SHAYKH MURTAZA'S LAPTOP, and then out the window behind it. The quad rooms didn't have views overlooking the Masjid al-Haram grounds, so what I saw were the bustling streets of Mecca.

Shaykh Murtaza, Sahaan, and Isa were either sleeping or resting, to prep for their second Umrah, resulting in a sense of calm around me. And, after searching in my e-mails, I'd downloaded some proposals I'd previously sent out, to now use as my template.

I was all set to work, but my fingers wouldn't start typing.

Maybe it was because I wasn't close to my work samples, in my workroom. I messaged Hanna to ask if she could go take pictures of the projects I didn't have on my website yet and send them over to me.

I realized right after I texted that she was at school, and by the time she got back home, it would be too late.

I was on my own.

I'd just started making the headings and writing my personal details when my phone pinged several notifications in a row.

A message on Instagram from Janna, of all people.

She was the kind of person who sent short, broken texts.

Salaam, this is Janna

Hope your Umrah is going well

I've been trying to get a hold of Z

I know you guys must be busy

But Sausun has been trying to get through

To Z but she's not answering

Z never told her

What time you guys were coming to see her

I was going to ignore her DMs to work but then figured that might mean more messages. And yup, she wrote again.

Also, look at this

She sent a photo of a carved two-seater with a cushion in a traditional pattern of burnt orange, sky blue, black, and white.

I decided to reply before she went on.

Nice. Sorry Z will be letting Sausun know that we won't be coming.

Why

The schedule is tight here

Sausun said Z told her you guys *were* coming

Sorry. I have to get to Medina to meet some people for a job

Oh cool

What job

Working to make little artistic models for store display.

That is amazing

Insha'Allah you'll get it

You're at the holy cities now

So pray hard

Working on the proposal now

Then I added, It's my first job in a while so gotta hustle

Ok I'll let you go

And will let Sausun know

I turned off all notifications and set my fingers in position above the keyboard again.

Nothing came.

I got up and took two steps to stand at the window, to look below at all the people moving around like ants.

Why were they all here? Why were *we* here?

Because the Qur'an told us to come: *And proclaim unto all people the pilgrimage; they will come on foot and on every [kind of] fast mount, coming from every far-away point [on earth], so that they might experience much that shall be of benefit to them. . . .*

Pilgrimage was a beneficial experience.

Beneficial experiences could be had anywhere people gathered. Like at a store.

And with this job I was trying for, I'd be making visiting the store a beneficial experience. I could tell stories through my models of various places around the world.

Seeing my 3D maps would enlarge a customer's world. Which would make them feel good at the store they were shopping at.

Which was good . . . right? To create happy shoppers?

I peered at the pilgrims below again to avoid thinking too much about creating happy shoppers.

My job was to make people reflect on the magnificence of the world, to then hopefully link that magnificence to the Magnificent.

I sat back down and, using a hotel pen, jotted that on the notepad by the table lamp.

I had my niyyah now.

I set my fingers atop the keyboard again.

Nothing happened again.

A cell phone rang behind me. "Hello?"

I turned to see Shaykh Murtaza sitting up in bed, his phone to his ear. "Zayneb, assalamu alaikum. Wait, let me go into the hall. We've got two people sleeping here."

Why was she calling Shaykh Murtaza?

Zayneb. She was why I couldn't write. She was upset for some reason, increasingly cold toward me.

All our strange interactions were getting to me.

And it had something to do with Sarina.

Was it because Zayneb remembered I'd liked her half a decade ago?

No, that couldn't be it. Zayneb was way stronger than that.

That would have been *me* if someone Zayneb had liked once upon a time was on this trip. Like Yasin.

Oh man, if he'd been here, always hovering around her, I would have been pretty miserable.

Because I'm the one who feels on shaky ground with Zayneb's feelings for me.

I had to get on a firmer footing, feel more worthy of her.

And that will happen if I get this next commission, after which I could also start saving up—maybe then I'd have enough to live with Zayneb.

I sat up straighter. I had to do this proposal in a way that would wow Sarina's brother Waleed.

I started typing.

I'd found my motivation: *Zayneb.*

At two p.m., Sarina knocked, and I brought the laptop out into the hall. She took it and sat down on the floor beside our hotel room door and immediately began scrolling on the track pad, reading. "Okay to adjust some things?" she asked.

222

Standing against the wall across from her, I nodded.

She began fixing and editing, her eyes narrowing at the screen sometimes and looking aside at other times as she considered something. Finally, she got up—carefully, due to her billowy jilbab—and turned the laptop to me.

I did a read-through and immediately found it better organized. Smoother. "Hey, thanks."

"No problem. Now e-mail it to me? I'll send it on." She started to back up, to get to the elevators. "And don't worry, Waleed knows I'm helping you with it."

"I figured so, thanks again." I waved at her.

"Oh, and he's okay waiting a few extra hours so we can stop at your friend's on our way to Medina."

"Friend's?"

"Yeah, Zayneb told Shaykh Murtaza about the invite from your friend who lives in Thuwal."

"Oh yeah. So everyone is going?"

She nodded. "Shaykh Murtaza talked to the family, and it seems they often host Umrah groups."

I nodded and then said salaam.

I went back into the room, where everyone was up and getting ready for Umrah, and sent the commission proposal to Sarina.

Now I had to get ready for some just-Zayneb-and-me time.

ARTIFACT TWENTY-EIGHT: ZAYNEB'S ORANGE HEADBAND
INTERPRETIVE LABEL: *IN TIMES OF STRESS, SOME BECOME BOLDER AND BRAVER*

EVEN THOUGH I HAD A THROBBING HEADACHE, IT FELT SO GOOD TO walk around the mall talking to myself.

It was Mila's idea.

During breakfast at the hotel, at a table for just us two, after I trained her on how to make sure nobody from the Umrah group approached us—by staring intensely at each other and our food, leaning in toward the center of the table so that our heads almost touched—I had told her about all the things I hadn't told Adam.

About the stress tics.

About being unhoused.

About Adam thinking Layth was taking care of Bertha Fatima just during this Umrah trip, not that Layth had been doing it for almost a month now.

About how I may not get into the externship program due to the allegations against me. How Adam knew about the campus insinuations but not how they would affect my aspirations at school.

I told Mila about how I'd been voice-recording my problems so I could tell him everything all at once when we had time to be face-to-face, touch-to-touch, hug-to-hug. And she said, "Why don't you try the same tactic to deal with what's happening now—now that you *still* can't be with each other face-to-face?"

I felt like crying at that moment, when she brought up that part. Because yes, we were in the same place, the best place on earth, actually, and we couldn't even be together. And then we'd go back to our respective homes at the end of the week.

But I'd decided to take her advice. After sleeping a bit on my return from breakfast, I left the room while Mila was getting ready for her second Umrah, which included organizing all her things to leave for Medina tomorrow morning. I'd decided I'd pack when I got back from seeing Adam tonight.

I'd taken the elevators down to the mall that made up the first four levels of the hotel.

I walked around and, with my earbuds in, recorded the new things I wanted to tell Adam. About how worked up I'd gotten when I'd realized who Sarina was.

While talking, I multitasked. I bought Mila some more headbands for her scarf or her hair, fun, colorful ones, more secure stiff ones, and bought one for myself too, a bright orange one, to remember her by after the trip. I bought Fatima better shampoo and conditioner for her hair because she'd forgotten to pack some, and the hotel shampoo wasn't good for her. I bought her Hodan's favorite brand of hair care products. I even bought Ustaadah Ramlah the kind of scarf she liked, to thank her for lending me some clothes.

I didn't feel guilty for not buying Sarina anything.

Then I sat at a coffee shop and people-watched while drinking an espresso, hoping the intensity of the caffeine would deal with the headache that had gotten almost unbearable now. I made a mental note to get a painkiller when I returned to the hotel room, which would, thankfully, be emptied of the others now; I'd made sure to deliberately exit the room before Sarina bustled around the place getting ready to leave for Umrah.

I wished Adam were sitting across from me right now.

He would have gotten a latte. He would have taken a quick glance at the table we'd be sitting at to make sure it was clean, and if it hadn't been, he would have gotten a napkin and wiped it for us. Then he would have set his cup down and looked at me and smiled before doing anything else.

In the pauses between talking, and in between playing with my fingers—which he loved to do because physical touch was his biggest love language—he would have shared a little something he saw around us in the café that I hadn't even seen, because my eyes were always zoomed out on the whole of something. But he would have noticed that little girl across from me, trying to give her baby brother bits of her cookie when her parents weren't looking.

I smiled at the little girl now on behalf of Adam and waved at her when she gave me a small smile back.

I missed him hugely and couldn't wait for winter break, when we could be with each other for days, just us two, insha'Allah, with a bit of time with my family woven in, that is. And we were supposed to spend the beginning of the holidays with his grand-parents in Canada, both sets, as his father's parents were flying in from Vancouver to be with Hanna and their dad, who'd be home in Ottawa for the break too.

It was all going to be so cozy.

I was about to take my earbuds off when I heard the ping of a new incoming e-mail. I clicked the notification from *Campus Daily*, headache so bad now that I was ready to bolt back to the room.

Investigations of misappropriation of funds to start in cases of several students accused of funds mismanagement, including treasurer candidate Zayneb Malik.

It was an article describing the college administration's decision to officially begin the process of looking into all the stories circulating on campus.

A wave of nausea filled my mouth.

I was going to puke.

Somehow I just barely made it back into the room and into the entrance of the bathroom before throwing up all over the tiled floor.

In the pause between heaving, I lumbered to the toilet and dropped to my knees.

Over and over I threw up and flushed, threw up and flushed.

I could feel chills. I was breaking out in sweats.

I was unbelievably sick.

And no one was around.

When I retched and retched and nothing more came out, I sat back against the tile wall. After taking shallow breaths for a bit, I pulled a towel and wiped my face, chin and neck with it. Then I crawled with a new towel in hand and shoved it all over the mess in the entrance to the bathroom.

I found where I'd flung my phone when I entered the hotel room and called Adam.

"Z, don't worry, I'm ready for dinner! Let's go early?" He sounded so giddy that a huge sword of guilt stabbed my heart to let me know that I was going to ruin our plans.

"Adam, I'm sick. Really sick."

"What? Are you in the room?"

"Yes." I heaved again and ran back to the bathroom, throwing my phone on the carpeting again.

Nothing was coming out, but I couldn't stop the waves of nausea.

Soon Adam was at the door, so I forced myself to crawl back out and reach up to yank the door handle so he could push in. Then I was back in the bathroom, heading again to the toilet.

"Oh, Zayby." He was in the bathroom beside me, already on his knees. He reached out and loosened my sticky hijab and flung it into the shower stall. Then he got up and wet a facecloth and wiped my face with it, while rubbing my back with his other hand, and I leaned my head back on the tile, waiting for the nausea to subside, but every few minutes it would start again.

Finally I was able to get into bed—dirty abaya off and in the shower, being showered on along with my hijab—with a cold wet facecloth on my forehead and Adam sitting at the side with a plastic bag he'd found in the room. He'd also taken a bottle of water from Fatima's stash that he kept trying to get me to sip.

But I wanted nothing to go down.

"Can I call the front desk for a doctor?" Adam asked, his face full of worry, though he was talking calmly.

"Can we just wait? I just want to stop throwing up."

"Okay, then let me call room service for a sports drink. You need electrolytes."

"Not now. Let me just sleep." As soon as I said that, another wave of sickness erupted in me, and I motioned for the bag. Adam held it out, but again, nothing.

He stayed by my side holding that bag out until I fell asleep.

· · ·

When I opened my eyes, he was sleeping beside me, an arm flung across my waist.

I felt terrible still and gently eased the plastic bag from his hand and brought it up to my mouth.

I heaved and threw up some more and more, until again nothing was left in me. I used the damp facecloth that had fallen off my forehead to wipe my mouth. Then I leaned my head back on the pillows Adam had propped up for me so I wasn't completely flat.

Was it what I'd read? That the college is investigating me?

Have I really become that scared of everything?

I couldn't help it, but tears started flowing as I thought of how I'd started law school—on top of the world, like I could do anything I decided to do, ready to take anything and everything on.

Now here I was in Mecca, crying about my fears and my insecurities. Throwing up, getting sick about it all.

I glanced at the night table, and there was a sports drink and a small bottle of acetaminophen.

Carefully, so that Adam wouldn't wake up, I uncapped the drink and sipped some and took a painkiller. My head was still throbbing, and I wanted to sleep.

At some point, Adam must have left. Because the lights were out and the rest of the girls were back in the room sleeping in their beds.

But another of his empty plastic bags was hanging on the drawer handle of the night table.

The pain medication had apparently worked for my headache, allowing me to actually sleep.

I got up slow and steady, and walked to the bathroom, afraid of the state I'd find it in.

It was sparkling clean, with new towels. My abaya and hijab were nowhere to be found.

Adam must have called for service.

I took my clothes off and took a long shower and washed my hair. When I got out, I was shivering, even after wrapping myself in two towels.

I was still sick. I pulled my tank top and pants on again and went back to take another pill and get into warm bedcovers.

Please, please, ya Allah, let me be okay to leave tomorrow morning.

ARTIFACT TWENTY-NINE: ADAM'S ORIGAMI FOLDED PLASTIC BAG
INTERPRETIVE LABEL: WHEN YOU'RE IN LOVE, YOU'RE ALWAYS AT THE READY

THE NEXT MORNING, WE GOT ZAYNEB DOWNSTAIRS, USTAADAH Ramlah and I, our arms wrapped around her from either side. She was still weak, having spent the entire night sick, but insisted she could make it onto the mini coach bus leaving Mecca.

Before we exited the room, Mila and I had packed her things for her, including the abaya and hijab I'd washed in the shower and asked the hotel to dry for me. Along with the jilbab I'd gifted her, I put some fresh clothes and toiletries in her backpack to be quickly accessible for her. Mila took Zayneb's things down along with hers on a luggage cart and was waiting for us in the lobby. Everyone else was already on the bus.

Zayneb pointed to one of the plush lobby chairs, and when we walked her over, she promptly deflated into a seat and, after breathing in and out for some time, put her head down on her knees.

"We can try to get you two a room for tonight, and you can meet us tomorrow in Medina," Ustaadah Ramlah said quietly to me. "The journey may be too hard for her now."

"I'm okay." Zayneb's muffled voice arose from her still-bent head. "Just taking a rest."

"How about resting on a bed?" I knelt beside her chair so it could only be us two conversing about this. "We could stay now and leave when you're fully recovered."

"But we're not going far."

"Medina is four hours away."

Mila, who'd wheeled the luggage cart over to us from near the automated doors, said, "I thought Shaykh Murtaza said we're stopping for lunch at Zayneb's friend's? That's just an hour and a half out."

"Yeah, an hour and a half," Zayneb mumbled into her legs. "I can rest at Sausun's. She sent me pics of her place. She has a huge bedroom. It has a kitty palace in it."

She sounded delirious.

I stood up. *I'd better check room availability here at the hotel. I could put it on my credit card and pay for it sometime . . . soon . . . insha'Allah.*

Ustaadah Ramlah and Mila stayed with Zayneb while I went to the front desk.

I was back quicker than I expected. Because it was last minute, and only the better suites were available, the cheapest one was currently over six hundred dollars.

Maybe I could find another hotel, farther away from Masjid al-Haram.

Zayneb stood up. She had a sports drink in her hand, its cap off. She took a sip and handed the bottle to Mila, who capped it for her before sliding it into the big purse she was carrying.

"I'm good now. Let's go?" Zayneb took a step forward but it was shaky, and I came to her aid quickly. Ustaadah Ramlah held her other side, and we walked her slowly out of the hotel.

When we got on the bus, I took a spot near the window right at the front, and Mila took the spot at the window across the aisle from me, and we lay Zayneb down so that her head was in my lap, her knees up, with her feet resting on the edge of the seat next to Mila's.

Zayneb had bad food poisoning.

Mila had figured it out after questioning Zayneb about everything she'd eaten.

Zayneb had thrown up again after recounting she'd eaten hours-old Albaik—in the Haram, of all places.

I stroked her forehead now, several thick plastic bags on standby, one in my hand, others origami folded small in the pocket of my thawb, in case she needed them.

We just had to get through the next two days in Medina.

And Sarina had arranged with her brother and his colleagues to come to the hotel to do the interview, so that I could have maximum time with Zayneb. Sarina had also said that she and Ustaadah Ramlah would be there for Zayneb while I met with Waleed.

Zayneb slept the entire way to Sausun's place. When we arrived and the bus driver entered the gate to park in the courtyard driveway, I woke her up.

She immediately dry-heaved, and everyone on the bus patiently waited for to finish, as they needed us off the bus to exit.

Sausun's home was two stories, except for a single-leveled central area that jutted out right in the front, covered in tall windows. Doubled-storied wings spread out behind it and on either side with smaller windows. Shaykh Murtaza went up the three low steps to the double doors leading to the house, but they opened before he got near enough to ring the doorbell. A man in a crisp white thawb and white shemagh stepped out, a big smile on his bearded face. "Assalamu alaikum, welcome musaafireen!"

He hugged Shaykh Murtaza and smiled at everyone in turn with his right hand on his heart, and then swept his left hand toward his open doors. "I'm Abdullah ibn Abdur-Rahman. Please come inside my home."

There was no foyer as we immediately entered the central area, and I realized it was another courtyard, a completely enclosed one, a glass ceiling crisscrossed with beams on top. It had so many grandiose sofas, dark burgundy ones with flamboyantly curved golden-edged arms and similarly gilded high backs and gold-and-cream patterned cushions, edging the walls that it felt like we were in a sofa emporium. Behind the sofas were ceiling-to-floor fancy cream drapes with long gold-tasseled fringes, presumably in front of all those windows seen from the outside of the house. In the middle of the room was a huge oval table in gold-veined marble, close to the ground with square cushions tucked under. The floor was cream marble with a square, gold-framed center filled with a design of large gold flourishes.

It was all very opulent and obviously the sitting room where guests were received. There was enough seating here for maybe forty people, and I realized Sausun wasn't kidding when she said they were used to entertaining pilgrims.

The double doors leading to the actual house opened, and a girl in black abaya and niqab entered the room. She went to each of the women and said salaam with a quick hug. When she got to Zayneb, she ended her hug by holding on to her arms. "I heard you've been sick. Shaykh told me. Let's go inside." She turned to me. "Assalamu alaikum. I'm Sausun. I take it you're Adam. If it's all right with you, I'll settle Zayneb into my room, and then when it's an all-clear inside, with us women in the house and our hijabs, you can come to be with her?"

I nodded and squeezed Zayneb's shoulder. "Love you, Z. I'll come as soon as I can, okay?"

She tipped her head and rested it on my arm for a bit and then followed Sausun.

I watched her go into the house and then joined the others gathered on the sofas. Sausun's dad was giving everyone an overview of his family, how his side was from Medina by heritage, how they divided their time between the US, South Africa, and Saudi Arabia. We spent a good half hour listening to him and asking questions, which he was kind enough to answer.

The doors to the house opened again, and four men in matching uniforms of white pants and safari shirts came in with huge platters of food and trays of drinks.

Each platter was rice with a different kind of meat on top. One mound of rice was smothered in chicken, another lamb, another fish, still another with shrimp, and there was one with roasted vegetables. There were also platters with fresh salad, yogurt, and dates.

Shaykh Murtaza showed us a solitary porcelain sink in a corner of the room, and we all went to wash our hands in turn. "We're going to be eating with our hands from the same platter, as is custom," he said in a low voice as we approached the oval table after. "For those unfamiliar with the tradition, please ensure you eat only from your side of the plate as per polite manners."

"Yalla, let's eat!" Sausun's dad exclaimed from behind Shaykh Murtaza. "Bismillah!"

He pulled out the cushions underneath the table, and we all sat down, me near the fish. Though my mind was mostly on Zayneb, wondering when Sausun would let me into the house to be with Z, I reached out with hungry enthusiasm to the nearest bit of rice on the platter and began eating with everyone else who'd chosen fish likewise, which was Alim, Sarina, and Suhaib's dad.

I'd eaten with my hands when I'd visited Zahid and his family before, so it wasn't too difficult, though I did find it messy.

The food was delicious—fresh grilled fish, its flesh soft and flaky, with flavorful rice—and I just had to add a whispered alhamdulillah right after saying bismillah. I hadn't eaten well last night or this morning because I was preoccupied with Zayneb's illness.

Now that she was resting properly, with good food at her fingers as well, I felt okay to eat.

Sarina did a mock interview for me while we were eating, and, periodically, her questions were so trivial—like which chocolate I liked the best in a Quality Street box—that I'd laugh, but then she said they were actual questions her brother told her his employers had asked him and others. That if anyone chose the chocolate flavor people at the office didn't like, they were told they got an extra point. It was all in fun, and it gave me a bit of insight into my potential workplace.

I gave Sarina a diplomatic answer to her mock chocolate question. "Is there any flavor that isn't good, though? Hey, just give me all the orange creams and coconuts you don't want."

But yeah, we all laughed a lot, and after a couple of weeks worrying about my future, it felt good to just enjoy the possibility of it all.

When lunch finished, I waited for a while, but still no Sausun emerged. I approached Ustaadah Ramlah and asked what I should do because I wanted to check in on Zayneb, but it was clear that men weren't allowed in the house freely.

Ustaadah Ramlah said she'd ask permission to see Sausun inside.

While baklava trays were being passed around in the sitting room, she talked to Abdullah ibn Abdur-Rahman. He called someone on his cell phone, hung up, and walked to the house doors to open them for Ustaadah Ramlah.

She went inside.

And came out ten minutes later, her face somber. "Zayneb's gotten worse, and Sausun is saying she should stay here while we go on to Medina."

"What? Can I see her?"

"No, Adam." Ustaadah Ramlah lowered her voice considerably and indicated I should follow her to the porcelain sink, where none of the members of our Umrah group were gathered. "I'm sorry to tell you this, but she doesn't want to see you."

"What do you mean?"

"She insisted, and Sausun got upset at me when I tried to tell her Zayneb's not thinking right."

"You must have heard wrong. I'm sorry if that sounds rude, but you've never heard properly whenever Zayneb talks." I shook my head, trying to clear the confusion settling in. "It's because of her American accent."

"Adam. It's not because of her accent. She said please go on ahead to Medina. Please make sure Adam goes so that he gets the job he wants."

"Oh, so she just wants me to not miss an opportunity." I took a deep breath of relief. "It's not that she doesn't want to see me."

"No, she doesn't want to see you."

That wasn't Ustaadah Ramlah speaking.

I turned around and there was Sausun, standing just behind Ustaadah Ramlah. I frowned at her. "I'm sorry, what did you just say?"

"Zayneb is resting, and she said she needs space for recovery. She asked me to emphasize to you that she needs the next couple of days to get over her illness, and then she'll catch up with everyone in Medina, insha'Allah." Sausun's arms were clasped behind her back, but now she brought them forward to cross them in front of her chest. "I'll bring her there myself. Women can drive here now, you know," she deadpanned. "But yes, she doesn't want to see you, or anyone, for that matter. She told me she doesn't need her luggage as she has a change of clothes and essentials in her backpack."

Then she turned around and went back into the house.

Ustaadah Ramlah looked at me, and her face was so full of pity, it made me upset.

So upset that I snapped at her. "Zayneb is not a vegetarian. We don't have any kids, let alone being pregnant with a second, and she's studying to become a lawyer, not a police officer. Please just listen next time."

I went back to sit on the edge of one of the ostentatious sofas and pulled up my phone and messaged Zayneb.

Zayneb, what's wrong?

Why can't I see you?

I can't go to Medina without you

Are you okay?

Please answer me

Please

I won't

Leave you

Here

I don't

Understand

What's

Happening

I'd turned into a Janna type of a texter, my fingers flying to get her to answer me.

Janna.

I calculated the time difference. She'd probably be in class now.

So I couldn't text her and find out what Sausun was all about.

I'd met Sausun only briefly at Janna's brother's wedding. But Zayneb had hung out with Sausun after—and it was obvious they'd become good friends here or something.

Sausun seemed fierce. But also caring.

At other times I would have found that an interesting combo.

Right now, though, I just wanted to see Zayneb.

After speaking to Shaykh Murtaza and Sausun's dad, Abdullah, it was decided that we would all leave for Medina.

Including me.

Shaykh Murtaza told me that he could arrange for someone to bring me back tomorrow so that I could visit and, hopefully, pick Zayneb up.

Abdullah said he'd confirm everything with Sausun, so that whenever Zayneb was feeling ready for the rest of the trip to Medina, she'd leave with me.

As the bus pulled away, I messaged Zayneb again and then dropped my hand clutching my phone with a skyscraper of unanswered texts onto the empty seat beside me.

The only thing to do now was succumb to peering into the same hole I'd carried inside me before I even flew to Umrah—because now it was unavoidable.

It had grown into a cavern.

• • •

We checked into our Medina hotel. I was so numb, I didn't notice anything about it.

As soon as we got into the room, I went into the bathroom, turned the lights off, and locked myself inside, leaning my forehead on the back of the door.

In two hours I was supposed to meet these fancy people for an interview.

For a job that, if I did well, could become a longer contract, as the parent company owned high-end stores all around the world.

My work could help make their stores cozy and inviting to rich customers.

Which wasn't really what I was about, but . . . maybe I could become committed to such a thing?

Maybe I could find the good in this type of work too.

Maybe on other days I would have.

But today, the cavern had split within, I'd been cut in two, and I just didn't know how to put myself back together.

So I just fell apart and back in time, to when I was a kid.

"The hospital is the best place for Mom right now, Adam," Dad told me when I'd asked where she was, when I'd come down to the kitchen to tell him that Mom wasn't in their room. "Grandma is with her now. And I'm just going to feed Hanna and go back to the hospital. Grandpa will stay with you."

"Can I come too?" At nine, I was just beginning to feel that if I participated in something, I could help shape its outcome. If I stayed by Mom's side, I could help her get better faster. "I can help with things."

"The hospital can do the best job helping her." Dad tipped the bottle and let drops fall on his wrist to check the temperature while Hanna clutched his leg, whining for her milk. "You can help Grandpa take care of Hanna."

"Can't Grandma help with Hanna?" I wasn't usually so bold, but the last time Mom had gone to the hospital, she was there longer than any of her previous hospital stays.

If she saw me there beside her, she'd know I was ready to do anything.

I'd encourage her like she encouraged me.

She'd get better faster.

I could even point out things around her, how awesome they were. That always made her smile, when I taught her what I'd learned from her.

"No, Adam." After settling Hanna in her seat to drink her bottle, Dad gave me a stern look. He was the firmer parent, but he'd always erred on the side of gentleness even when being strict. But now he was unrelenting in his gaze and tone. "Mom can't see you now. She needs to get better. I already told you that."

I nodded and went to stand at the living room window that looked out onto the darkening street.

I hadn't seen Mom leave for the hospital, but I was going to wait as long as I needed so I could see her come back.

But I never saw her come back.

Yes, the cavern split inside me.

In the space revealed, I saw the ugly truth: I'd been desperate for a job, any job, even a job I didn't believe in, because I was afraid of losing Zayneb.

I canceled my interview and slept.

ARTIFACT THIRTY: ZAYNEB'S LITTLE JAR OF HONEY AND GINGER
INTERPRETIVE LABEL: LOVE COMES IN ALL SORTS OF LANGUAGES, INCLUDING FOOD

I WAS A MESS. INSIDE, OUTSIDE. IN ALL WAYS.

Besides throwing up more, I'd also broken down after seeing Adam and Sarina from Sausun's sitting room, which had a window overlooking the courtyard living room.

The drapes had been drawn tight in the sitting room—a space outside Sausun's bedroom to receive guests—and she'd told me to lie down on the sofa while she prepared things for me in her own room. But I'd stood up and considered the window and decided to watch everyone downstairs through a small opening in the fancy curtains.

Everything had been okay until the food came—I'd even been thinking, *That looks amazing and I'm hungry, so maybe I'll go join them after a bit of rest.*

But then Adam and Sarina looked at each other and went straight for the same platter of food, sitting across to eat from the large plate between them, their hands reaching toward the other. Adam, facing the house, in direct sight of me, had laughed and laughed.

It seemed like Sarina was telling jokes. Exclusively to him.

I felt awful staring like that but couldn't tear myself away. I'd been so engrossed that I didn't even notice that Sausun had come to stand at the other end of the curtain. And that she'd been watching too.

I began heaving immediately after Adam smiled big at Sarina a third time, before throwing his head back to laugh.

Sausun ushered me into her bathroom, where she'd set a big steel bowl on the counter. I motioned for her to leave, and when she did, I threw up—the electrolytes I'd drunk before.

When I started shivering, I wondered, again, if it was really food poisoning.

Or, like the tics, stress.

"It's food poisoning, not stress. You ate old chicken. And now you're throwing up," Sausun told me, tapping away at her phone after she settled me under the duvet on her bed. "I'm just chatting with my bestie, who's doing her residency at the Mayo Clinic." She stuck her chin out to indicate the tray on the night table. "Now eat that."

I nodded and reached for the toast she'd brought up along with a banana, a bowl of white rice, and a sealed plastic cup of applesauce. She'd also brought up her grandmother, who stood silently by the bed holding a little jar of something, with a spoon resting on top of the lid.

I smiled at her and said salaam.

"Walaikum musalam, child. Take this. I made it for you like I make for my kids and grandkids. It's crushed ginger mixed with special honey. It will stop the nausea," Sausun's grandmother said in an accent I couldn't place. Her hair was dark and parted in the center to meet at the back and descend in one thick braid.

She reminded me of Daadi, who'd only ever given me the best

food, so I let her spoon some of her concoction into my mouth.

I closed my eyes when swallowing, afraid that it would be gross, but it tasted surprisingly good.

When I opened my eyes again, it was like Daadi was standing there, with her right hand reaching out to feed me as she'd done many times after school when I was little.

The reach of love was the same.

I instantly teared up, because there were so few times I felt those snatches of boundless love.

And because Daadi's life was taken by those who didn't see her as a loving, loved being.

"Thank you, Nanni," I said to Sausun's grandmother, using the term for maternal grandmothers, assuming she was from Sausun's mom's side.

Nanni stroked my head and said a shifaa dua over me. Then she left after reminding me to finish the ginger "medicine," the container of which she'd left on the bedside table.

"Thanks, Nanni," Sausun echoed me, tilting her head to call out before her bedroom door closed behind her grandmother.

Then Sausun turned to me. "Now, let's get you better."

In response, I nibbled the edges of the toast in my hand.

"Eat in bits and keep drinking. Alternate between water and electrolytes," Sausun read off her phone. "But Ruqi also said this is not medical opinion and, I quote, in capital letters, NOT THE MAYO CLINIC'S OPINION, but simply friendly advice based on surviving bouts of food poisoning herself." Sausun typed into her phone and then put it facedown beside her at the foot of the bed. "I had to confirm to her that I shouted the Mayo Clinic disclaimer out to you."

I grinned weakly.

She smiled back and said, "You'll be fine, insha'Allah. If you stop wearing that doomed look on your face."

I scooped some more gingery-honey goodness with the spoon and lapped it like a cat. "Your grandma is cute. What's her accent?"

"South African. With a touch of Gujarati and Urdu from way back." She stood up and unwound her hijab and removed her face cover. Then she pulled off her under-scarf band and unclasped her hair and tossed all of her niqab and scarf stuff onto a chair. She kept her abaya on and came back to sit at the foot of the bed again.

I remember seeing Sausun without niqab at Sarah's henna party, before Sarah's wedding to Janna's brother, but it was still surprising to glimpse her face. It was very striking, with long features and sad-looking eyes. Her hair was also super long and straight with severely even bangs.

I realized it was easier to talk to her with her niqab on.

Because her un-niqabbed expression was deadpan, while her eyes were searching.

It was the type of face that saw through BS.

With a careful set of questions, she got these horrible truths out of me:

I hadn't wanted to come to Umrah.

I was wildly jealous of Sarina.

I'd treated Adam like shit for most of the trip.

I didn't try to connect with anyone in the Umrah group because I hadn't wanted to. Except Mila, but only because she brought me fried chicken.

And, finally, that I felt like a soulless beast.

As soon as I got those facts out, my stomach started to feel better. Which made me muse out loud that maybe it *was* stress, and now that I'd confided in someone, an actual friend, things were clearing up.

"No, it's my grandma's ginger and honey that's clearing you up," Sausun said. "Now tell me why you were spying on everyone from my sitting room window."

"Like I said, I'm a soulless beast."

"When I first met you two summers ago, you were confident and powerful." She leaned back on the footboard, drew her legs in to cross them, and rested her hands on top of her knees like they were the arms of a throne. For some reason, that move of hers made me feel more under the magnifying glass. "I got long-lost-sister vibes from you. And every time we met up with Janna in Chicago, you were the same. Strong. What changed?"

"I started law school?"

"No. Something else."

"Something bad? Sad?"

"Something big."

"I got nikahfied?"

She didn't say anything and stared at me unflinchingly.

I looked at the banana. And reached for it, even though I wasn't hungry.

"You said you were treating Adam badly. Why?"

The question came out of the blue, and I dropped the banana on the bed. "Because he acts like he likes Sarina. And he's oblivious to her attempts to focus on him. And—" I swallowed. "Because he's hung out with her more than he's hung out with me on this trip. And acts ignorant about it."

She didn't say anything again.

I picked up the banana and peeled it. Took a tiny bite and closed it up.

"Can you stay here? While the rest of them go on to Medina?"

"Why?" I furrowed my eyebrows.

"Because you need rest. And space."

"Space from what?"

"From him. Adam."

I frowned at her. "All I've had is space from him. That's the problem."

"Space here, between Mecca and Medina."

When she said that, my stomach clenched for a moment, but it wasn't due to being sick. The sensation was a bit higher, right under my diaphragm.

It was anxiety.

What did I think was going to happen if I wasn't with Adam?

Why had the potential of being apart from him during this break almost driven me into a frenzy of fear and then almost to depression?

That fear-fuel had catapulted me to hop on two international flights.

And now here we were.

"I can send a message to your Umrah chat if you're good with staying with me for the next while. Or a private one to your leaders. The shaykh. And Adam, of course."

"There's an Umrah chat group?"

"You're not on it? The shaykh added me yesterday after I talked to him. Because *you* were never picking up my messages or calls." Sausun scrolled on her phone. "You *are* on the chat. It says your name right here on the list of participants. Zayneb."

I picked up my phone from under one of the pillows and opened the group chat app I rarely used. Yup, there *was* a chat. *Autumn Umrah Group.*

I scrolled through the messages quickly, but all the photos and videos I'd previously missed slowed me. They'd been added by various people and included a bunch that were extreme close-ups of Adam's 3D Hijrah map, some so well shot that it looked like photos of a real place.

There were a *lot* of pictures.

But my fingers paused to tap and enlarge only select pics.

One after another, Adam and Sarina showed up. Mostly with others but also sometimes just them.

In front of the Kaaba. At the base of Jabal Al-Noor, beside a juice stand, laughing at Sahaan's attempts to do a pinch-the-clock-tower pose.

And the worst: sitting at the mall coffee shop I'd wished him to be sitting at *with me*.

He had his latte, and I saw a used napkin crumpled beside his cup, confirming he had cleaned the table before putting down his drink.

They were with Shaykh Murtaza and Ustaadah Ramlah, but this pic hurt so much, I started crying.

Sausun came to stand beside me and whispered, "That's why I said take some space. I'd seen those pictures. And I also saw from the window in my sitting room."

I nodded. "I can't be with him right now. I don't want to."

"I'll go tell him."

When she left, to avoid going back into the chat, I mindlessly clicked my e-mail app.

I'd turned off notifications from it, so this was the first time since I got sick that I'd be seeing new developments.

All the articles on *Campus Daily* about the administration's investigations featured or referred to me—even though there were several student groups under scrutiny.

I raced through the pieces.

It seemed that Murie had worked overtime while I'd been away. Many of the articles quoted her saying seemingly innocuous things like, "Let's wait to hear the results of the investigations" and "I'm glad someone else is running for the position against me because it gives me the opportunity to share the difference, the integrity, I'll bring as treasurer."

And, again, green-sweatshirt guy, Tyler, had glowing pieces about Murie's vision in the *UpBeat*, but, in his favor, at least he hadn't restarted a focus on me and the MSA fundraising money, like the *Campus Daily* had.

I should have stayed in Chicago.

I should have faced everything head-on and made sure to win.

Instead I was lying in someone else's bed, throwing up in their bathroom, while mourning all the ways Adam and I were falling apart.

A new e-mail came in.

Professor Mumford.

Re: Your Statement of Interest in an International Human Rights Externship

I was about to click it open, but my mind conjured Daadi's hand reaching out to feed me again. Her face was kind but earnest. *Sabr, Zayneb. Say a dua. This is important, and you're between two of the holiest places in the deen, so pause to remember and be reliant on Allah.*

I bent my head and whispered a prayer—*please let it be that I've gotten in, that I can help my daadi and all those innocents like her through such an opportunity*—and then opened the e-mail.

Dear Ms. Malik,

Thank you for your interest in participating in our prestigious externship program, the first of its kind in the country. In your Statement of Interest, you indicated The Hague as your "first and only choice" for placement should you get into the international human rights program.

I'm writing today to inform you that student positions at The Hague are limited and quite selective. This year, we managed to place only two students; last year, it was one. While we are working to increase those numbers, please note, the likelihood of securing this achievement is rare.

For that reason, I ask that you consider the current on-going investigations of your tenure as a student club leader and choose a more achievable goal from the list of externships we traditionally connect students to. As the facilitator of the program, I pride myself in matching all students interested in the international human rights stream with their top choice of host organizations, and thus, ask you to withdraw your "first and only choice" and opt for a more realistic and suitable match.

I also ask you to refrain from listing only one position. It limits your possibility of entry into the program itself.

I await your adjusted list.

Sincerely,

Professor Lincoln Mumford

I dropped my phone.

ARTIFACT THIRTY-ONE: ADAM'S EMPTINESS
INTERPRETIVE LABEL: SOMETIMES THERE IS NOTHING TO DISPLAY

Every time I opened my eyes, I remembered Zayneb and my gut twisted.

She didn't want to see me?

I didn't get it. What did I do?

I'd given her time to rest. I respected her. I remembered she was coming on this trip on the heels of a challenging time at school.

And I tried my best to get a new commission so I could "stand on my own two feet," as Zayneb's parents would be saying forever, it seemed.

Even though right now I felt so exhausted that "standing on my own two feet" was something I couldn't even think of doing.

It felt like I couldn't even *physically* stand right now

Please, Allah, don't let me face an MS challenge now, I prayed.

I'd been taking all my medications. I'd been trying not to overdo it.

But now, as though an avalanche of pent-up fatigue had felled me, I was winded.

I pulled the bedcover up over my face in case someone else was also awake in the hotel room.

If they turned this way, they'd see I was bawling. Silently but with

pain, such deep pain that wrung my insides, because I couldn't understand how everything had gone from looking up to *you're a fool, Adam.*

*Something changed between you and Zayneb, and you didn't even
know it.*

She hadn't replied to even just one of my messages—from the
ones I'd sent at Sausun's house, to the ones I'd shot off while lying
here when everyone went to dinner.

> **Zayneb why**
>
> **I need to see you**
>
> **What happened**
>
> **Please?**

. . . and on and on.

I'd even tried to message Sausun at the number Janna had
given me. But Sausun, too, had acted like I no longer existed.

I didn't like her. Sausun.

Thinking that awakened something in me.

Anger began flickering its eyelids open.

Maybe this wasn't Zayneb's doing; maybe it was Sausun's.

With the blanket stretched taut over my face and tucked under
the back of my head, I pulled up my phone and searched "Niqabi
Ninjas."

As soundlessly as I could, I reached onto the night table to
grab my earbuds.

I speed-watched a few videos, noticing how Haytham, the guy
Sausun was married to, only made one appearance the entire time.
One clip showed that Haytham lived in Arkansas, while Sausun
"divides her time between Eastspring, Chicago, Little Rock, and
Mecca and Medina like the boss she is."

*What gives her the right to feel so sure about herself? Why does she
act like she knows everything?*

She didn't know about me. She didn't know I absolutely loved Zayneb.

She didn't know that I would turn into stone if Zayneb didn't like me anymore. That I'd feel moored to one spot, like I couldn't look forward or behind me.

Anger opened its eyes completely.

Then it lumbered up from the floor of the darkness inside me, straightened, and tipped its head back to look all the way up.

Sausun didn't have the right to tell you what to do.

Only Zayneb did.

I let anger take its proper space within me.

Because I've never let it fully unleash.

I'd always sent it away—to avoid the fallout. To be responsible.

It's something I first learned to do when I was young.

Three days after Mom went to the hospital, I woke up to an eerie silence. After searching the whole house and not finding anyone, I kept knocking and knocking on Mom and Dad's door.

But no one answered.

Even though I could hear something sort of moving inside. It was a shaking sound—but not from a thing.

From a person.

Then Hanna started crying and saying "dada" in the pauses in between her bouts of sobbing. She slept in a crib in their room.

Was she the only one inside?

I opened the door, even though I'd always been told to never ever open doors without someone letting you.

The room was dark, but the baby monitor light shone.

Dad wasn't on the bed. It was still made. I knew he'd come back from the hospital late last night—I'd heard him come in.

I stroked Hanna through the bars of her crib to try to soothe her and waited for Dad or Grandpa or Grandma to come up.

They always came when they heard Hanna through the monitor. But no one came.

Should I go heat Hanna's bottle?

I was afraid to pick her up by myself because she was now starting to try things, and I was afraid she'd try to dive out of my arms as soon as I lifted her.

I turned around to go flip the light switch on so that I could see Hanna better, and that's when I saw the shaking in the room.

Dad was curled up on the floor in the corner, crying soundlessly, his shoulders shuddering, the edge of a wicker hamper he was leaning against thrumming, his face buried in his arms.

I stood there for so long while both Hanna and Dad cried, paralyzed by the fear of finding out what I already knew.

That fear nudged awake an anger within: *Dad never let you see Mom.*

I narrowed my eyes, my shoulders beginning to curve in, a million wings beating at my heart: *Stand up! Stand up for yourself! Stand over him!*

My fist unclenched as I heard "dada" again behind me. As I saw Dad take a deep breath, still curled up tight.

I couldn't get mad at Dad now, because then Hanna couldn't be taken care of properly, and she liked Dad the best of us all.

Dad and Hanna.

They were the most important people in my life now.

I slumped down on the floor at the foot of the bed and extinguished that small flare of anger with my tears.

• • •

A new e-mail notification popped with the subject line *URGENT* as I was getting ready to turn off my phone, spent from all the emotions I'd finally allowed to take over.

The message was from my bank.

Telling me to take action immediately as my bank account was in overdraft.

And you walked away from a potential job, Adam.

ARTIFACT THIRTY-TWO: ZAYNEB'S EMPTINESS
INTERPRETIVE LABEL: [BLANK]

I PULLED THE BLANKET RIGHT OVER MY HEAD AND CLOSED MY EYES. I needed something softer than this duvet to cocoon in, but *my* blankets were at home, some at my parents', one packed in my box of things at Mariyah's, and a small one tucked into my sleeping bag rolled up by my rental couch.

And I'd lost Scarfy in the shuffle from Mecca to Medina, having tucked her away under my pillows, and then, because I'd been too sick to pack my own things, she'd been left behind.

I couldn't sleep, but if Sausun came back into the room, I'd fake snore convincingly so she would, hopefully, leave. She told me she was going to be sleeping in her sister's old room, as her sister had permanently left Saudi. Apparently their dad kept the bedroom in pristine shape in case she decided to come back one day.

But sometimes people leave because things don't make sense anymore.

Everything can fall apart without notice.

Like one moment you're feeling secure in the one thing you didn't doubt: your relationship with a person who understands you like no one else does, who lets you be yourself like no one else does, who looks at you like no one else does and has ever done.

In a way that shelters you in the warm wrap of just one glance.

And now he doesn't even see me anymore.

When we got our nikah done, I'd promised Adam that I wanted him to always feel completely loved. That if he didn't feel that at any moment with me, he'd just have to tell me.

It was *that* easy to be clear with me, I'd told him. "Just say, *Z, I don't feel it from you. That you completely love me.*"

He'd smiled at that and said, "That's never going to happen. Me telling you that. I just know it from the way you are all over me, Z, you animal."

We'd laughed, but then every time we lay together, before we drifted off to sleep, I'd whisper, "You feel completely loved, right, Adam?"

I'd even asked that on our night in London before we flew here. My words had been slurred because I'd been drunken with sleep, but I'd held his hand and said it again. "You feevcomfleetheely woved, wight, Assam?"

He'd said yes, and we'd fallen asleep holding hands.

Instead of texting other things, I wish he would just ask me that back right now.

Because I'd tell him, *No, Adam, I don't feel it from you. That you completely love me.*

Tears streaming down my face, I blocked him on my phone.

I read Professor Mumford's e-mail again, this time with a critical eye.

Not at his letter, but a critical eye aimed at *me*.

I couldn't remember why I'd thought I'd even get into The Hague.

If there hadn't been a risk that someone might come into the bedroom at any moment, I would have let out a loud, long maniacal laugh.

Recently, I'd lived as though I could be blessed with the best. Which was so funny.

Who even am I, to think my life would turn out how I wanted it to?

After I met Adam, and learned how to take more charge of my emotions from Auntie Nandy, and to fixate on a goal, I began to believe in possibilities again.

When I shouldn't have.

When too many of my past experiences have taught me that I'm the type of girl who gets shoved aside by society.

A visibly Muslim girl.

A brown girl.

A you-don't-count girl.

But I constantly try to deny this truth. And think if I just hustle harder than everyone around me, I'll be worthy, finally.

But I'm not.

I'd been playing a caricature of a girl on top of the world, with an assertive personality that got her places, who'd landed the cute guy, who was getting ready to walk into her future with him, believing she could avenge the injustice of innocent lives taken for greed because she had a fire in her.

But I was actually a limp puppet lying in a box of discarded toys, spent, suppressing a villainous laugh for trying so damn hard to be lovable.

It was grotesque.

ARTIFACT THIRTY-THREE:
ADAM'S LITTLE MASJID AN-NABAWI SOUVENIR
ON A GLASS STAND
INTERPRETIVE LABEL: ARRIVE AT THE AWAKENING READY TO SEE

THE ONLY THING TO DO WHEN YOU'RE LYING IN PAIN IN THE CITY OF Light is to get up and move toward the light.

I remembered during Sa'i, I'd pledged to keep moving.

Even if it was in worry. Pacing.

At least *do something*—like Hajar.

I decided to join the group in their itinerary for the day.

With our hotel being just a block away from Masjid an-Nabawi, Shaykh Murtaza, Isa, Sahaan, and I walked to Fajr prayers together at the Prophet's masjid.

The adhan filled the massive grounds, and again, like in Mecca, we joined a flow of people headed toward the masjid. In between the call to prayer reverberating and the quiet hum of those of us repeating the words to the adhan, there was also the sound of birds flitting around the minarets.

The beauty of Medina was instantly apparent as we approached the masjid. There was an ambiance here that differed vastly from Mecca.

Looking around, I realized one of the major reasons why.

There were no behemoth buildings overshadowing the masjid.

The horizon was just purely masjid and rising minarets, etched against the still-dark sky.

We made it inside the building before Fajr started, and after finishing our sunnah prayers, I sat and let my gaze trace the rows upon rows of pillars as far as I could see, pillars that held arches between them, striped dark gray and the same sandy-beige color that filled the patterned, niched ceiling. Huge but sparse circular chandeliers hung above our heads, spaced apart evenly.

I took it all in from the floor to the ceiling.

It was a study in beige, gray, gold, brown, and white, seemingly repeated infinitely in every direction I turned—repeated in spectacular, breathtaking harmony, such that I'd never seen anywhere else.

I was surrounded by subdued, serene colors.

Welcomed by a subdued, serene aura.

I lowered my head, overcome with emotion.

Because I remembered the biggest reason I was Muslim.

And why I chose to become one so close to Mom's death.

And why I needed to remember it now.

For two years after Mom passed away—after I never got to see her when she went to the hospital, after I never got to look at her again—I got caught in a prison in my head.

The prison doors would only open when I remembered details of Mom. Her smile, her frown, the way she nodded very slightly when she noticed something wrong I did, as though she was storing it away in her brain to be addressed at a better time, when it was just me and her.

The way she chewed quickly and then slowly, like, mid-chew,

she'd remembered it was a better way to eat. The way she spread her food out on her plate so that nothing was heaped too high. The way she wore her shoulder-length brown wavy hair down except when she worked on something with laser focus. Then it was all swept up with a giant claw clip.

When a visual of her arrived in my head with full-blown, HD accuracy, I'd be filled with elation, like I'd successfully caught her gossamer self.

But very quickly, I'd retreat into the prison when I couldn't examine her more, when it became evident I'd had a fleeting memory, that there was nothing to keep her anchored in my heart's eye.

I'd always been quiet, but in the years after Mom died, I became even more so. I knew Dad was worried, leading him to make frequent attempts to check in with me.

But he was also busy with school, and trying to single-parent two kids the best he could, which involved arbitrary rules like if there was a weird weather occurrence, I could game all day. But if not, then it was an hour only, like Mom's rule.

Soon I convinced him weird weather was happening often. And I disappeared more and more into gaming.

I'd succumbed to the comforting lure of a world where reality didn't matter.

That's when Dad suddenly woke up and broke me out of my virtual world *and* the prison in my head. He went back to the firmness he'd abandoned when he became the sole parent.

He forced me to pay attention to the universe. We went to museums, parks, wadis, dunes, architectural wonders, all in Qatar.

Slowly, by looking once again at the world around me, I came to understand the reason for existence at a basic level.

That there was so much to notice if you looked with quiet eyes.

As I learned more about the things I'd become interested in, like stars, like rocks, like trees, I started seeing the connection between the things I observed, the things we think they are, and what they *actually* were. And, most importantly, the truths they carry for us humans.

Our sight, our perception, the reality, and the enduring essence behind it all.

Like bees. Like how Mom saw them at first, as something to be feared, but how they're actually living beings working together to produce honey, keeping the world green for all of us. Reminding us of working for the good of all.

Like stars. How we see them as twinkling lights, but how they're balls of gas that look like they're fixed in the sky, helping us navigate for thousands of years. Thus reminding us we are connected through space, time, and that which is beyond us.

Later, Dad had introduced Qur'anic verses to me, and it felt like my mind blew open, allowing me to emerge from the cage I'd constructed, to begin to understand there was a blueprint holding everything together, there was a reason for us, for Mom to be here and then gone.

"[Bees] take your habitations in the mountains and in the trees and in what they [humans] erect. . . ." There emerges from their bellies a drink, varying in colors, in which there is healing for people. Indeed in that is a sign for a people who give thought.

And it is He who has set up the stars so that you might be guided by them when the land and seas are dark. . . .

At the time I needed it, these words were comforting to me. To know that there was something more to it all and I just had to pay attention.

Knowing that I could do something to make sense of my world was the deepest relief.

And I was finally able to hold and carry Mom in the best place of all—in my heart—because I finally understood her essence.

Mom. The most important person at the beginning of my life on earth, who, before she left this world, pointed out a way for me to be, pointing at the stars, at the bees, at the details.

The essence of Mom was her ability to live in profound awe at the simple beauty of life.

Before she left me, she'd shown me how to carry on. *Adam, you'll always be all right if you see and cherish what is immediately around you.*

That's why, shortly after her death, I'd begun to collect the marvels I saw, noting them down in notebooks. That's why I kept my circle of love small—my family and long-time friends—people I could actually pay real attention to.

But, during this Umrah trip, I'd fixated on and cherished what wasn't here.

I'd ignored what was right in front of me, the details of me-and-Zayneb, because my fear of being jobless conjured a seemingly better but false reality.

I'd also ignored the fact that Dad had always been there for me and that I had the privilege of asking him to lend me money until I had things figured out.

I could stand on my own two feet to ask him for help.

Because I knew I'd try my best to repay him and that I'd always be ready to give him whatever help he needed back too.

• • •

After Asr, after we'd visited the Prophet's grave, its location marked by the one distinct bright green dome of Masjid an-Nabawi, I made a decision.

I made the decision after lots of duas for guidance.

I was going to go back to Sausun's house tomorrow. To see and talk to Zayneb.

Shaykh Murtaza had told me before we left the hotel for Asr that Sausun had called him and given him the update that Zayneb was almost 100 percent recovered.

But Zayneb still hadn't replied to me.

I didn't lie to Shaykh Murtaza, I didn't say Zayneb had told me to come, but I asked him to arrange the hired car he'd promised early in the morning to take me back to pick her up.

I also needed to get away from the group for a bit.

Due to being organized and separated by our room groupings to fit into the time slots for visiting the Prophet's grave, and due to segregated prayer spaces, I hadn't seen Sarina all day, and I was glad for that.

I'd heard she'd been upset that I'd canceled the interview, and while I wasn't too bothered, it was a relief to not have to be in the vicinity of the vibes she'd be giving off.

And I was dumbfounded by something else.

Something I found in the Umrah chat group.

Sahaan had mentioned that the photo adds in the chat had significantly dropped since we left Mecca, and I realized I hadn't even checked the chat to see if Zayneb had added anything—either before or, what I really hoped for, since we'd separated.

My hope wasn't fulfilled, but I also discovered that there wasn't a single photo with Zayneb in it.

And that there were so many—too many—of me and Sarina.

Had Zayneb seen these? I clicked on some of the more glaring examples of where it looked like someone—well, Sarina—had added pics focusing on only us and checked their viewership info.

All of them showed that Zayneb had clicked on them.

So had Dad—who I'd asked to be added to the chat group so he could see Umrah-progress updates on his own and wouldn't worry about me.

Was that why Dad had asked me if I was spending time with Zayneb?

Was that why Zayneb had called Sarina a homewrecker?

I didn't even process that word fully when she'd said it, thinking she'd been too upset to be lucid. Like when she went on about snowflakes versus sand.

I can't believe myself.

I glanced up from my phone at the slow opening of the huge umbrellas over the plaza in front of the masjid, a vast marbled space teeming with people walking around, sitting on the ground in clusters talking, or moving singly or in unison while praying.

Or me, standing there with eyes wide open.

I suddenly understood why Zayneb was so upset.

The realization didn't strike me gracefully, like the umbrellas unfolding above me, but hit me hard.

I'd been so busy fixated on securing a future, that I hadn't seen what I already had in my hands.

I should have paid attention all along to the truth of Zayneb exhausted, sick, and alone, observing me all caught up with someone else—someone I'd seriously fallen for before.

I texted Zayneb again. I didn't care that she wasn't replying to anything. I needed her to know that she was more important than anyone I'd ever met before or I'd ever meet again.

I sent the huge message composed of a strange mix of love poetry and confession and sappy thoughts and sexting and immediately sighed with relief.

I'd let fear drive me to believe my hands were empty, but they'd been full of love.

Tomorrow, insha'Allah, I was going to go get her and bring her back to Medina to spend the final days of our break together.

ARTIFACT THIRTY-FOUR: ZAYNEB'S
BLACK ABAYA
INTERPRETIVE LABEL: CLOAKING IS POWERFUL

SOME CATS SLEEP WITH THEIR FACES PRESSED DOWN. SOME CATS like to be curled up with a friend, their limbs around each other. And other cats lie conked out on their backs.

I observed all this in the "cat therapy room" Sausun prescribed for me. It was essentially one of the two closets in her bedroom. This one didn't contain clothes and instead had a cat flap hatch on one of its double doors.

The closet was carpeted with a very faded Persian rug and housed a weird contraption Sausun and her brothers had made when they were little, comprised of pieces of carpet glued onto various crates, boxes, and platforms, all screwed in haphazard fashion on top of an old bench with the words "Cat Palace" written in black Sharpie. There were four cats living in the Cat Palace currently, and they were all sleeping.

Freshly showered and in one of my three sundresses I'd brought on Umrah, a pale green one, with one of Sausun's abayas, black, always black, unbuttoned on top like the thinnest coat, I crossed my legs and watched the sleeping cats for a while and decided this was a good time to call my own Bertha Fatima.

Today was a new day, and after sleeping all through my first night here and then most of today, Wednesday, I wanted to forget about everything in my life right now except the good things.

And Bertha Fatima was one of the few remaining good ones.

Sadia was another good one, but, it being four p.m. in Indiana, she was most probably already at my parents for Thanksgiving eve, so there was a high risk they'd overhear the stress in my voice. My brother Mansoor and his wife Hodan were leaving town to spend their Thanksgiving break at Hodan's parents and then were coming over to my parents on the weekend.

So Bertha Fatima was my only family who'd be available.

I lifted the black shayla I had around my neck and wound my head with it before FaceTiming Layth.

He picked up on my third try. "Sorry, I'm in the middle of something I don't usually do. And thus didn't want to wreck it." His jaw was half-covered in shaving cream. "*It* being my face."

"You have a date or something?"

"Yup. Hey, are you at Umrah or a cat shelter?" He peered into his phone, at me and my surroundings. "The only reason I picked up your call was because I thought I'd see the Kaaba behind you or something."

"I finished Umrah."

"How was it?"

Mine wasn't good. "It was great. Just at Sausun's now, stopped on the way to Medina. Where's my baby?"

"Pooping. For some reason, she insists on using the bathroom when I'm in the bathroom."

"As soon as she's done, let me see her." I looked at the dark shelving behind the chair he'd just taken a seat in. "We saw Janna."

"I know." He wiped his face with the towel around his neck. The swiping revealed a combination beard: partially scruffy and partially trim, barely there. Even without being completely cleaned up, he was a Zayn Malik doppelgänger, but with longer hair. Janna had told me once she hated One Direction when she was a kid, when everyone else was wild about them. And now here she was, falling for a Zayn clone. "Janna's why I'm fixing my face right now. Dania and Lamya think I should join them when they go see Janna's mom and their dad tomorrow. The polite thing to do and all that."

Janna's mom had married Layth's maternal uncle, the father of Dania and Lamya, good friends of mine, which must be awkward all around. "I endorse. Polite things win over old folks. Note this: Janna's mom loves basbousa. Take some over."

"I was going to try to make kanafeh."

"Make it? What are you, some kind of chef?"

"Have you ever lived in a remote sanctuary in Ecuador? Cooking is entertainment."

"And where are you doing this thing?"

"Right here." He got off his chair and walked to point out an induction hot plate resting on a wooden cart, under which was tucked a mini fridge. A single saucepan sat on top of the toaster oven behind the hot plate. A bunch of packaged ingredients—most likely for kanafeh—cluttered the top of the cart, the toaster oven, and even the saucepan.

"You have a kitchen?" I'd never actually seen his place before because he'd come to pick up Bertha Fatima from me on campus.

"Yes, I live in luxury."

"Seriously, don't be rude. It's mini, but it's a real-life kitchen, Layth."

"I'm not kidding. This is amazing." He spun his phone around the room slowly to give me a tour. And then walked to the bathroom, at which point he stopped and knocked on the open door. "Hey, Berths, are you done? May I enter?"

"Ber*tha Fatima*," I emphasized. "She needs to know and respect both her heritages at all times."

He stepped into the bathroom and showed me the lay of the land inside. Basic but clean.

With a shower. Lucky Layth.

Bertha Fatima meowed, and Layth lowered the phone.

"Bertha Fatima baby! It's Mama!" I squealed, hoping Sausun wasn't outside the closet door, in her room, hearing me shriek at one a.m. She'd think I had succumbed to illness again.

Bertha Fatima didn't look at me and instead looked beyond the phone and meowed again.

"Wait." Layth lifted the phone back up and left the bathroom to go to another set of shelves, to get a phone stand. *More shelving?* This bookcase surrounded the door to the room. "She wants me to clean her litter, so I'll just prop the phone up for you to talk to her."

"Just how many bookshelves are there in your place?"

"This house is literally like the house in *Knives Out*. This room I'm in is like the murdered guy's office, except there's not as many books here. And look," he said, moving to the window. He turned the phone around and tilted it, and now I was looking down on a leafy street, but it was from high up. "This is the only room they rent out on this floor."

After I'd seen my fill of the view outside, he walked back to the bathroom and set up the phone stand in front of Bertha Fatima so I could see her while he tended to the litter box.

I cooed and baby-talked to her and tried to show her the sleeping cats, but she didn't pay attention. Instead, she stood alert to supervise the way Layth cleaned up her poop.

Maybe she missed Adam more than she missed me.

The other good ones I called were Kavi and Ayaan, but I made sure to stick with Umrah updates and general pleasantries. We agreed on a firm date to meet during winter break. Our friend Noemi was going to join us too.

After I hung up with them, I replied to messages from Mila and Fatima checking in on me. I also followed them on their socials.

I knew Mila was the real deal, my squad, when I saw her Twitter feed. Her most recent tweet was the resharing of a graphic that said, *Women deserve to walk the streets knowing they will make it home.*

Yes. I immediately liked it and retweeted it.

I decided to add Ava to my good-ones list. She'd sent me a few messages, hoping my trip was going great, and I hadn't had a chance to reply to them. It was five p.m. in Chicago during break week, so I knew I'd get a hold of her if I called now.

She picked up immediately, lying in bed, hair center parted and woven into two high French braids. She actually yelped with excitement. "Zayneb! Guess what! I have good news for you." She smothered her enthusiasm to add, "Well, sort of. But first, you tell me about Mecca! I've been looking at pictures online, and it's stunning. Can't imagine how amazing the real thing must be."

"It's so good. So full of light, the aura." I shifted the conversation. "What's going on with you?"

"I talked to my parents, and they think I should stay home this year. And commute. So if you still want a place?" she said, smiling.

"Just remember that Lars continues to come by with Sasha. But there's a lock on my door."

I couldn't believe it.

I hadn't even prayed hard for my stuff going on at school. And just like that, Ava was giving me her room.

"I'm not scared of Lars." *And I'm not scared of Murie, either.* She'd be livid when she found out I'd be around. "And anyway, I'm planning on telling Sasha what he's up to."

"I've been wondering why I'm so chicken to. Maybe it's because Murie and I didn't like her boyfriend before Lars either? And Sasha might think we're just piling on her?"

"Well, she needs to know. It's a big to-do on my list." I looked at Ava carefully. "Thanks so much, Ava. But are you sure?"

"Yes, a million times. You can even use my furniture. Actually, it would help me if you did. Then I wouldn't have to deal with it until the end of the year."

All that dark moody goodness being mine made my eyes light up. Ava must have seen, because she laughed.

"Oh my gosh, I love the vibes in your room. Thanks again." I couldn't stop a smile from breaking out and taking over my face. Even if I didn't get The Hague, even if I didn't get into the international human rights stream, I had a bed to sleep in for the rest of the year. "As soon as I get back, we'll write something up to sign, and I'll take over your payments. I can't believe it."

"I told my parents how you had to put up with the couch. That was one of the reasons they suggested I offer it." She tugged the end of one of her braids and twisted it. "Two birds with one stone. You get a room. I get away from Lars."

I nodded gratefully and we chitchatted about other things, but something about her "getting away from Lars" bothered me.

It didn't make sense. For her to drop her room so quickly.

But my inner voice slammed me immediately. *Stop analyzing and just accept your bonanza! As if you don't have enough to stress about as it is. When you fly back, besides studying nonstop for exams, you have to reconfigure your externship. Figure out if you even want to do it anymore.*

And you have to figure out the something else that's cropped up that you don't want to think about: you and Adam falling into an abyss.

Maybe it was time to finally do what Mom and Dad have always advised me: *Put less on your plate.*

Live a balanced life. Whatever that means.

No, it means something good.

It means you only do enough.

And don't bother with all the other things not meant for you.

I closed my eyes. Could I? Just say no to things?

Take everything off my plate except school?

I imagined flying back home. And meeting Ava at Houston, We Have a Problem again. Signing an agreement to take over her lease. Then moving my things—currently in a corner of Mariyah's room in my old apartment, bless her soul—into Ava's cute room. Setting up my stuff to study at her desk.

And then only studying. Nothing else. Not trying for the externship or anything extra.

I took a long breath in, but it was shaky all the way down.

I decided to sleep off my nerves. Tomorrow I'd go to Medina, insha'Allah.

And then, on Friday, I'd fly back home.

The next morning I emerged from the cat therapy room after another session and found Sausun ironing an abaya. She looked up and gave me a brief smile. "How are you feeling?"

"Better."

"Better physically or mentally? Or both?"

"I think both. I'm ravenous. That must mean I'm better, right?" I sat at the side of her bed and grabbed one of the applesauce cups still on the night table from my steady diet yesterday of BRAT: bananas, rice, applesauce, and toast. And Nanni's ginger honey. I peeled the top of the cup and picked up the ginger-honey spoon to shovel the applesauce into my mouth.

"As soon as I'm done with this, let's go to breakfast. Nanni always makes the best eggs and paratha when we have guests."

Ah man, again, her nanni was just like Daadi.

Did they all go to desi grandma school or something? To turn out the same?

But it wasn't only desi—yesterday, Ava had just mentioned how her bubbe had been sending freshly cooked delicious food for her on the weekends to take back to school on Mondays because "she lived on her own" and how her parents were sharing in the eating of it, while discussing when to tell Bubbe the truth that Ava was actually now spending more than the weekends at home with them. "My parents are enjoying receiving *my* food," she'd said, laughing.

And Adam's grandmas on both his Chinese and Finnish sides were similar; the latter wasn't a cook but would always buy us a little something sweet and tuck it into our pockets as we were leaving at the end of visiting her.

I could actually feel my face muscles scrunching when he came into my head, on top of remembering Daadi.

I will not allow myself to cry.

I started to cry. Big ugly sobs.

· · ·

Sausun let me bawl while she completed her ironing. Then we went downstairs and ate as Nanni hovered by the table watching us with satisfaction. Apparently she was going to leave for South Africa on the weekend, to go back to Sausun's nanna, and had only come to Saudi because Sausun was here visiting.

"Nanni wants to do another Umrah before she leaves," Sausun said. "She always does two. One when she first gets here and one before she leaves."

"Is your dad going to take her?"

"No, I'm taking her." She ripped off a piece of paratha and scooped up some of the eggs loaded with onion, tomato, cilantro, and peppers. "That's why I was prepping my clothes. I'm going to do Umrah too."

I nodded and drank super-strong chai to wash down the meal—the second of only two full meals I'd eaten since I got to Saudi. I decided to take a second helping.

"Why'd you come on this Umrah trip?" Sausun asked me. "Janna told me a month ago you and Adam were going to be in England for a week and how you guys had made a dinner catch-up date with her."

I forked a piece of mango from a bowl of cut-up fruit and put it on my plate. "That was the original plan. Then Adam brought up Umrah."

"Why'd you say yes?"

"Because it's Umrah?" I didn't tell her my initial feelings about the trip. Which, I now realized in hindsight, I should've paid more attention to. My gut had been smart enough to know that doing an exhausting Umrah was a recipe for disaster. "And it was our nikah gift from Adam's dad."

"Did he want to go? Adam?"

"Of course. He was really excited. He felt good physically, so it made sense to go when his MS is stable. And I wanted to do Umrah when Adam felt good." I closed my eyes, remembering his idea to split up. Even though I was having a miserable trip, being on completely separate trips would have been more miserable, truly. At least now I'd learned things about him. I opened my eyes and looked at Sausun. "So that's why I said yes."

She tilted her head, and her bangs all neatly fell to one side. "So you did Umrah for Adam."

"No. What do you mean? I did Umrah for me." I frowned at her. I didn't know her well, but I knew she was self-assured, which had always come across previously as confident and badass. But I resented it now. "Why would I do a spiritual thing for someone else?"

"Right?" She speared a piece of papaya, dropped it on her plate, and then did the same with pieces of pineapple, mango, and guava. It came across as very stabbing-like. "That's what I always say."

She looked at me triumphantly.

I considered her. She was obviously being sarcastic.

I didn't need her sudden weird vibes now. "I feel a lot better. Thanks so much for your healing powers," I said with sincerity. I was grateful for her hospitality and kindness. I just needed to get a move on. "I'm ready to go to Medina whenever it's good for you. Or I can also arrange a taxi or Uber on my own."

"I'm free. I was going to offer you a ride on the back of my motorcycle if you are okay with that."

"You have a bike?" I sat up. "I ride."

"You're kidding me."

"No, really."

"Okay that means we can take turns sitting behind." She grinned huge. "You can use your American license here."

"I also have an international license. I got it because of traveling so much to be with Adam." My voice faltered when I said his name. I shoved the mango piece in my mouth to have something to chew and swallow to dislodge the lump of pain in my throat.

Memories of riding in California on my brother Mansoor's bike, with Adam's friend Connor beside me on his bike, Adam seated behind him, came to me. We'd done the trip after we'd gotten engaged.

Mansoor had been with us, me and him sharing a hotel room, and each night, he'd let Adam come over to our room so we could all watch a movie together, but it had always ended up as Adam and me talking about the future with Mansoor interjecting his cynical takes on things.

I stopped chewing.

I remembered something.

About last year, in California.

ARTIFACT THIRTY-FIVE: ADAM'S ANT-MAN ACTION FIGURE
INTERPRETIVE LABEL: *"INDUSTRIOUS" LOOKS DIFFERENT DEPENDING ON ONE'S PURPOSE*

AFTER ASR, AS HE AND I WALKED BACK TO THE HOTEL FROM THE masjid, Shaykh Murtaza asked me how I felt.

I told him the truth: *exhausted*.

When we got to our room, Shaykh Murtaza indicated I should go in but that he had to make a phone call in the hall.

He came back in two minutes later and said that Dad was expecting a FaceTime from me. "Yes, I called your dad."

I didn't ask him why, but I was unnerved about being treated like a kid on a field trip whose parents needed to be called.

I shouldn't be so harsh—maybe Shaykh Murtaza felt the duty to do so because he'd promised Dad that he'd take care of my health.

I'd meant I was *emotionally* exhausted, but maybe he'd seen something else on my face.

Shaykh Murtaza told me Dad had asked if he could talk to Zayneb as well, and Shaykh Murtaza hadn't said anything about her, that he was going to leave that part to me.

Before calling Dad, I debated internally on what and how much to share.

I would have to tell him the truth. Besides the fact that Dad would see right through me, Shaykh Murtaza was also sitting on his bed looking at his phone, obviously able to hear everything I said.

While pacing from the room door to my bed, I FaceTime audio-called Dad.

After I caught him up on Medina so far, and my health, he asked about Zayneb. Why he'd never heard or seen us together. How he was in the chat group and he'd wondered why she wasn't even in there . . . no messages, no photos.

Aha, so I was right. He *had* begun worrying about us due to evidence from the chat group.

That was my cue to reveal all.

I turned away from Shaykh Murtaza and sat on the edge of my bed. When I started talking about Zayneb becoming sick and then seemingly refusing to see me at Sausun's, my voice shook, and Shaykh Murtaza got up from behind me and nodded before he left the room. He mouthed, *Keep going. I'll be in the hall.*

As soon as he left, I broke down.

I felt like a little kid, sobbing, telling Dad things I'd never talked to him about, even when I *had* been a little kid.

How I felt we were disintegrating, Zayneb and I.

Again, that assertive voice that always reminded me to be mature and pragmatic popped up: *Hey, why are you making his life hard with your problems? When you've held it together for so long?*

Dad and Hanna. They're the most important people in your life, along with Zayneb.

You're the easy child, remember? What if he can't handle it all?

But Dad just kept encouraging me to cry and talk, crying with me when it was too much for him to bear too.

It was a good thing that Isa and Sahaan were out shopping with the rest of the group, because the gates holding everything in for so long had opened, and it all gushed out like from a broken pipe.

I was the opposite of Mom, though, in sharing my vulnerabilities.

There was no wisdom, no trying to make sense of it all.

It was just me telling him the truth. About not having a future, about wanting to live with Zayneb but not being brave enough to tell her, in case she got disappointed by my inability to find work.

About feeling like if she found out the truth about me, she'd get quiet with the realization of what she'd actually walked into when she'd agreed to a relationship with me.

Like how she'd acted in California.

Last year, in July, in a hotel in California, Mansoor lay on his bed, a bag of chips on his chest.

Zayneb sat cross-legged on her bed.

A visitor to their room, I sat on the desk chair that had been spun away from the desk so I could see the TV screen too.

We were watching something Mansoor chose, and I don't even remember what it was, just that it brought up a bunch of "would you rather" questions.

"Would you rather lose your memory or lose your ability to work?" Mansoor asked.

"Easy, lose my memory," Zayneb said. "I'd never be happy if I couldn't work."

"Yeah, me too. Imagine no income but rich in memories," Mansoor said, combing his beard with his fingers to get chip crumbs out. "Your turn, Adam."

I opened my mouth, about to say *lose my memory*, but then imagined not remembering Mom. "Lose my ability to work."

"Really?" Zayneb tilted her head back. "But you're an *ant*. Always busy building stuff."

"Huh?" Mansoor scrunched his face, confused.

"Ignore. It's this thing Adam and I have. He's an ant and I'm a beetle. Beetles are hard but soft inside and—"

"You're soft inside? Since when?" Mansoor raised his eyebrows.

Zayneb threw a pillow at him, the third she'd thrown since we started the movie. "And Adam is industrious like an ant."

"Ooh, a carpenter ant. Nice." Mansoor nodded at me.

"Carpenter ants damage wood, actually," I said, laughing.

"He's more like an Ant-Man sort of ant," Zayneb offered.

"But let's go back to not working. That's not going to fly too well with Mom and Dad," Mansoor said. I couldn't tell if he was joking, the way he was looking at me, shaking his head slightly.

"Relax, it's a game," I said.

"But I'm being serious. They're all about holding down a job. Drilled it into us kids from the moment we were born."

"Who said no to that? I just said I'd rather keep my memory. And, again, it's a game."

"I understand the memories part. Why you'd choose to keep that. But yeah, jobs are super important too," Zayneb said, before lowering her head to stare at the bedcover she was sitting on, like she was thinking deeply about something.

About me not being able to work?

I was irritated that Mansoor was still shaking his head as though it was serious. "I'm all for working. While I can. And will do whatever job I get." I looked at Mansoor. "So pass that on to your parents? That I'm not planning to live off Zayneb?"

Mansoor switched his tune as though he had just woken up to the fact that I wasn't amused, like he was offended by my tone.

"Hey, I thought we were just playing a game. Why suddenly so serious, dude?"

I shrugged, wondering why exactly I felt so wounded. As soon as Zayneb's parents and jobs were brought up, I immediately got my sword and shield ready.

"Okay, can you drop it, Mansoor?" Zayneb said, looking at me, even though she was talking to Mansoor. "Would you rather lie in a bed filled with spiders for one night or eat a single centipede?"

The questions petered out soon after, and the game ended in a slow descent into silence.

Everyone stayed quiet as we watched the rest of the movie, but the message was loud in my head.

And the seed of worry about securing steady income was planted.

I was already all about that—independence even after an MS diagnosis—but now, on top of proving it to myself, I had to prove it to Zayneb and her whole family.

Dad asked two things of me: for me to rest and recuperate, and to pass the phone to Shaykh Murtaza so he could talk to him. In the hall.

I decided to go to sleep early again—this time not from sadness but to get enough rest so that I could go bring Zayneb to Medina tomorrow.

Previously, Shaykh Murtaza had asked if Suhaib and his father, Khaled, could accompany me, as they'd wanted to get more footage of the area for Suhaib's Umrah TikTok chronicles.

Of course I'd said yes, but I was also wondering what kind of a scene Suhaib would capture with Zayneb.

And with me confronting Sausun.

AFTER BREAKFAST, I WENT OUT INTO SAUSUN'S BACKYARD AND eschewed the deck chairs to sit on the eerily trim lawn, so perfect it resembled Astroturf. Sausun had gone with Nanni to the shops to get some things for Nanni's trip back to South Africa, and I'd decided to stay to get rested before we left for Medina.

Now that I had recovered from food poisoning and been stuffed with hearty meals, blanketed with sleep, and was feeling healthy again, I considered everything that had happened between me and Adam in such a short time—with an even shorter time left to decide what to do about it.

While the rest of the Umrah group stayed on for one more day, I'd be flying home from Medina tomorrow as I had the farthest to go.

Adam was leaving for Doha on Saturday. Everyone else in the group would be flying to London.

In my head, when I'd made the decision to come, I'd imagined Adam and I would be spending the last few days in Medina, just us.

Ayaan had pumped my head full of the peaceful noor of the city, and that's how I'd wanted to end this break: me and Adam surrounded by that light.

When I got back home to Chicago, I had to hit the ground running. Get settled in Ava's room, bury myself in books for exams . . . and decide what I wanted to do about the externship.

There would be no bandwidth left to untangle this thing happening with Adam.

It took so much time, and we didn't have any, in each other's physical presence.

I couldn't do it over the phone.

Either I needed to wait until Adam came over for winter break, if he did come over for winter break now, or I . . .

I got up.

On the low table between the deck chairs was a shallow glass bowl full of sand, with a rake in it. It had a fake little bonsai in the corner surrounded by a few large pebbles.

I sat on the floor beside the table and raked the sand in the bowl, trying not to think of Sarina's hand clutching her precious sand for Adam's project.

Before today, I'd been bothered that it was just another example of how she'd been so fixated on Adam throughout this trip. And then I'd evolved to wondering why Adam had been so fixated on her as well.

But now I thought I knew why.

When I remembered his face crumpling and falling in the hotel room in California, when Mansoor brought up working, I could see how things must have unfolded in Adam's head: *Here's Sarina promising me a job. I'd better do everything I can to make sure she's happy with me. So she'll get me the job.*

It became all about the job for him.

I picked up some of the sand and dribbled it through my fingers.

And what had it become all about for *me*?

Everything the last few days?

About Adam.

It had become all about Adam for me.

I secured the shayla Sausun had lent me tight around my head and walked to the end of the lawn. There was a tall, solid-concrete wall at the border of the yard, the same one that went around the entire villa.

But there was a door in the wall, and I knew from Sausun that the path outside it eventually led to the water, to the Red Sea.

I unlatched the gate and stepped out.

I was met by the opposite of the artificial perfection behind me.

Here the sand was polluted-looking, with debris—human-made, like plastics and paper, and other garbage—and pockets of wetness and rocks and other beach detritus.

I walked through it until I got to the water. It was still early and a school day, so I was the only one here.

I sat down right on the beach, unmindful of my abaya getting covered in wet sand, and looked across the water. This was the sea that some of the very first Meccan Muslims had crossed to escape persecution, to seek refuge in Africa, at the benevolent hands of the Christian king of Abyssinia.

The Meccan persecutors, the Quraysh, had sent people across the sea too, articulate leaders who tried to sway the king with words and precious gifts to return the "foolish youths" running away from their "customs" and "families."

When the king asked the refugees their side of the story, I've never forgotten learning of the way their leader, Ja'far ibn Abi Talib, responded.

The way he set up their reason for turning their entire lives around, causing upheaval to affect almost every single household in Mecca—a revolution, the fastest and longest-lasting the world has ever seen.

O King, we were an ignorant people. . . . We committed all types of disgraceful acts and did not heed our obligations to neighbors and relatives. The strong among us devoured the weak through power. . . .

And then he went on to describe how the Prophet had taught the opposite of this order. How all those who'd wanted a new status quo based on justice, all those who had joined the Prophet's movement, the majority of whom were the most oppressed in Mecca, had been subjected to torture, economic boycott, starvation, murder.

Upon hearing this, the Christian king had been moved and immediately vowed to protect the refugees and provide them with peace and security for however long they wanted to stay in Abyssinia.

I stared at the horizon above the water, tears filling my eyes as I remembered I was on the same land that so many of my seminal stories came from, how it was true, like Adam had once said to me before, that this piece of earth I was sitting on had witnessed such rich histories.

Like the Hijrah from Mecca to Medina Adam had captured through his map and the first Hijrah those early Muslims had undertaken from these shores, all journeys to peace and safety and freedom.

Which was what I wished for everyone.

As I wiped my tears away with the ends of Sausun's shayla, another set of teary eyes invaded my thoughts.

Ava's face under her bucket hat as she sat on the front stoop beside me last week.

I stood up. Because I remembered something the most important human to me—the Prophet himself—had said so long ago. He said he would continue to struggle with his mission until a woman could travel on her own from Syria to Mecca without a single fear for her safety.

Like Mila's tweet: *Women deserve to walk the streets knowing they will make it home.*

Ava deserved to walk around and live in the safety of her *own* home.

I needed to call the green-sweartshirted *UpBeat* reporter, Tyler, immediately.

I was done running away from him.

Because, writing all about Murie, he was focusing on the wrong things.

There was other breaking news he needed to cover.

Do justly now.

When Sausun returned an hour later, I'd finished speaking to Tyler and had my things packed in my backpack.

It was time for the *walk humbly* part.

I asked Sausun if she could take me to Mecca instead of Medina.

PART FOUR

And it is He who has set up the stars so that you might be guided by them when the land and seas are dark.

—Surah 6:97

ARTIFACT THIRTY-SEVEN:
ADAM'S BOTTLE WITH SAND FROM THE RED SEA
INTERPRETIVE LABEL:
SITTING BY THE WATER IS SOUL EXPANDING

SUHAIB, KHALED, AND I LEFT TWO HOURS AFTER FAJR AND GOT TO Sausun's late in the morning.

It was only after we'd been deposited in front of the closed gates to the villa's courtyard that I remembered no one knew we were coming.

Shaykh Murtaza had assumed the pickup had all been arranged between me and Zayneb.

The taxi left while we were still pressing the buzzer in a console set into the huge concrete wall skirting the property. There was a quiet and still air around the entire place, and I tried not to look at Khaled's face after he buzzed long and hard for the fifth time, in case we ended up being shut out.

With a rumble, the gate mechanism began working, and I let out a breath.

As we went up the shallow steps, Abdullah ibn Abdur-Rahman opened his door wide to us again.

"Ah, assalamu alaikum, you are back." He waved us in. "Yalla."

We entered the sofa-covered sitting room once more, and, after some catch-up talk, Khaled asked for permission for Suhaib to film. Suhaib had been recording parts of our trip from Medina with his phone sticking out the window to capture the terrain, and now, when Sausun's dad assented to the request to film the sitting room and the outside of the house, he broke out in a big smile, his braces flashing.

While Suhaib and his dad busied themselves with their work immediately, not even waiting for the tea Abdullah said was coming, I leaned forward in the sofa beside the one Abdullah was seated in and asked to see Zayneb.

"Zayneb?"

"Yes, she was staying here with Sausun." I hoped the expression of confusion on his face didn't mean anything ominous. "Remember she was sick? On Tuesday, when we were here for lunch?"

"Yes, I know Zayneb." His eyebrows were still curled like sideway question marks. "But she is not here anymore."

"She left?" I stood up. "She went to Medina already." I uttered this as more of a statement to myself.

"I don't know where she went."

"What do you mean, Uncle?" I let my voice fill with the irk I felt rising in me. Why was he being so relaxed about it?

And why was I getting so worked up?

"She didn't leave on her own, right?" I sat back down, worry driving me to approach this with an uncharacteristic action I felt like taking: rebuking him verbally. *How can you* not *know where Zayneb went?*

But I returned to myself. "Did Sausun go with her?"

"I don't know. I wasn't in the house when they left. But I know that Sausun and her grandmother are not here either," Abdullah said. "They must have told someone in the house where they were going. I can go inside the house and find out. But, son, why are you so worried? There's no need."

I stopped moving and stared straight ahead, again resisting the urge to succumb to atypical emotions erupting inside, urging me to talk back to him. *Hey, can you just stop policing my feelings and find out where Z is?*

I'd gotten prepared for a fight with Sausun, and it seemed like confrontation was all my mind was offering now.

Meanwhile, it was fear and worry underlying it all.

I was worried because Zayneb makes quick decisions. And sticks by them.

Leading to the fear: *What if she decided she's done with you, Adam?*

"I'll go get the tea and find out for you." He got up and patted me on the shoulder. "Put your trust in Allah."

I nodded and leaned into the sofa and tipped my head back. The sky above the sitting room was hazy blue, and I remembered all the times Zayneb and I had looked at the same sky from our respective cities and taken pictures at simultaneous moments to share with each other.

When mine was star filled, hers had been cloud filled.

When mine was dulled by sand-dust, hers had been flecked with snowflakes.

Mine, a somber afternoon sky like this one above me now, hers, the same searing night blue as the hijab she'd been wearing when I first saw her at Heathrow.

I just wanted to look at the same sky as Zayneb for more than a vacation, a break, a pause in our lives.

I wanted to lie under the same sky forever, with her lying beside me, marveling.

I closed my eyes now and imagined it.

"Really? More stars than grains of sand on earth?" Zayneb would ask me incredulously. "How? And how does anyone even know that?"

"Have you heard about this thing called science?" I would point at the night sky with my chin, because my hands would be occupied. My arms would be completely encircling her as she snuggled into my side.

"Okay, but you can actually count the grains of sand? If all seven billion people in the world got involved in helping do the count, that is. But who can verify that there are that many stars?"

"Again, science." I would kiss the top of her head—she'd be wearing her favorite dark-green-and-turquoise pashmina as a hijab, a scarf that used to be her daadi's, because it would be winter. And, um, we'd be lying in the snow. In Chicago. *Maybe even this winter?* my heart whispered. "And also, the Qur'an. Which teaches us about the ever-expanding universe, remember?"

"How do you do that, Squish?" She'd look up at me. And a fluffy snowflake would fall in the space between her eyes. "Just slam-dunk prove something? Like I'm ever going to argue against the Qur'an."

"Why do you always feel the need to argue?" I'd ask her playfully before kissing that snowflake away. "Everything's not moot court."

"Adam, speaking of sand, why didn't you tell me about the *Grains of Sand* exhibit? Why did you tell Sarina so much about something I don't know anything about? You know I always listen to you when you talk about your art, even though it doesn't always make sense to me. Why—"

The daydream was wiped clear by the squeegee of reality.

I flipped open my eyes. And straightened my head.

Abdullah had just entered the sitting room with a silver tray in his hands, stacked with glass teacups, a teapot, and a plate of dates, the door behind him being held open by one of the servers I'd seen on Tuesday.

Abdullah set the tray on the table, separated the teacups and poured tea into them with exaggerated flourish, and beckoned me to the floor cushions before heading to the front doors. He opened them and called out to Suhaib and Khaled. "Tea, the very best in all of Saudi."

He came back in and waved a hand at me to start. "Drink. Eat."

I took a glass and sipped the hot amber liquid flavored with cardamon and cinnamon. Then I took a date. "Did you find out about Zayneb, Uncle?"

"Yes, alhamdulillah. Zayneb, Sausun, and her grandmother went to Mecca. But they left a message that Zayneb will be getting to Medina tonight, insha'Allah, so not to worry. They left half an hour before I got home, so maybe an hour before you arrived."

I put my tea down. So she *had* made a sudden decision.

I wondered what else she'd decided.

After eating a late breakfast with Abdullah at his insistence, Suhaib and Khaled asked if I wanted to see the beach behind the house before we left for Medina. They'd taken lots of video of it already but felt they could use a few more shots.

I agreed nonchalantly. There was no use in rushing back to Medina now anyhow.

We stepped onto a shore exactly like many of the Doha beaches I'd been to that weren't connected to hotels or part of housing compounds, like the one I lived in.

If it weren't for the evidence of people living nearby through the litter scattered here and there, this would've been simply a shoreline left to the whims of nature.

I found a cluster of rocks to sit on while Khaled recorded Suhaib walking into the water, his pants rolled up.

I'd found out something that added to my worry about Zayneb. Apparently she'd left on a motorcycle, Sausun's, while Sausun had taken her older brother's bike with her grandma seated behind her.

I couldn't believe it.

Abdullah had chuckled at my face during breakfast when I'd learned this and assured me that Sausun's grandmother was okay, that she'd taught Sausun to ride in the first place. "Just to be sure, it *is* her grandmother you're worried about, right? Not Zayneb?"

I hadn't said anything—because I hadn't been worried that she was riding, but worried about her doing so in a new place. Especially with the traffic I'd seen en route to Mecca from the airport when we first got here.

Even though I didn't reply, Abdullah had explained that Sausun rode a lot and knew all the ways to avoid getting into trouble.

I couldn't shake the worry, though.

Now, on the beach, I pulled out my phone and scrolled my messages until I found the staccato ones from Janna.

She was the link between me, Zayneb, and Sausun.

She had to help me.

Janna was kind enough to cut short our texting and call due to my inability to communicate clearly via messages what I actually wanted.

I, who hated talking to strangers, who didn't pick up phone calls unless they were from Zayneb, Dad, Hanna, or Connor, proceeded to dump everything on Janna, including what started my wanting to please Sarina so badly: my quest to move to Chicago and be with Zayneb full-time. "I thought if I just got a job, it would all work out. That I'd be able to convince her."

"Okay, so you know what the most profound thing I've

learned this past year has been? That I still struggle with, but I'm trying make peace with?"

I had Janna on speaker because Suhaib and Khaled had walked off toward the single palm tree in the distance, and her question hit the air as I was staring at the water and sky. "What?"

"That we're not tasked with the outcome of anything. A lot of my anxiety in life came from thinking that it was all in my hands." She paused. "But only the effort is in our hands, Adam. We can't force or focus on what the end looks like; that's in Allah's hands. I don't know how that feels to you, but for me it's been freeing."

I gazed at the horizon above this body of water, remembering the almost despair with which I'd stared at the horizon above Doha Bay just a few weeks ago.

To think I wasn't in charge of what was at the very end of my gaze *was* freeing.

But it was also a thing I'd understood at my core before. Janna was telling me something I'd told Zayneb many times over the years. But with other words, words shared around us already: *Focus on the things you can control.*

The way Janna put it was more deen centered, though. More spiritual.

You're not tasked with the outcome. That's in Allah's hands.
Yours is the effort.

I had let what I'd instinctively known before completely lift out of my mind's grasp as I sank further into the embrace of fear.

I'd put aside the here and now in order to materialize the happily-ever-after I wanted so badly.

While Janna talked about how her newfound realization helped her make peace with herself, her family, and her past, I listened the way I listen to my favorite podcasts—being inspired by the strength and confidence in her voice floating around me while I paid close, minute attention to my surroundings.

The air, the sand under my shoes, the waves moving rhythmically. *With hardship will come ease. With hardship will come ease.*

With hardship will come ease.

I narrowed my eyes.

Was that a trail?

With Janna's voice still streaming onto the beach, I got off the rock and went to a spot near the sea, where the sand was saturated with water. I turned toward the house.

Yes, it was a trail. A litter-free trail to the gate at the back of Sausun's house.

Zayneb had been here. She'd most probably sat here next to the water, because she loved water, and then, while walking back to the house, picked up the garbage on her way.

That was her. Action with impact, without fanfare. But always action.

An hour later, as I sat on the steps alone waiting for our late taxi to take us back to Medina, Janna called me again.

I guess Janna had moved onto my list of pick-up-right-away people, because I picked up.

"Assalamu alaikum." Her voice came out on speaker again. "Adam, something amazing happened since we last spoke! You must have prayed really hard back when you were in Mecca!"

"Your parents said yes to Layth?" I perked up, happy to hear the spark in her usually steady voice.

"No," she said, laughing. "That is not happening. At least not yet. You guys did pray for it though, right?"

"Yes, I did for sure. And I'm sure Zayneb did too."

"Thanks. But this amazing thing is something for *you*."

I became quiet, my mind pinging all the possibilities—all involving Zayneb saying she loved me and never wanted to leave me. But I tempered that and said, "Did Sausun explain things?"

"Remember I said I learned that profound thing? About us humans not being responsible for the outcome if we put in an honest effort?"

"Yeah?" I played with some pebbles in the soil of a plant urn. *Where is this going?*

"But the honest effort—you gotta do that part, Adam!"

"I lost you, Janna." I didn't know her enough to say, *Can you just spill it? Please!*

"'Cause if you don't do the effort, and the outcome doesn't turn out how you like it, you can't say it wasn't meant to be. Basically, I lost things like that. People I'd liked, opportunities I wanted." She paused before going on. "So I have an opportunity for you."

I stood up. A job. She had a job. "Thanks so much. Is it a contract? I'm willing to take a look at anything. Even if it's not making stuff."

"No, not a job." Then she told me her amazing thing, all laid out with all the details.

And it was amazing.

But, yes, while it involved effort, it also involved something I wasn't too keen on: *risk*.

A second call beeped, a notification flashing simultaneously. *Zayneb.*

"Janna, I gotta go. Zayneb's calling."

I picked up the call faster than I'd ever picked up anything in my life.

BERTHA FATIMA ASKS THE CURATOR TO INTERRUPT AND TAKE OVER AS SHE DOESN'T TRUST THIS PART TO BE DELIVERED HONESTLY BY EITHER OF HER PARENTS

AFTER THE INITIAL SALAAMS, A SILENCE LASTING TWO SECONDS BUT feeling like an hour passed between Adam and Zayneb. Both were scrambling to get out their first declarations to clear the air, but of course Zayneb was faster.

With the barely brilliant "Squish."

"Zayneb." Adam's voice, tortured and weirdly slow as molasses. "You called me."

"I think so?" She laughed, and, to Adam, it felt like that laugh melted away the last bit of frost on the windowpane between them.

Now he could open the window and climb in.

"I'm sorry! For ignoring you!" He paused these quick, staccato-like outcries, so unlike him, so like Hanna, and added, equally as swiftly, "And I ignored you a lot!"

Zayneb resisted the urge to ask him to go on listing his sins— as her nafs al-ammara told her to—and instead confessed her own shortcomings. "Will you forgive me for shutting you out?"

"I know why you did it, Zayby."

"It doesn't matter; I still did it."

"I saw the pictures she'd posted. Sarina. I blame myself for not paying attention."

"Adam, I realized neither of us signed up to be in a relationship with perfect people." Zayneb leaned on Sausun's parked bike, the one she'd ridden to Masjid Aisha, on the outskirts of Mecca. "And asking you to please not be a flawed human doesn't allow me to be one either. And I'm the humanest human I ever did see."

Adam, struck quiet by her simple brilliance, couldn't think of what to add to the truth of her statement. Except: "Will you forgive me for being a flawed human, then?"

"Yes," Zayneb whispered, before commanding, "Now forgive *me*."

Adam ignored the taxi that had just arrived to take him back to Medina, turning his back completely to it, to say loudly, "You're forgiven."

"I have to go. I'll see you in Medina tonight, Squish."

And then she hung up before he could ask her where she was right now, where she was going, where she'd taken his heart to.

ARTIFACT THIRTY-EIGHT:
ZAYNEB'S YELLOW SUNDRESS
INTERPRETIVE LABEL: HEALING YOURSELF SETS YOU ON THE BRIGHTEST OF PATHS

AFTER I HUNG UP WITH ADAM, I CALLED SHAYKH MURTAZA AND Ustaadah Ramlah and even Sarina.

I asked them all for forgiveness for my outbursts, for my cold fronts, for actively ignoring them.

Then, at Masjid Aisha, I made ghusl and changed into ihram, this time into my own yellow sundress paired with a new black abaya on top, unbuttoned, a gift from Sausun, and walked out with Sausun and Nanni onto the asphalt covered with pigeons.

We took a coach bus humming with pilgrims to the Haram.

Sausun told me not to worry about Nanni, that she'd take care of her, and to only concentrate on my Umrah, that we would meet after four hours outside the bathroom palace.

I wanted to do a new Umrah because my first one had been for Adam.

I'd even agreed to come to this holy place *for* Adam. Keeping him happy being my main goal.

But *this* Umrah was between Allah and me.

As soon as my bare feet hit the cool floor around the Kaaba, I started crying when I spoke the same words I'd said before but without letting their meaning penetrate my heart. *Labbayka llāhumma labbayk, labbayka lā sharīka laka labbayk, inna l-ḥamda wa n-niʿmata, laka wa l-mulk, lā sharīka lak.*

You have no partner.

Everything I wanted had jostled for a spotlighted place in my heart and pushed out the source of all in my life.

Even things I didn't want—like running for treasurer—had supplanted my reasons for being here: to connect with Allah, to remember my purpose, to ask for strength in continuing my pursuit of justice, to continue the revolution begun here so long ago.

I didn't need to take things off my plate. I needed to put the right things on it.

If I'd learned anything from my obsession over Sarina, it was that my mind occupied by stress, by default, would begin fixating on the wrong things. Things I thought I could control, because the things I couldn't were bigger than everything I had in me.

I *was* conflict prone. If something needed challenging, I gladly stepped up.

But I didn't need to see challenges that weren't worth my efforts.

I mean, I didn't know what Sarina's deal was. I—and Mila—saw that she'd acted strange, but that was between her and Allah.

My focus, a long one: Using my courage and bravery for bettering the world. For fighting for the sanctity of life. Every single life, but especially those tossed aside like foam on the ocean, like the Hadith says.

Like those refugees fleeing nightmares constructed by the collusion between the palaces of tyrants and dictators, and the democratic corridors of power in the "enlightened" world.

Like Daadi, eliminated by the decision of people who hadn't seen her as completely human.

That's why I'm here.

After performing an Umrah full of prayers directly from my heart and from the little book Sausun had given me at Masjid Aisha, *A Pilgrim's Prayers*, I sat on the floor across from the bathroom palace and drank bottled Zamzam.

I knew I'd finish earlier than Sausun and her nanni because I'd been doing it all solo. I still had over an hour left before they got here to meet me.

I people-watched until I felt strong enough to do what I had to do.

I'd already told Tyler, who'd just been made news editor, I learned, that I'd quit running for treasurer, but now I needed to officially withdraw my name.

I hadn't wanted to be treasurer.

I had wanted the truth about my time as MSA president, that Murie had recast so suspiciously, to be shared.

I didn't know if my interview with Tyler this morning would play out online how I'd wanted it to.

But at least *I* got to represent myself, not Murie deliberately misrepresenting me.

After sending the election-withdrawal e-mail off, I took a deep breath, looked up at the minarets of the holiest masjid in the world rising high just yards away from me, and said bismillah before starting to compose another important e-mail on my phone.

I didn't want an externship at The Hague for the sake of an externship at The Hague. I wanted to work toward international justice. I wanted to help hold warmongers, war criminals, and oppressors accountable.

So I wasn't going to quit my pursuit of working at The Hague. That goal would stay firmly on my plate.

After obsessing over the wording of my terse but respectful e-mail, I sent a message to Professor Mumford telling him that I wanted to keep The Hague on as my first choice but that I'd added two more organizations as a backup should I not get in.

Then I turned around, held up my phone, and FaceTimed Ava with the Masjid al-Haram behind me.

"Wow, that is stunning." Her eyes widened. She was lying on her pillow, so I was looking down at her face.

"I know it's really early there, so let me keep it short," I began. "I don't want your room, Ava."

"What, why?" She pulled herself up from under the covers and sat leaning against her headboard, the phone lifted high in front of her. "Did you find something else?"

"No, I want you to stay there."

She was quiet, just blinking at me.

"I saw the way you'd decorated your room, girl. You planned on staying there. That's a lot of little knickknacks you've collected over time."

She sighed. "Yes, it's true. But honestly, Zayneb, it makes me happy for you to have somewhere to live."

"But it makes me happier for you to feel safe." I spoke gently before adding firmly, "So I'm taking care of things. Of the Larseho—" I looked around, remembering I was on holy grounds, remembering I was trying not to descend. As much as I humanly could. "Of Lars. In a way where there won't be any fallout for you. I promise. Keep an eye on the *UpBeat* tomorrow."

"Really?"

"Really. And I also sent Sasha a bunch of links and screenshots about her quote, unquote 'brief hookup.'" I'd messaged Sasha after my interview with Tyler this morning, before we left for Umrah.

"Oh wow, that's why she called me after midnight crying." Ava's own eyes glittered with tears. "She was apologizing over and over, and I thought she'd suddenly learned about him. On her own. But it was you."

"I want you to eat your bubbe's food all by yourself in your coolest room," I told her. "Without having to share the delish with your parents."

She laughed, and her eyes sparkled with fresh tears again, and I decided I liked people who cried spontaneously.

It showed they had hearts they hadn't buried too deeply inside.

I'd have to look for another place, but at least I had the rental couch for another two weeks.

And I'll make sure to hold on to it until the very last second of December tenth.

Now, because Layth was flying back to Ecuador this week, I just needed to find Bertha Fatima a place until I could bring her home to me again.

BERTHA FATIMA PAUSES THE STORY TO PUT HER HEAD FACEDOWN ON HER PAWS UPON HEARING THAT LAST STATEMENT—THAT SHE MAY NOT END UP LIVING WITH EVEN ONE OF HER PARENTS, LET ALONE BOTH—BUT WE COMPEL HER TO PLEASE GO ON WITH THE STORY

ARTIFACT THIRTY-NINE:
ADAM'S WATER BOTTLE WITH SAND, GIFTED
INTERPRETIVE LABEL: LOOK BEYOND THE GIFT TO SEE WHAT YOU CAN MAKE OF IT

ALL THE WAY BACK TO MEDINA, I RODE IN THE FRONT PASSENGER seat of the taxi with a smile on my face.

Zayneb was coming to Medina tonight. Sausun's dad was going to drive her and Sausun after they rested from their Umrah.

We were going to meet after Isha at the Prophet's masjid, by a certain pillar umbrella Sausun specified.

While I was ecstatic, there were two things I needed to figure out still, the first one to be answered before Zayneb and I parted ways tomorrow, the second before I got back home.

1. How I was going to get a bit of time with Zayneb alone?

2. How I was going to explain my financial situation to Dad?

"Whoa, there are a thousand likes already!" Suhaib burst out from the back of the taxi.

I turned around. "Nice!"

"Alhamdulillah. Which one?" Khaled asked.

"The before-and-after-Umrah-hair one!" Suhaib's voice was bubbly. "Dad, we have to edit the other ones right away!"

"I'm on it. AirDrop me the palm tree videos."

"No, can we do the Mecca to Medina one? We got good clips for that." Suhaib peered at his phone, rubbing his bald head with one hand absentmindedly like he'd been doing ever since he got it shaved. "Or wait, let's do the Mecca chicken one! I can't wait for it to go viral!"

I smiled again and turned back, missing Hanna, missing that confident energy.

There was a plastic bag on my bed when I got into the hotel room. Inside it was a mini water bottle that contained sand.

Sand from Jabal Al-Noor was scribbled on it. It was from her, Sarina.

I was more interested in the special item folded under the bottle.

The more I stared at it, the more an idea grew in my head.

It sounded wild; it sounded impulsive; it sounded like something Zayneb would be able to totally pull off but I never would. That I'd take a week or so to consider and work out before coming near it.

I had to talk to Dad.

I needed a loan to make my plan work.

I'd never heard Dad say yes so emphatically before. "But it's not a loan. It's a thank-you gift."

"For what?"

"For being you, Adam." The phone was quiet. I hadn't Face-Timed him because he'd been in his office at school. It was parent night, so his door was open, and the school had a strict policy on parents and students being recorded without their permission. "I can't get into it now, but as the years go by and Hanna grows into the age you were when you grappled with Mom's passing, I can't believe the maturity with which you dealt with everything."

"I'd rather work for it, Dad."

"Again, I can't get into it now, but I feel like I took your sense of care and consideration for granted. You probably suffered quietly through a lot of it." He pulled in a breath. "I have an appointment in five, but don't worry about anything. I'll work it out, insha'Allah. And update you." When I didn't say anything, as I absorbed his kindness, he added, "I'm here for you until you can set out on your own. And I'm grateful I can be here for you."

"Thanks, Dad," I said, my mind zooming in on what a gift of a father I had.

After dinner and Maghrib, I slept for an hour before showering and getting ready for Isha, and to meet Zayneb.

And Sausun.

My anger at her had dissipated because she'd taken Zayneb to do Umrah, but I didn't know how I'd look at someone who'd drawn a line between Zayneb and me.

I didn't know the full story, and Janna wasn't able to provide any more clarity, but I knew that Zayneb was grateful to Sausun, so I guessed I should be too.

Our Umrah group gathered in the lobby to head to the masjid together, and, on the way, I asked Mila and Fatima if they wanted to see Zayneb before she left tomorrow. They'd asked about her repeatedly the last couple of days. And I'd answered, "She's still recovering," as though I knew it for certain.

"Yes!" Mila enthusiastically replied.

"We have to take her shopping tonight!" Fatima said. "She'd mentioned wanting some gifts for people, and I'd told her to wait until Medina."

Sahaan stuck his head between Fatima and me and grinned. "Did someone say more shopping?"

"How okay do you think she'll be about eating Albaik again?" Mila asked, her eyebrows lifted, a stiff headband on top of her hijab. "I've been craving it. And Suhaib's Albaik TikTok just landed, and it's him just eating fried chicken over and over."

"Just ask her." I told them to meet us after prayer in another location than where I'd be meeting Zayneb. I wanted some time with her first.

She was standing by the pillar umbrella to the left of the main gate.

In a black abaya, open at the front, under which she wore a yellow dress.

On her head was a black hijab; on the shoulder of one arm, the strap of her backpack.

I took all these details in hungrily, like she would disappear any minute.

I was tired, but I sped up until she could see my smile, until I could see her smile back, until I knew we were maybe going to be okay, insha'Allah.

I wanted to run to close the final gap between us, but she was standing with her fingers entwined in front of her, sort of in a nervous pose, and I didn't want to scare her.

So I took one big step toward her until she was within arm-reaching distance, and with my own hands awkwardly in the pockets of my thawb, I just stared at her.

Drank her all in as she stood there, her smile turning shy for the first time in a long time, actually, since the first time I'd met her in Doha so long ago.

Her fingers began loosening their hold on one another and started to reach out, but my hands were already out of my pockets, moving.

And then we were hugging, my eyes closed as I sank my face into her hijab above her shoulder, the thin cloth of which didn't hide her lavender-coffee smell.

I couldn't stop tearing up, smelling that.

It was only after we parted after hugging that I noticed Sausun just a few feet away. "I come in peace," she said to me. "And I delivered her to Medina, so cut me some slack."

"What do you mean?" I asked, confused.

"Your expression is what I mean. When you looked at me just now."

"She not only delivered me. She also nursed me, took me to Umrah. And lent me her grandma," Zayneb said. "She's not a big fan of hugs, otherwise, she'd be glued to me right now." Zayneb flailed her arms at Sausun in a play at trying to hug her.

"Away, away. Begone." Sausun flicked her hands at Zayneb and then looked at me. "Anyway, I should apologize. I shouldn't have been so harsh the other day. Apparently, you're 'the best.'" She used air quotes.

"It's okay. I don't think anyone would call me 'the best' the last few days." I looked at Zayneb when I said this, before turning to Sausun again. "If Zayneb is in, a few of us from the group wanted to take her shopping and for a meal. Would you like to join?"

"I don't know, Zayneb. Do you even want me to come? Or are you sick of me?"

"Come on." Zayneb laughed. "You lent me your ride. Now we're literally ride or die."

Sausun laughed. "Oof, true."

"Are you in, Z?" I reached out for her hand. "Or did you want to get some sleep in before you fly back tomorrow?"

"I'm in." She smiled at me and threaded her fingers through

mine. "But only if we don't stay out too late. Because remember you were going to pick me up for Fajr?"

I let go of her fingers and put my arm around her shoulders and led her to the others in our little group.

And, after Fajr at the Prophet's masjid, we rode the hotel elevators without pressing our floors until everyone got off one by one, and, when it was just us two, I reached up and covered the camera, and she reached across and pressed the door-close button, and we kissed for so long with one arm around each other that the elevator alarm started ringing. We both let go—of each other, of the camera, and the elevator—and it went down one level to pick up new people.

I hoped we didn't look too guilty, but we couldn't resist trading goofy glances with each other the entire way down to the floor both of our rooms were on.

ARTIFACT FORTY: ZAYNEB'S BOARDING PASS
INTERPRETIVE LABEL: RETURNING YOURSELF,
MORE WHOLE, IS THE POINT OF A JOURNEY

I'D HAD TO SAY GOOD-BYE TO EVERYONE AT THE HOTEL, LINGERING on Mila and Fatima, but not bypassing hugging Ustaadah Ramlah or Sarina. I thanked them and the shaykh for all their help. Sarina gave off slightly snobby, oh-you-who-are-you-again vibes, but I shrugged it away as her problem.

Adam and I tried to go up in the elevator again for our exciting Elevator Kisses™, to say good-bye properly, but it hadn't worked, even though we'd tried a few times. Every single floor had new people enter. We'd settled on hugging each other outside my taxi three times.

We promised to make time to talk it all out properly when Adam flew to my parents' for winter break. Until then, I'd be swamped with school.

I took the bullet train from Medina to Jeddah. At the airport, as I rested my head on the wall next to my seat near the boarding gate, I tried to think of the positive.

I would have wanted to have spent more time in Medina, but, except for the brief time shopping for gifts, I did stay at the Prophet's masjid for most of it.

One day I'd come here with Adam, just us two, insha'Allah.

And we'd start our Umrah trip in Medina as Sausun had advised me to—though spending the afterglow of an Umrah done right in the City of Light had been beautiful too.

After boarding, I got buckled in my seat and picked up my phone to refresh the *UpBeat* website again.

Tyler hadn't published anything.

Well, it *was* still morning in Chicago.

An hour after takeoff, I checked again. Nothing.

Just as I lifted my head from tucking my phone into the seat pocket in front of me, I saw him.

Adam.

Walking toward me on a plane the same way he had that day my life had lifted to soar.

**ARTIFACT FORTY-ONE: ADAM'S BOARDING PASS
INTERPRETIVE LABEL:** *RETURNING YOURSELF
CHANGED FOR THE BETTER IS EVEN BETTER*

THERE SHE WAS—SITTING IN AN AISLE SEAT, BESIDE A BOY IN A THAWB and a man in a business suit next to him by the window.

She had just looked up after tucking something into the seat pocket, and her eyes grew large on seeing me.

I nodded at her. And said the same first words I'd risked saying to her, a stranger, one day, words that had brought love into my life. "Assalamu alaikum."

"Ad—walaikum musalam!" She unbuckled and stood up swiftly, her arms already going around my neck.

Well, this part is different from when we first met.

I'd wanted to re-enact the whole thing in slow motion, but Zayneb was already snuggling into my chest. "Whoa, calm down, tiger. We're getting a lot of astaghfirullah gazes right now."

To her halal credit, she dropped her arms and just smiled huge at me. "What is going on? *Whoa, tiger,* yourself? What are doing here, Squish? I thought your flight to Doha was tomorrow from Saudi!"

"I switched things up. Flying out of London now."

"Aw, so we can get more time together?" She started to reach out to me again.

"Yep, because, Zayneb Malik, I have a plan to share. Actually, plans, and we're having a meeting, you and I." I pointed to the rear of the plane "Will you do me the courtesy of joining me all the way at the back? I talked to the flight attendant, and she is totally okay with you switching to the empty seat beside me."

Zayneb whipped around and grabbed her phone and small purse and flipped open the overhead compartment to look at her backpack. "Nah, I'll just leave that here. Time is of the essence! We get a few hours to ourselves finally!"

I let her think that, that "time was of the essence." That we had only a few hours.

I wouldn't share *that* part of the plan until we landed in London.

I turned quickly so she wouldn't see the giddiness taking over my face as I thought of finally having Zayneb beside me *on a flight*.

When we got to my seat, I indicated the empty seats around it with a flourish of my hands. "All yours, my lady."

"How?"

"These are the worst seats, and I deliberately chose mine here knowing that this flight was not at capacity." I let her go in first so she was near the window. "And did you know that I walked by you several times? First when I boarded, with my head down like the worst spy undercover in existence, with this very obvious hat of Sahaan's on my head. Second time, when I went to the bathroom near your seat and came back hoping I'd catch your eye then. But you were engrossed in your phone. And so then I just paced a few times by you until you looked up. Pacing actually works." I smiled to myself, remembering having that eureka moment during Sa'i. *Just do something; move; get things going.*

Zayneb, settled in her seat, laughed. "No wonder everyone on the plane was like, *haram*. They probably thought you were trying to pick me up, and then I shot out of my seat into your arms, like, baby, just take all of me!"

I grinned and opened the overhead compartment to take out the blanket the flight attendants had handed out at the beginning of our flight. I opened it up, sat down, and spread it over us. "So we can snuggle in peace," I said, linking our fingers under the blanket. "What were you staring at so hard on your phone?"

With her free hand, she lifted her phone from under the blanket and face-unlocked it. The phone revealed her campus media website. She pulled the screen with her thumb to refresh it, her eyes opening wide at the results. As she read, a smile grew on her face.

She turned her phone around to me.

An Exclusive Interview with Zayneb Malik: Student who briefly helmed club under investigation points to double standards, bias, and inequity in current scrutiny of student activities on campus

I reached for her device, but she pulled it away suddenly. "Wait, Squish. Before you read this, can you listen to something? Things may make more sense if you do."

I nodded, and she let go of my fingers to pick up her purse from under the blanket. She unzipped it and took out AirPods, handing one to me, sticking the other in her ear. "This has been my life for the past couple of months. I couldn't tell you everything because it felt like it would take so much explaining, and that if I told you everything over the phone, we'd fall into a rabbit hole of negativity. I couldn't touch and comfort you like this to make sure you knew you hadn't gotten together with a complete wreck." She threaded her free arm through mine and rested her head on my shoulder.

Leaning my head on top of hers, I listened to the voice recordings. All of them began with *Dear Adam, if you were here with me, this is what I'd tell you.*

When I finished listening, before I read the interview with her, I pulled the blanket over our heads and lifted up her chin and kissed her so softly in the dark that she trembled. Then I kissed the sides of each of her eyes. "That's to take care of the tics. And I'm going to do that every night, insha'Allah. That's part of my plan."

She turned on her phone flashlight in her lap like she was getting ready to tell a spooky story, and an eerie circle of light pooled on her chin and mouth and tip of her nose. God, how could her face be beautiful even when it looked creepy? "You'll kiss my tics when you come at winter break?" she asked, tenderly touching my lips with a finger.

"No, when I move to Chicago. As soon as possible." I took her finger gently and turned it around to fit it in front of her own mouth. "Wait. Before you speak, listen to me. My turn now. Okay?"

She nodded.

"I won't move in with you, Zayneb. I can see that it stresses you to live together right now. I never want to stress you, ever. But I want to be where you are. Always." I put my own finger on her lips, as her finger had dropped and she was beginning to open her mouth. "I haven't told you things going on in my life too. The biggest being that I've been without contracts for a while now. But I have ideas. I just need to connect with the right people or the right opportunities. Until then, I'll live away from you in Chicago. And we can go on dates and be there to tell each other things while we hold hands. And kiss." I leaned forward again to—

"Excuse me, sir, but we've received a complaint from the gentleman sitting across."

I whipped the blanket off our heads and looked up, stricken, at the flight attendant peering down at me and Zayneb.

"I'm sorry, but what exactly is he complaining about?" Zayneb drew herself up. "How does someone else get to police our behavior in *our* seats?"

"It's okay, Z." I clutched her hand, then spoke to the attendant. "For sure, we won't bother him. Thanks for letting us know."

She nodded and walked away.

Zayneb stuck her head out and looked across the aisle at the complaining passenger, a frown on her face. And then she sighed and leaned back into her seat, muttering to herself. "When am I ever going to learn to pick my fights."

"A lot of people on this flight are returning from Umrah. They probably don't want a hanky-panky-in-a-blanky situation happening," I said, and Zayneb laughed.

I glanced at the man I didn't even remember sitting across from before.

But it was okay. We would have time to ourselves soon enough, insha'Allah.

"Are you done with your turn?" Zayneb asked.

"No. I just wanted to tell you not to worry about me. My dad said he's going to help me out. Lend me money until I settle into something in Chicago." I put my arm around her. After which I looked across the aisle at the complaining man.

He was gone.

That was strange. Was he a passenger from up front who'd come back here just to tell us off?

Zayneb frowned. "But I wasn't worried about that. About your money situation."

"I meant you don't have to figure things out for me. I'll do it." I wondered if I should bring up Janna's suggestion. About the makerspace studios—renting one out to develop some of my project ideas. Just using that as my space to "go to work," even if it meant I wasn't making money for the first little while. Dad had said he'd invest if I decided to start a business.

Maybe I'd tell Zayneb all that when I figured out how much that would cost, when there was a plan in place that I was actually going to embark on. After I put in the effort.

"Now can I talk?" she asked.

I nodded. "Wow, you've been pretty patient."

"I wanted to ask where you were going to live."

"So, that's the best part of my plan! Layth had booked his room for another month for his mom to come visit his uncle in December but she's only coming to the US very briefly, a day or two at a hotel. She's going to visit Layth in Ecuador for a couple of weeks instead. So he checked with the landlord if he could switch it over to me and they're okay with it. If I like it, I have the option of staying on for a year's lease." I spoke fast, pulling Zayneb closer to me. "Janna and Layth worked it all out. I get the key next week, but I'll only be able to move in in a couple of weeks, after your exams, anyhow. So you don't have to stress about anything, Zayneb."

She mumbled something so quietly with her head bent down, completely unlike her, that I couldn't hear anything at all at first. "Sorry, what?"

"Can I live with you?" she whispered.

I tilted my head so my ear was closer to her. "Did you just ask me—"

"Can I please live with you? We can split the rent. I might need to take a bus to school, but it will be okay. And can I move in next week?"

I let go of her and pumped my fists in the air. "*Yeah!* My Zayby just asked if she can move in with me! *Me!*"

Then I stuck the blanket back on our heads and quickly kissed her, before pulling it off again, glancing across the aisle to check if anyone had seen.

What in the world? The guy was there again. Full-blown frowning.

"You never answered, Adam." She lifted the blanket to shield her from the passenger while she adjusted her hijab.

"Why wouldn't I want to come home every day to the best thing that's ever happened to me?"

ARTIFACT FORTY-TWO: ZAYNEB'S SNOW GLOBE ENCLOSING A COTTAGE IN THE WOODS
INTERPRETIVE LABEL: IT'S HERE ALL ALONG, WHAT WE GO OUT THERE TO FIND

WHEN WE LANDED, I THOUGHT ADAM WOULD GO ON TO CATCH A flight to Doha. While I waited for my flight to Chicago.

But he had another surprise waiting for me.

He and his dad had arranged with Shaykh Murtaza, who'd booked all my travel originally, to change my flight to the day after tomorrow.

Apparently no one had taken Hidden Bloom when Adam's dad canceled it after I joined the Umrah trip, so Adam had re-offered the deposit money, and they'd been happy.

Adam and I had one night and one day at the cottage. And we made the most of it.

The night we arrived, we spent it exactly how I wanted it—exploring each other, tenderly, slowly, lovingly, until we couldn't stand it any longer, and we wanted each other completely.

After, we lay in each other's arms, and Adam traced my face with his finger again, his favorite thing to do while he stared at me. Then he informed me that he was going to tell me things about the stars while we lay in the night snow in Chicago this December. "You have to wear your favorite green-and-blue pashmina.

And any snowflake that falls on your face, I'll kiss away."

"But I like snowflakes. I want them to stay on my face."

"Okay, then keep your snowflakes," he said, amused. Then he gazed behind me, with thinking eyes, the light of the bedside lamp hitting his face just so, leading me to reach my own finger up to trace *his* face. His considerate eyes, his mouth full of kindness, and the way his jawline—firmly Muslim, always trying to grow a beard but always failing—touched his deeply listening ears. He looked at me again. "Actually, that's my first project in Chicago. The link between snowflakes and Islamic geometric designs—in particular, the hexagonal source of each, like much of nature, like the hive of a bee. The earliest geometric forms on a masjid being . . . "

He went on, and I fell asleep listening really hard.

Before we walked to the village nearby to get lunch, while Adam was changing, I remained in my yellow sundress and sat with my legs under a quilt on the periwinkle-blue sofa in the living room to look at the new comments on my interview with Tyler.

I was surprised the *UpBeat* had given so much space for it. As they would say in the news world, it was a "far-ranging" interview.

It covered a lot of things, such as the fact that goalposts were always moving on the way we were supposed to view entities in different parts of the world. How there were organizations in Afghanistan that had been seen as collaborators with us at one point while they were fighting *for* us, but then, with one sweep of the pen, had been designated as terrorists—after having been used for our proxy war purposes over the years. How grassroots charity organizations in so many Muslim countries, who'd done the work for the people they served for generations, had been designated as criminals when they affiliated with political groups we didn't want in power—because they wouldn't allow our stronghold on their economies or governments.

The Palestinian group that I'd sent money to, something Murie had skewed, was one such organization, I pointed out. They'd been doing work on the ground for years and years.

And I told Tyler that this was why I wanted to work in international law, so that international systems could be strengthened and not based on the whims of the powerful. I even shared the story of Daadi.

Tyler kept Teju Cole's term, "unmournable" body, to describe how I felt about my grandmother, and I teared up about that.

Tyler was all right—he was clearly willing to listen and be open.

Most important for me at school, he'd kept his promise about the interview: to include my analysis of how certain student groups were being singled out.

To bolster my thoughts, he'd added his own research on how fascist groups on campus were not facing the same scrutiny as the MSA and other clubs. I'd called out Lars and his group by name and pointed to his online postings, particularly his questioning the Holocaust and sharing antisemitic posts, and Tyler provided the screenshots from Lars's social media accounts to accompany the interview.

The receipts don't lie.

It would just be a matter of time for Ava to be comfortable enough to hang her mezuzah outside her door once more, insha'Allah.

As I was liking all the positive comments about Tyler's piece, I got a Twitter notification.

I popped over to Twitter, and my mouth dropped open.

Professor Mumford, Professor Lincoln Mumford himself, had shared the interview and tagged me in it! *"Double standard norms*

in campus policies and International Law are symptoms of bias"—
Zayneb Malik makes links between latest campus investigations &
global inequities & inconsistencies.

I lowered my phone. I couldn't believe it.

I didn't know what this meant, if it meant he agreed with me, or he was letting me know he'd seen it or whether it even meant he was subtly pointing out how ridiculous my link was.

I did, however, know one thing for sure: It meant that I had taken a firm step forward on the map that led to my goal. I didn't know if I would reach it. But, like Hajar did while she strived, I knew I'd always take pauses along the way and ask for guidance.

I'd been so engrossed in reading Professor Mumford's other tweets to ascertain his views that I didn't realize Adam had come out of the bedroom all dressed in the chunky knit gray-blue sweater and jeans he'd worn in London before we left for Umrah, and that he was now leaning on the doorjamb of the bedroom, looking at me.

I only knew of his presence when he moved forward suddenly and lifted the end of the blanket near my feet to get on the sofa, under the quilt with me. He tucked his legs beneath mine and said, "Go on, keep doing what you were doing."

"While you stare at me?" I rested my phone in my quilted lap and tipped my head, my eyes scrunching in suspicion.

"No, while I drink you in, my water. My snowflake water."

"That sounds even more creepy?"

"Zayneb Malik, did you know you're a bumblebee?"

I looked down at my yellow torso sticking out of the quilt, the straps of my sundress falling off my shoulders. Maybe this outfit was actually sexier than my tiny clothes from Macy's. "Because I'm wearing yellow?"

"And your hair is black."

"Okay. Am I supposed to be blown away by this poetic observation? Zayneb Malik, you are my bumblebee?"

"I didn't say *my* bumblebee."

"Whose bumblebee am I, then?"

"Yours. Because you're not a beetle. You're a bee who works hard for all the world, who loves work, who works without expecting reward or extolling, but just because you want to see a beautiful world for everyone, because that's what bees do." He reached out for my left hand resting on top of the quilt. And played with my fingers. But then, suddenly, looked down. "My mom loved bees. And I know she would have absolutely adored you. Because I completely do. I wish she'd met you."

I got off the sofa and went to his end and tucked under the quilt beside him and kissed the left edge of his mouth.

He turned his head and my lips weren't at the edge anymore but fully on his hungry mouth, and then he slipped his fingers under the shoulder straps of my dress to slide them down farther so he could kiss-trace my neck and shoulders.

I helped him by pulling the dress completely off.

And we ended up being very late to go for lunch.

In the village, after lunch, after I'd purchased a little snow globe with a cottage in the woods as a souvenir of this beautiful trip, *the whole of it*, I noticed some late-blooming roses growing on a small bush in front of a quaint charity shop, and we went over to look at them.

After we stared quietly, reverently, and Adam had taken a picture of me smelling them to send to my parents, I made him promise to never buy me roses. Because they deserved to be visited out in the world, and I'd always try to go out and find them.

As I took a video of him on his phone pledging to never buy me roses, he got a notification.

It was an e-mail through Adam's website asking about his availability for a 3D mapping project.

Then another message, this one via Instagram, showed up as we were reading the first e-mail.

Then another one? "Whaat?" he asked. He read through one of the messages. "It's because of Suhaib. His TikTok."

We huddled against the stone facade of the charity shop and watched Suhaib's latest TikTok, called "Mecca to Medina," that tagged Adam and had his website listed with a comment: "This guy can make things you wouldn't believe."

The TikTok was a stills-come-to-life one with photos of Adam's map of the year 622 as transformed today, with Suhaib standing in each spot.

Khaled was awesome at editing, and the video had racked up twenty-two thousand likes already after a day. "The boy is going viral!" Adam said, excited.

"Um, you're going viral too?" I said, as the top of his phone kept lighting up with notifications—people following him on his socials, making comments tagging him, just connecting with his talent.

"Insha'Allah, I can go to work now." He beamed and told me about his idea to rent space at a maker collective. How having a flexible schedule he was in charge of, instead of a full-time job, would work the best with his MS reality.

He also told me that he was learning to make peace with the fact that he may grapple with the loss of some of his abilities, like his vision and mobility, in the future due to MS. But Umrah had helped him realize he wasn't going to wait for things to happen *to* him, and instead, would make things happen *for* him, as much as he could.

Remembering the scene in the hotel in California, how Adam had shut down when Mansoor had pushed him about working at a job, I told him something I'd wished he'd known then: When I agreed to solemnizing our relationship, to doing our nikah, I'd agreed to enter an oath with him to face hardships together. "We're bonded like H_2O, Squish. We flow when we're together. And if you need a break, I'll keep flowing for us." I turned to him. "I promise you that."

In reply, he threaded his right arm through my left one and wove his fingers through mine.

On the way home, we decided to take a walk through the old-growth forest that the cottage was nestled in, the Winnie-the-Pooh forest, and I asked him to put his arms around me because I was cold and he stopped and told me to wait and speed-walked ahead to the cottage, which was a far way down from where we were.

I stood there, hugging my arms around my own chunky sweater, perplexed.

While waiting, I tipped my head back and stared at the tops of the trees around me. It was exactly how I'd imagined it—crisp with a nip in the air, a few remaining leaves of pale yellow and rust brown and burnt orange poised to fall from above.

I traced the trees down to where their roots were covered in an autumnal carpet and thought of Layth's room.

No, our mini apartment.

I closed my eyes and allowed myself to dream of how it would look, with me and Adam living there.

I'm totally going to go with a dark, richly colored, antique, and cozy aesthetic—but not full-blown dark academia. I'm going to ask Adam's help to translate that look with Islamic art and design so it reflects our heritages. Maybe I could get a hand-me-down Turkish rug from my parents. And beg for one of the woven wall hangings from Somalia that Mansoor and Hodan have all over their place. And next time Sadia goes to Malaysia to visit her in-laws, I could ask her to bring me some traditional art from there. Maybe a batik bedspread.

Or I could just ask for one of hers, because we're tight like that.

Mila, who I'd already invited to visit me with her husband Jack when she next came to the US, could bring us something Balkan Muslim, and Haytham and Sausun, something Syrian and Saudi and South African.

We could have an apartment that paid homage to our ummah, insha'Allah.

I allowed myself to believe that I was worthy of such a pretty place, a place to share with the love of my life, where I'd work on a world that opened the doors of dignity and beauty to every human.

The sound of Adam approaching made my eyelids flip open. He had something in his hands behind his back, and when he got close, he brought it forward with a tender smile on his face.

And then he wrapped it around my neck.

My big blanket scarf, the one I'd bought for our trip.

"I slept with it in Medina," he confessed. "I missed you so much, and it was the closest thing to you."

"Aw, Adam. You found Scarfy!" I'd been sure I'd lost her forever. "Where did you find her? I thought she was gone for good."

"Um, uh, someone brought it to me. I guess she'd found it when they were doing a last sweep of your hotel room in Mecca."

"Sarina." I brought the scarf up around my face and sank into it. "You can say her name. She doesn't do anything to me anymore."

I'd actually decided to share her info with Ayaan to introduce her to Yasin. He wanted someone passable to the haram police in him, and maybe that was Sarina.

Who knows, maybe they'd find love and comfort and friendship in each other.

Maybe my first intense crush meets Adam's first intense crush and it all works out somehow and it all makes sense in the end.

"About that . . . you know I'm sorry, right?" Adam said, his hands tucked in the pockets of his jeans, his shoulders tightening.

"You texted me that a million times. Before I blocked you, so it must have been two million." I put a hand on his chest and looked up at his eyes. "*I'm* sorry. Again."

"I'll show you those two million texts still on my phone." He nodded and then said seriously, "But you know what I'm *not* sorry about? Buying you that jilbab like hers. You said you loved it, the color, and the jilbab itself. In London, before we left."

I grinned sheepishly, not recalling this small piece of information. "I did?"

"Yes." He reached his arms out. "But forget about it. You never have to wear it."

"No, I will. When I went back to Mecca with Sausun, we changed the color." I thought of wearing it in Chicago sometimes, on the days I wanted to take a break from fashion-policing myself. I'd wear it with boots and the warmest flannel long johns ever and this blanket scarf. And I'd remember to look beyond what I saw immediately.

Adam can take in the details, peer to find the beauty in everything, and I'll keep trying to concentrate on the bigger picture of life itself.

I turned around and leaned back against Adam and he hugged

me, and we took a funny selfie with Scarfy wound around both of our necks to send to Sadia.

More things you can do with blanket scarves, I texted her.

Then, as we stood in the middle of this most beautiful place, the most beautiful thing happened: snow started falling.

Snowflakes.

Ice flowers.

Masterpieces of design and miracles of beauty, Wilson Bentley called them.

Overwhelmed, I tipped my head back to feel them fall on my face, the miracles, the hardships, the pacing, the climbs, the falls, and the soars, and Adam whispered,

الحمد لله

And I added,

على كل حال

Alhamdulillah for it all.

EPILOGUE

Under the microscope, I found that snowflakes were miracles of beauty. . . . Every crystal was a masterpiece of design and no one design was ever repeated. When a snowflake melted, that design was forever lost. Just that much beauty was gone, without leaving any record behind.
—Wilson Bentley

No leaf falls without His knowledge, nor is there a single grain in the darkness of the earth, or anything, fresh or withered, that is not written in a clear record.
—Surah 6:59

TO THANK YOU FOR YOUR ATTENTION, DEAR READER, BERTHA FATIMA REQUESTED THE CURATOR RECORD ONE LAST CHAPTER

BERTHA FATIMA SLEPT ON A SCENT CLOUD ARISING FROM THE MIX OF fir wood shavings and cloves scattered into the crisp cool air of an ocean, upon the shore of which paced a girl who used lavender soap regularly, a mocha in her hand.

That is to say, she slept on Adam and Zayneb's bed. On a black, burgundy, brown, and orange floral batik bedspread from Malaysia, that matched the burnt orange lamp on the bedside table perfectly.

"Cat: *MEOW!*"

Bertha Fatima opened one eye at the eerily precise catlike sound emanating from someone with her face covered in a black veil, one of the humans who gathered every Friday night at her home, bringing with them junk food that messed up the healthy-home smells of the rest of the week.

Friday night was something called "cheat night," apparently.

Friday night was also *loud* night.

Bertha Fatima tolerated it, though. The humans were intelligent enough to recognize that the bed solely belonged to her—and her parents, of course—on such a night and that they must sit on all the other available seating in the place, including the floor, should they need to.

Tonight was louder than usual, and Bertha Fatima opened her other eye to ascertain why that was so.

There were, including Adam and Zayneb, eight people gathered this time, and not the regular six. And then there were eleven more people on the screen of the laptop set on the round pedestal table.

And half of this party, the ones in the room, were shouting animal names and making animal sounds while flailing or jolting, and it was neither pretty nor cultured.

Bertha Fatima sat up and placed her paws together on the bed and pursed her mouth and watched sternly.

But then her gaze was caught by the dark teal bookshelf across from her.

It was now more filled with books, yet her eyes landed on the story box, as they often did when she was peeved about something.

One glance at it restored her soul, reset it to its default now: that of gratitude.

The lid of the story box was closed, but it was empty—all the artifacts it had previously contained, except the clothing, of course, now artfully arranged on the shelf.

Like all good stories, this story box had opened up, for its owners, a new way to live.

For Bertha Fatima, it was the deliciousness of gratitude that she was home with both her parents now.

For Adam and Zayneb, it was a realization that love doesn't have a destination.

That they had to wake up every day and decide to travel to each other again and again, even if their paths were twisty, or slow, or stalled by a huge avalanche, or cracked in two by an earthquake.

Because their hard travel days also created days when they flew to each other. *With hardship comes ease.*

And that truth was the bigger part of the story.

Adam turned to Zayneb, sitting cross-legged beside him on the floor, and rested his hand holding a phone on her thigh. "Hanna's calling. It's super early in the morning in Doha. Must be something important. Let's pick up?"

Zayneb nodded and swiped his phone to receive the call.

Hanna was in her prayer dress, the one Zayneb had bought her in Mecca, and sitting on her prayer mat, the one Adam had bought her in Medina. "Guys, I just finished Fajr and remembered I'll be at your house *in two days.*"

Before they all gathered in Ottawa at Adam's grandparents for the first part of the holidays, Hanna would be spending a day with Adam and Zayneb. And, in case they forgot this amazing thing, they'd been getting a call from Hanna every few days reminding them.

Zayneb shouted with glee over her friend Ava, who was trying to whinny like a horse but failing miserably, "We know Hanna, and we can't wait! And remember you're coming with us to see my baby nephew, Hassan!"

Next to Ava—on the wooden settee she'd acquired and set up as a surprise gift for Adam and Zayneb in the apartment—Janna bleated like a terribly weak sheep, while a friend of hers and Zayneb's, Bilqis, sat on the floor by Janna's feet, laughing uncontrollably in the midst of quacking.

"What is happening?" Hanna sounded concerned. "You guys are at home, right?" Adam lifted up the phone, and she saw the dark teal wall behind them and the faded Turkish rug under them but wasn't sure due to the farmlike ambiance.

"It's games night. Winter break version. Hence the pajamas."
Adam pointed at his, covered in snowflakes (a gift from Zayneb),
but also covered with a traditional black sleep robe, in deference to
his more subdued sensibilities.

Zayneb proudly wore a loose black-and-yellow-striped shearling onesie. She'd even pulled the antennae hood on top of her
hijab to complete the look.

"Ahhhh! Can you do games night when *I* get there?" Hanna
looked eager.

"Actually, we have something better planned for you," Adam
said. "We're taking you to the mecca of basketball, United Center.
For a game! For our first out-of-town guest ever!" He'd been adamant about that, that Hanna would be their first real guest, and
Zayneb had agreed.

Hanna, for her part, was about to yell, *Hey,* that's *not the mecca
of basketball!* but decided to just act excited. She'd straighten Adam
out when she landed in Chicago.

After they hung up with Hanna, Adam and Zayneb turned
back to the game, Outburst, but were informed by Ava that it
was now over. The online team had won by cleaning up the dairy
products category.

Zayneb nodded at Mariyah, who got up and went to get the
cake she'd taught Zayneb to make before everyone got there.

"Janna, Layth, surprise!" Zayneb held the cake high so Layth,
online in Ecuador, could see it too.

It said J + L, and Janna immediately pulled her black pajama sleeves
over her hands and lifted both to her face to cover her blushing.

"Oh no you don't," Sausun rebuked. "The news was already
posted online, so it's in the public domain now."

Janna lowered her hand and pulled the sleeve back and showed the ring Layth had bought her and sent back with his mom from Ecuador. Before she'd left for the UK, Layth's mom had done a traditional rishta visit to Janna's dad and stepmom, with Janna's mom and stepdad present. She'd presented the news that Layth was now the assistant head of the animal sanctuary and, more importantly, how much he was in love with Janna. She'd also brought laddoos *and* basbousa.

It had worked.

Claire clapped, Bilqis got up and hugged Janna, who was already being side-hugged by Ava, and, from the laptop, Nuah and Sumayyah, who knew Janna well, burst into mabrooks; Kavi and Ayaan, who knew Janna a bit, said congratulations; and Mila, Jack, Sahaan, and Fatima, who didn't know Janna at all, beamed.

Connor, who also didn't know Janna, hooted because he was Connor.

Layth, using his precious Wi-Fi, laughed as Janna's hands kept finding their way to her face again and again, to cover her happiness.

And the final person online waited for Sausun to text him.

She picked her phone up and sent Haytham a thumbs-up, and then addressed Janna. "So, my precious Janna, we have a second surprise for you. Haytham, my other precious, remembering how much you looove country music, has a song to commemorate this special occasion. A song without any music, just his voice." No one could see that she beamed proudly under her niqab after saying that.

She was also proud that, besides Adam, who'd learned to lower his gaze, no other guy was in the room. She just felt more relaxed in such a space and now leaned her back against the foot of the bed behind her, ready for Haytham's performance.

"Wait, you love country music? Hey, I didn't know that, and this might affect things . . . ," Layth interjected.

"I don't!" Janna lifted her hands off her face to state this emphatically, leading everyone to laugh. She realized her obvious and un-shy eagerness to prove herself to Layth, and joined them in laughter.

"Don't worry, this one's your favorite, Janna. And I made sure it was pitched perfectly with no twangs," Sausun said, her voice full of love. "Hit it, Haytham."

Haytham smiled and counted down softly as everyone quieted, and then began "Bless the Broken Road."

Zayneb leaned against Adam, surrounded by friends, filled with hygge happiness, and Adam put his arm around her. He shut his eyes, listening to the lyrics, and, as he rested his head on hers, he marveled at how the words of the song fit him and Zayneb perfectly too.

Zayneb was at peace; he could feel it.

He was energized; he could feel it.

So many ideas whizzed in his head, he constantly reached for the small notebook he tucked into his pants pocket daily, filling it with drawings and diagrams, labels and blocks of text. They were just sprouts for now, but he'd water them whether they blossomed or not.

His domain was just the grand effort.

And he would make his efforts grand, insha'Allah.

Meanwhile, Zayneb marveled at this: how necessary to life it was for her to be surrounded by the heartbeats of kind humans.

It gave her the hope that she could work toward a world where everyone felt this loved.

This worthy—not to simply survive—but to thrive.

• • •

Bertha Fatima, still holding herself aloft, tried not to be disturbed by this fresh new noise. *Bless the broken road?*

Musically, she preferred "You Are My Sunshine," the song Adam sometimes sang to Zayneb, and "I Don't Want to Live on the Moon," the song Zayneb sometimes sang to Adam, both songs being more to the point than the one emitting from the laptop currently . . . but then she remembered something.

She remembered what the story box revealed: *Sometimes humans needed to set out on a journey to find their way to the point of it all.*

They did not, after all, possess the superior intelligence of cats.

Bertha Fatima lifted her head, sniffed once, and then folded her limbs to settle down into the softness of home.

She closed her eyes on the humans and their antics and decided she would allow them to continue their ways.

Adam and Zayneb looked content, their friends looked content, and that was all that mattered in her world.

AUTHOR'S NOTE

Love, romance, and *Mecca*? Do those even go together?

Before we get there, let's talk about my job.

My job as an author is to tell you a story.

I take this job seriously—which means first carefully deciding on the tale I want to tell.

I always end up choosing the same kind of story when I set out to write: the type I wish I'd had as a young reader spinning around in libraries in joy at ALL. THE. BOOKS . . . but with a gap inside, a growing one, wondering where my life experiences were to be found on the shelves around me.

I felt only a bit real.

Only the bits I saw stamped by society to be "okay" were valid, it seemed.

But what about my Muslim pieces? Did their erasure mean I couldn't bring my whole self anywhere? Did it mean I had to deny experiences that had profoundly impacted my life?

As a young writer, these circumstances caused me to feel like I wasn't permitted to kindle myself fully on the page, that I was to shut access to the vivid images and indelible marks my Muslim experiences had left on me—even though they provided me a deep creative well to draw from, to put my readers right *there* in the settings I felt confident to conjure palpably, in the swirl of emotions, in the blur of pains and losses and the heights of loves and joys.

That seemed unfair.

That I wasn't to dip into the consciousness I carried within if it was *particularly Muslim*.

It seemed especially unfair that ALL. THE. BOOKS in those libraries I'd spent time in allowed other authors to bring their whole selves in for generations, so much so that Muslim-me knew Greek and Roman myths, Biblical stories, historical accounts and mysteries and romances told through the lens of colonialists and their apologists, classics with faith-based allegories, fairy tales rooted in medieval European religious mores, and I can go on.

Books that are preserved and reissued and still taught in schools, still fill libraries.

Reflecting on this, I grew up to decide, *I will never contain my Muslim-self.*

Impactful experiences for me included going to Mecca for Umrah, the lesser pilgrimage, and visiting Medina, the City of Light, seven times beginning when I was nine years old through senior year of high school, to my twenties, after graduating university, to my thirties, young kids in tow, to recently—when I made dua while clutching a hope that the next time I visited Mecca would be for the greater pilgrimage, Hajj, insha'Allah.

An additional impactful experience: meeting another Muslim in a serendipitous way and falling into deep halal-love; this relationship became the springboard to a commitment to write Muslim-love as romantic, spiritual, tender, real, and, of course, fluffy and funny.

While writing, I vowed to always approach Muslim topics the way I'd learned to from the Muslim communities I was nurtured by: candidly and kindly, with the understanding that our deen was a loving, living one, not to be kept in a curio cabinet, too "sacred" to touch.

These are the reasons I chose to write a romantic story set during pilgrimage to Mecca.

So, love, romance, and *Mecca*? Do those even go together?

As together as the whole person who told you this story.

ACKNOWLEDGMENTS

This book is full of trip souvenirs. So, of course, in the tradition of my acknowledgments style, I must pass out souvenirs to special people.

I give a little Kaaba to my parents, who taught me deen: to my father, whose well of Islamic knowledge astonishes me, whose guidance is deep and wise, who never wavers from tawheed, and to my mother, who exemplifies taqwa. Thank you, Ippa and Imma, for answering my Umrah questions and for always making dua for me.

I give a goose pendant, gold, to Heba Subeh-Hyder for her input into Adam's MS scenes. Heba, I appreciate that you melded your MS experiences with spirituality while doing your authenticity read. Your insight was so important and I thank you for taking the time to provide it.

I give crystal snowflakes to my husband and my kids, my siblings and their spouses, and my nieces and nephews, for their constant love and support. And for the Umrah memories that helped shape this book. I want to go on Umrah with all of you again, insha'Allah! Another crystal snowflake to my sweet mother-in-law. Johanne, thank you for your unwavering encouragement—for saying from day one that, along with Louise Penny, I'm your favorite author (insert sobbing emoji). I want to go on Hajj with *you*, insha'Allah! (And, of course, additional crystal snowflakes to more in-laws—father, brother, sister—for being there in love and kindness.)

A snow globe with a cute cozy cottage to my beloved agent, Sara Crowe. Sara, I'm so thrilled to be working with you, and that this special book is our first one together! Another snow globe to Kendra Levin for editing such an unapologetically Muslim novel with tender respect. I cherish your words about this story so very much. More snow globes to Justin Chanda for helping start Salaam Reads and maintaining the "Muslimness" of Salaam titles; to Lisa Moraleda, Alex Kelleher, and Rita Silva, publicists extraordinaire; to the brilliant cover team of Lucy Ruth Cummins and Mary Kate McDevitt; and to managing editor Jenica

Nasworthy and copyeditor Brian Luster, both *so* important to the continuity of Adam and Zayneb's story; to Michelle Leo, Amy Beaudoin, and the rest of the school and library team; and to Chrissy Noh, Karen Masnica, Emily Ritter, Anna Jarzab, Ashley Mitchell, and all involved in the marketing of my novels. Thank you for being on team #AdamAndZayneb.

Bee bracelet charms to the Muslim crew of writers who kept me smiling while writing this book. Like Zayneb says, it's essential to have kind hearts surrounding you, and I'm grateful to have them. Safiyyah Kathimi, Aisha Saeed, Jamilah Thompkins-Bigelow, Huda Fahmy, Nevien Shaabneh, London Shah, Huda Al-Marashi, Sabaa Tahir, Zoulfa Katouh, Shannon Chakraborty, Hena Khan, Tahereh Mafi, Samira Ahmed, Ausma Khan, Haneen Oriqat, Zaynah Qutubuddin, Fartumo Kusow, Ashley Franklin, Asmaa Hussain, Hajera Khaja, Ream Shukairy, Nafiza Azad, Somaiya Daud, Hafsah Faizal: thank you for being there either as pre-pub readers and cheerleaders, and/or supports to lean on and share with, or for simply being sister-souls in publishing.

Now, this is a bulky item to pack multiples of, but I *must* do it; I must hand out thick, big brown knit scarves to the community of readers who have shared and maintained their love for Adam and Zayneb since *Love from A to Z* released in 2019. I know many of you by name, which is so beautiful to me. I hope your scarf envelopes you in the cozy warmth of a community you've created on your own.

Finally, gift boxes of my favorite dates, Ajwa, to all the new readers discovering the world of Adam, Zayneb, Janna et al. for the first time. Welcome to this universe I wrote for you to feel comfortable in, to feel beloved as you are, to marvel at the ultimate beauty of life in all its minutiae and its grandeur. I hope, insha'Allah, you go on to read all the books I write centering those of us who never got to star in our own stories—the books I write with love for us.